VICLAS

Richard Norbert

Viclas

C&A Publishing

RichardNorbertBooks.com

This is a work of fiction. Names, characters, places, and incidents either are the product of the author's imagination or are used fictitiously. Any resemblance to actual persons, living or dead, business establishments, events, or locales is entirely coincidental.

Copyright © 2020 by Richard Norbert

All rights reserved. No part of this book may be used or reproduced in any form or by any means, or stored in a database or retrieval system, without prior written permission of the publisher except in the case of brief quotations embodied in critical articles and reviews.

ISBN: 978-0-9919912-3-5
Kindle edition ISBN: 978-0-9919912-5-9
E-pub edition ISBN: 978-0-9919912-4-2

To Annette:
Thank you for your unwavering love, encouragement and wisdom.

To Edith:
Thank you for believing in me.
I'm so sorry I never finished this book in time for you to read.

"to the hard of hearing you shout, and for the almost blind you draw large and startling figures."

~ Flannery O'Connor

Prologue

Hamilton, Ontario - July 1979

Although the hippie movement had been reduced to a tiny blip in history by the early seventies, some of the country's disenchanted youths maintained their attraction to the subculture's sexual revolution and its pursuit of self-awareness through psychedelic drugs and orgies and continued to wage war against institutions that stifled their freedom and protested anything capitalistic in nature. Paula, who went by the name Summer, and her latest live-in boyfriend Stewart, who called himself Leaf, were no exception.

Neither Summer nor Leaf could hold a job for more than a few weeks, and when they did manage to land something, the work wasn't about getting a better life or becoming responsible, contributing members of society. It wasn't even to put food on the table for her eight- and six-year-old boys or even to cover rent and power. It was a means for Summer and Leaf to support their increasing tolerance to LSD.

When the need for it became greater and the money scarcer, both Summer and Leaf began selling their bodies to strangers in their home for a few measly bucks while the boys watched Saturday morning cartoons on a stolen black-and-white television set in the run-down living room of the rented, dilapidating, story-and-a-half house in Hamilton's Stipley area.

Once belonging to practicing Catholics who fell on hard times, the house ended up in the hands of a slum lord after the bank repossessed it. Still, the house managed to keep a few vestiges of its former self. There was a large print of the Sacred Heart in the living room and a holographic picture of the Last Supper in the kitchen, but—as evidenced by the cigarette butts in the holy water font on the wall by the front door—the new residents couldn't care less about the once-cherished devotionals, keeping them out of laziness rather than any sort of religious piety. Truth be told, many jazzed discussions were had about them, sometimes even *with* them, when the acid trips were exceptionally groovy.

"How much longer do we have to wait for breakfast, Peace?" the younger brother asked.

"Stop calling me that! You know that's not my name," his brother complained. "Come on; I'll get you some cereal."

"But Summer said to wait."

"Her name's Paula! I told you to stop using those stupid made-up names, Peter!"

"But if we don't call her that, she gets mad."

"Shut up and get in here!" he ordered as he opened the pantry door and reached for the only box of cereal.

"Here," he said as the last few morsels tumbled into the bowl along with the sugary dust from the bottom of the box.

"I want milk with it."

"There is none."

"But how am I supposed to eat cereal without milk?" the younger brother whined.

"With your hands, Stupid!"

Peter's bottom lip quivered.

"Sorry," the older brother said awkwardly, acknowledging the pain he'd just caused, but unsure of how to deal with the hurt feelings.

No one had ever taught him compassion, except his mother's grandparents who once had custody of the pair . . . until the old folks' untimely deaths in a tragic car accident, which prompted their immediate return to this hole—to Summer's discontent. He couldn't be sure that he preferred living with them, though. They were very different from his mother. They had some of those religious decorations all over their house as well, but *they* went to church. Even dragged him and his brother along with them. They tried to talk to him and Peter about someone they referred to as Jesus Christ. Although the name was quite familiar to him, frequently used by his mother in anger, he was reasonably sure they were not the same individual. To listen to the grandparents, their mother was going straight to hell—which, in times like these, the memory of those words made him smile.

"Here's a spoon," he offered with more patience.

His brother grabbed the utensil, then quickly shoveled the dry cereal into his mouth and coughed to clear up a bit of cereal dust that had made its way down the wrong pipe.

Angry voices originating beyond the ceiling made the children look up.

"Sounds like they're almost finished," the older brother observed.

"You call that oral?" a muffled-yet-audible voice resounded from upstairs. "Your boyfriend gave me a better one last week. Maybe he can give you lessons," the man's voice chuckled.

"Screw yourself!" the woman cried out.

"That's not enough for the back-rent you owe me, Summer, you know that," the man said, his insistent voice growing louder as he made his way down to the main level with the boys' mother in tow.

Her eyes were bloodshot, her long, blond, dirty hair was a mess, and her filthy t-shirt barely concealed her nakedness from her children. Seeing her sons staring back, she sneered. "Whatcha looking at?"

"I need another fifty bucks, Summer, or I'm kicking your sorry ass out of my house," he cautioned, his smile showing off a decaying set of teeth.

"What else do you want from me?" she pleaded.

He scratched at his shaggy, lice-infested mess of hair. "Your deadbeat boyfriend is crashed out on your bedroom floor, and you haven't got anything left in ya," he said, then flashed a twisted smile in the young boys' direction. "Maybe they can help you out with the payment," he suggested, unbuckling his pants with a grin.

"Wait!" the mother stepped in, to her eldest son's relief. "Wait," she added, her desperate voice trembling and her puffy eyes pleading. "There's no way those two are only worth fifty bucks. Gimme another couple of hits of Purple Haze, and they're yours," she bargained.

"Deal!" he snickered and produced a small paper envelope from his shirt pocket.

"No!" the older brother screamed. "You're not touching us, you filthy son of a whore!" he roared, borrowing the words he'd once heard from his great-grandfather.

Grabbing his brother by the arm, he raced them up the stairs and into their bedroom, locked the door, then shoved him under the bed and followed behind him.

Whimpering and heaving, the little brother's distress was unstoppable.

"Shut up!" the older brother ordered in a loud whisper, wrapping Peter in a headlock and holding a hand over his face. "They're gonna find us if you don't keep quiet!"

"Peace! Get down here!" his mother boomed. "The man already paid me. Get down here right this minute with your brother!"

His brother had finally stopped crying. At least now they had a chance.

***

"Peace!" she cried out again from the bottom of the stairs after setting the purple tab under her tongue. "Don't you dare make me come up there and get you, you little bastard!"

"You really needed that, didn't you, Summer?" the landlord heckled. "You better get me those kids now that you've already taken those hits. You better hurry, too, before you start tripping and pass out like your chum upstairs."

"Peace!" she yelled, stomping up the creaky wooden stairs. "Peace!" she screeched then lost her footing and tumbled down the stairs, splitting her head and snapping her neck as she hit the living room floor at the landlord's feet.

"Shit!" the man cursed in a panic and hurried out of the house.

For several hours, the two boys laid motionless under the bed, but did not hear a sound since their mother's earlier commotion.

"I think we're safe now, Peter," he whispered, finally releasing his grip off his little brother's face.

"Peter," he repeated, shaking him, but his brother remained unresponsive.

"Come on!" he demanded.

Pulling himself out from under the bed and reaching for his brother's arm, he dragged him to the center of the room, but Peter's limp arms fell to the floor with a thud as soon as he was released.

"Peter," he called out. "Peter!" he repeated forcefully, then—leaning in closer—he pressed his cheek against his brother's mouth and nose to feel for a breath, but there was none.

He rose, cautiously opened the door to the silent hallway, and strained to listen for any hint of a sound. Reasonably sure there was no one left inside the house who could harm him, he climbed down the stairs and found his mother lying face down in a pool of blood from an open head wound.

For a long moment, he stared at her, then slowly made his way up to her bedroom, where Leaf was lying unconscious on the floor. He grabbed the granite doorstop on the floor and struck Leaf at the back of the head, then dipped his fingers into the freshly made puddle on the carpet. Stepping over the lifeless body of his first homicide victim, he climbed onto the bed and, with his bloody little fingers, scribbled the only scripture passage's chapter and verse he knew. He had looked it up after hearing his angry great-grandmother reciting it from memory while condemning her granddaughter. Leaving the bloody numerals VI:XXIII on the wall, he wiped his hand on the bedsheet, made his way down the stairs, and waited on the front porch for several hours until a concerned neighbor spotted him and called the police.

August 2012

1

Halton Hills, Ontario - August 2012

Barely noticeable from the road, half a kilometer down an unpaved driveway and hidden by overgrowth from years of property neglect, the old two-story limestone-and-mortar house which sits on ninety-four acres of farmland serves as his sanctuary.

It is located no more than four kilometers west of Georgetown and less than thirty minutes from Toronto's boundary on a good day, but 6th Line is seldom used by anyone other than its few local residents, the occasional farm tractor, or the odd traveler looking to find their way back to civilization without the use of a GPS.

He inherited the old property—you could say—years ago from the previous owners who, he had decided, no longer needed it. Why should they have a comfortable house when their decayed body remains are perfectly fine in the septic drain field's fertile soil in the backyard?

Although it's been years since he last heard it, the voice, like fingernails grating across a chalkboard, has begun tormenting him once again, and only by inflicting pain, suffering and terror will he be able to squelch the shrill voice. The need for blood has returned. Unlike all of his previous works, however, for this production, a theme will be chosen, a character developed, and victims carefully selected. He'll need a name, something with an ominously religious tone this time. Hmm, that would fit nicely with his evolving plan. Maybe he'll call himself "The Light Bearer" or "The Messenger" or something along those lines. Still plenty of time before he commits to any of those minute details.

The light breeze flowing through the cheap, sun-faded horizontal blinds covering the partially opened window does very little to alleviate the humidity and resulting stuffiness of the hot August night, and so the sweat beads glistening over his already pale skin render his complexion to a sickly, nearly translucent state. As instructed by the voice, he kneels before the full-length mirror in the dimness of his secluded lair. Like the aura of a saint, his pride radiates from the reverence with which he adores his naked reflection. According to the voice that lives through him, it is gracious and beautiful and worthy of homage.

O most glorious plan taking root in his mind. World Youth Day in Rio next summer, eleven excruciatingly long months away. How will he ever be able to harness the anticipation until the ultimate climax in Rio? The excitement builds and spills over and down his cheeks from the corners of his red, swollen eyes. It will be a most memorable celebration indeed! This will be his masterpiece—and, as usual, no one will ever even suspect him.

Infiltration strategies bloom in his degenerate mind. He smiles. Would he dress up as a cardinal? Hmm, probably not. He sighs; people tend to know those clowns by name. Perhaps not every one of them, but certainly any of those old geezers still young enough to make it to the Pope's party. No, he will most likely dress as a bishop or a priest. That would make it much easier to blend in.

His eyes light up. Maybe he'll take it to a mind-blowing level and dress like a nun. His thin lips part and a wicked smile materializes. He has the shape and the look that allow for an easy transformation into a beautiful woman; in fact, he recalls effectively doing so when circumstances had made it necessary a few years ago. He shudders at just how close that one had been, but shakes that uncomfortable memory from his head and the smile returns.

Could it be time to bring Jezebel—, or Jezzie, as he likes to call himself in a dress—back to life? His face contorts as the thin-lipped smile gives way to the terrifying sneer only ever witnessed by his victims sucking in their final breaths.

It's time to get back to work. It's time to silence the voice once and for all.

He bows reverently before the mirror one last time, then seats himself at the computer, where he logs on to the airline's website and purchases an advanced, one-way fare to Rio de Janeiro for Mr. Jude S. Cariot July 2013.

January 2013

2

Teulon, Manitoba - January 2013

"Look, I didn't ask to be here. The locals in the squad room across the hall invited me for my input," Inspector Rafe Kellar states, sitting at the head of the table in the small boardroom with Winnipeg's eight-member Tactical Support Team. The officers and their ornery leader were on loan to the small rural municipality, and it was obvious that everyone staring back at him in the tiny space did not enjoy being told how to do their job, especially by an outsider.

It doesn't happen as often as Kellar would like, but police departments in remote areas of the country with limited resources occasionally call upon the RCMP's Behavioural Sciences Branch in Ottawa to request on-site assistance from a ViCLAS (Violent Crimes Linkage Analysis System) Specialist who linked their serial case. Having investigated several other potentially related cases by studying victimology, eyewitness accounts, and behavioral and forensic data found at the various scenes for similarities, these ViCLAS Specialists have an intimate knowledge of the case and can provide valuable insight in bringing the suspect to justice.

With his piercing blue eyes fixated on the sergeant, Kellar insists. "Sergeant Nepinak, my job is to provide you with a usable profile of the suspect so you can do your job and take him into custody, not to get in your way. I'll be like a ghost. You won't even know I'm there."

"If you don't even plan on being seen, then stay here at the detachment!" Nepinak, a proud, second-generation Indigenous cop with a significant chip on his shoulder, fires back.

"You need me on the ground," Kellar insists.

"What for? My men know exactly what they're doing."

"Your men don't even know what he looks like."

"So? Neither do you!" the heavy cop argues. "For all we know, this guy is probably just a figment of your overactive imagination."

Kellar smiles. "Oh, there's a guy, alright. I may not know *exactly* what he looks like, but I know how he thinks. I've studied the other cases, and they all point to this building on 3rd Street—tonight."

Rafe Kellar is correct. Although he's only been there for three months, no one else at ViCLAS can connect seemingly unrelated crimes into a serial pattern as quickly as he can, but this one was a no-brainer—at least for him.

"We're probably just chasing our tails here. The brass in Winnipeg and these local officials might have bought an extra heaping of your load of crap, but it'll take more than your silly little sales pitch to convince me. And let's say, for shits and giggles, that your boy really does exist; what makes you think he's even gonna show? You just threw this plan together based on a hunch," the tactical boss says, his words thick with sarcasm.

"Not a hunch," Kellar corrects. "An educated inference, if you prefer."

"Waste of good, hard-working people's tax money if you ask me," Nepinak scoffs and shakes his head. "Where do we find these nerds anyway?" he sighs loudly in his usual unsubtle way.

Rafe bites his tongue, ignores the jab, and continues unfazed.

"The things that link this suspect to what I believe are four other unsolved arson cases here in your province is that in every case, the local fire marshal had just signed off on the sprinkler system in some sort of re-purposed old structure, just like our target building. None of the fires were ignited in the same manner, and no accelerants were discovered. The first incident was electrical, the second was caused by a heater that had apparently been left on over the weekend, the third one started in the roof assembly after the roofing crew had left for the day, while the fourth was started by an apparent faulty gas line that ruptured, and by all indication, accidentally ignited. Every crime scene was completely different."

"Without any evidence of arson, you have no crime and no crime scene, so again, you've got jack!"

"You didn't let me finish," Kellar replies patiently. "You're right. On the surface, that would appear to be true. If all you had to consider were the fires themselves, you could say these were just a string of bad luck. But I suggest these fires were, in fact, the work of a highly intelligent arsonist," he argues. "What you need to consider is that you also have unidentifiable human remains at every fire. Your coroner's office confirmed that, in every case, the victims were already dead before being consumed by the flames, which likely means that the fires are staged to cover up body dumps or possible homicide scenes. Plus, what you probably never noticed is that a missing person's report for a teenaged Aboriginal girl from a neighboring reserve was filed the previous month. Every! Single! Time!" he emphasizes with a searing glance directed at Nepinak.

Kellar takes a moment to appreciate the impact his words are having, seeing new understanding in each officer's face.

"One!" he rattles off with a finger. "The lack of comparable physical evidence in otherwise identical cases. There is absolutely no common denominator linking any of the fires other than the fact that a fire marshal had signed off on a construction site. Two! The charred human remains at every scene. And three, the missing person's reports. There's your evidence that points to a very high probability of a serial pattern that must be presumed and therefore investigated."

He surveys the sullen faces around the room and wraps up his discourse. "We could be dealing with anything from a serial arsonist who might be involved in sex trafficking to a serial killer using fires to clean up after himself."

"So, you figure he kills those girls and uses the fires to cover his tracks?" Nepinak asks with skepticism, but somewhat more decorum.

"It's not like I get the Serial Killer Monthly newsletter. I'm just linking similarities between cases. The missing girls and the fires might be coincidental, but it's my job to look at all the information police departments across the country provide us for the national database and come up with plausible scenarios. The bodies in the other fires were ravaged to the point where they couldn't be forensically identified. I can't say for sure that the dead bodies are those of the missing girls. I can't even confirm that your suspect is the one perpetrating the killings or if he's only a hired hand. But I can tell you with absolute certainty that something is going on that needs to stop. I'm ready to wager my next month's paycheck that your suspect is paying you a visit tonight."

"I'll believe it when I see it," Nepinak replies, not entirely convinced.

"Oh, he's coming," Rafe assures the team.

"This guy you say we're going after," Constable White, the team's newest member, speaks up with a grin. "Let's call him the Teulon Torch," he suggests to a few chuckles from the guys and a scathing glance from his boss. Recovering quickly, he asks, "Is he a fireman or something?"

"He's probably connected to the fire department in one capacity or another," Kellar affirms. "So, when the latest missing person's report for another young Aboriginal woman was filed a couple of weeks ago, it hit me. I contacted your fire marshal and had him sign off on the bogus sprinkler installation for this building."

"What if it's the fire marshal himself doing all of this?" Nepinak counters.

"Different marshal in every jurisdiction," Kellar points out.

"I'm still not sold on your hunch, but I'd rather prove you wrong than miss an opportunity to stop this guy in his tracks if he really does exist," the boss states. "Grab your stuff," he orders his men, then to Kellar, "You can come along, but you're staying in the truck!"

3

The driver of the cramped armored vehicle kills the headlights and comes to a full stop half a block from the repurposed warehouse, and all his passengers rush out into a freshly fallen blanket of snow. They hasten their way toward the building, splitting up on route with Team 1, led by Sergeant Nepinak, converging on the north side at the front and Team 2 flanking the south . . . with Kellar trailing behind, despite the multiple orders not to get involved in the action.

The lookout team observing the place all afternoon from the adjacent strip mall had established that a dark figure had made several trips between the parked van at the loading dock in the rear and the target building thirty minutes before the TST's arrival. They also confirm that he is still inside.

Originally an old grain mill and warehouse, the three-story structure was being converted into luxury condominiums until construction, nearly three-quarters completed, halted without warning when the builder's wife left him, taking his money and his brother along with her four months ago.

"Bradford, you get to work disabling the elevator as soon as we breach," Nepinak re-instructs. "Johnson and White, when we're done clearing the lobby, I want you at either end of the hallway to secure the stairwells and grab the suspect if he tries to make a run for it while Bradford and I sweep every suite from west to east and meet up with Johnson at the other end."

His team signals their understanding. "Hawkeye!" he calls over the radio. "Any movement from over there?"

"Negative," the lookout responds. "No sign of the suspect since we observed him entering the premises approximately half an hour ago."

"Roger that!" Nepinak snaps and looks to his team. "Team 2 will be coming in through the loading dock in the basement and securing it, then making their way up to the third floor to sweep and clear that area. Both teams will converge on the second floor at opposite ends, apprehend the suspect, and then call it a day. Any questions?"

Predictably, there are none.

The abandoned construction project is quiet and dark as Team 1 enters through the glass entryway at the front, their wet tactical boots surprisingly quiet on the marble-tiled floor. At the control panel, Bradford disables the elevator as instructed while the others secure the lobby. Constable Johnson slips into the security office and discovers an aluminum container concealed under the desk – an incendiary device comprised of a thermite composition of magnesium, polytetrafluoroethylene and fluoroelastomer equipped with a cellular activated high-temperature igniter.

"I've got something in here, Sarge," Johnson cries out.

"What is it?" Nepinak asks, glancing over his subordinate's shoulder.

"Looks like a home-made firebomb that's wired to a remote cell phone detonator. How do you want to handle it?" he asks.

"Just leave it alone for now," the leader replies. "He's not gonna trigger this thing while he's still inside. We'll handle him first and come back to deal with this after."

The four tactical officers conclude their inspection of the lobby, activate their night-vision goggles, and advance inside the darkness of the long, carpeted hallway.

Nepinak signals Johnson to take his post while he, Bradford, and White make their way to the other end.

As planned, Team 2 had penetrated the building's basement and, having discovered nothing suspicious in the mostly wide-open and unfinished area, the two pairs scale their respective staircases up to the third floor.

"We're now on three, Sarge. Nothing to report so far," resounds the voice of one of the constables on the third floor through the team's earpieces.

"Keep your eyes open," Sergeant Nepinak instructs. "We found a firebomb in the office just off the lobby. Is Kellar with you guys?" he queries.

"No. Isn't he with your team?" comes the surprising reply.

"Dammit!" the sergeant curses. "I knew it! Kellar!" he whispers forcefully over the radio, "where are you?"

"Kellar!" he repeats unsuccessfully over the airwaves. "Keep sweeping and clearing!" he finally orders. "To hell with that prick" he huffs and resumes the search for the suspect with his men.

After nearly forty-five minutes, Nepinak and Bradford have cleared all the units on the first floor, finding two more cellular activated pyrolants along the way, but no sign of the suspect or his alleged victim. Together with Johnson, the three tactical members hasten up to the second floor while White takes the west stairs with his assault rifle poised.

A small explosion resonates, and the flash of light illuminates the entire hallway through the metal door's window. Three successive, unnervingly recognizable pops follow the flash and bang, and Constable White falls down the flight of stairs and onto the landing, already dead from the bullet wounds.

"Shots fired! Shots fired!" Nepinak screams over the radio as he and his men race across the corridor. They burst through the door in combat position and find White's body. "Officer down!" Nepinak barks. "Suspect just escaped through the west stairwell! He's headed to the lobby. Back-up team, intercept! Go! Go! Go!"

**

The suspect hurries through the lobby, fully expecting heavy reinforcement to emerge at any moment. Drawing his weapon, he shoots his way through the locked tempered-glass doors, anxious to remote detonate the igniters. The high-temperature accelerants he was using this time would light up the old building in a flash. He sprints past his van and skips over the train tracks skirting the property in the rear and slows his stride long enough to retrieve his phone tucked inside his coat pocket. He grins as he looks back at the building, eager to admire his work, but a sudden, burning sensation sears through his forehead. The phone slips from his limp fingers, and the last thing he would see in the last moment of his life was the silhouette of Rafe Kellar perched against the parapet of the roof. His lifeless body flops to the ground, the snow beneath his corpse absorbing the blood—a dark crimson in the freezing, moonless night.

February 2013

4

Ottawa, Ontario - February 2013

With the Teulon Torch case a month behind him, Rafe Kellar, hailed as a cop's cop and the one who stopped a serial killer no one knew existed, strokes his face where her hand had left its imprint, a lump forming in his throat and a knot growing larger by the second in the pit of his stomach.

Just as an approaching storm is noticeable in the distance, this moment has been brewing for quite some time; in fact, he's surprised their marriage has lasted this long. But still, it pains him.

"So, there's nothing else I can say that would make you change your mind?" he whispers hoarsely, extending his hand for hers. She shakes her head and slowly moves away from him.

People gathered around the couple look away in embarrassment, as much for his sake as for their having to witness the drama developing firsthand. She could have waited until everyone left, but in pure Annie Kellar fashion, she needed to make an attention-grabbing production of it. It helps her feel like the victim. It could have been worse, though; she could have dumped him right in front of their son's casket. She turns and retreats there now, reverently taking position on the kneeler and stroking her son's cheek, weeping silently.

From the doorway in the funeral home's foyer, Rafe looks on as his in-laws gather around his wife's side and Jake's peaceful remains. They're already talking about moving her back to Montréal. The pain in his chest intensifies. Not even a week ago, he had a wife and a son, and now, he has neither. Life was never perfect, but rarely is it so for anyone. They were still a family—the only one he has that really matters to him, unless you count the close-knit bond he shares with his friends on the force. Although they also live in Ottawa, he and his parents hardly visit, none of them making a concerted effort to communicate except for the occasional call at Christmas or his birthday, and always initiated by his mother.

"You okay?" a tall and muscular, fashionably dressed Black man asks, wrapping a thick arm around his friend's shoulder.

"Yeah," Rafe confirms, drying his eyes, as people he doesn't recognize try their best to avoid his gaze. "She doesn't even want me at the funeral. Can you believe that? She says it's my fault," he sniffles, his eyes moist and his cheeks still red. Deep down, he actually shares her critical reproach, and he suspects that's what bothers him the most.

"This ain't on you, man. Look, you know you loved your son," he reassures him. "Come on. Let's get out of here."

But Rafe doesn't budge.

"Come on, look around, Arch!" his friend calls him by the nickname he's had for him for years. "You're not welcome here. Let's grab a coffee—or a beer."

"I'm really not up to it, Juice," Kellar declines.

"Yes, you are," he persists, shepherding him through the handful of people in the foyer and out onto the parking lot. "There's nothing you can do for Jake tonight. Place is locking up in ten minutes anyway."

Kamarre Toure, affectionately known to his friends as Juice, had flown to Ottawa from J Division headquarters in Fredericton as soon as he had gotten word about the suicide of Kellar's seventeen-year-old son. They call him Juice because of his likeness to O.J. Simpson in his former years—minus the big hair and scandal. The two have been best friends since their days as fellow A Division constables attached to Parliament Hill, shortly after graduating from the RCMP training academy internally referred to as "Depot Division" in Saskatchewan. Juice had successfully climbed the ranks while Kellar, to his friend's dismay, had declined promotions that would have confined him to full-time desk duty.

"I'll take you back here tomorrow for the funeral, and we'll sit in the back if we have to. They can't stop the kid's father from attending the funeral, man, that's just stupid talk!" Juice fumes while leading Rafe across the lot to his Equinox, then opens the front passenger door for him.

"Hop in, Arch," he orders, his breath visible in the deep, numbing Ottawan cold.

Rafe complies without a fuss, and they ride in silence for a few kilometers.

"So, how's ViCLAS treatin' you?" Juice says, breaking the silence. "You catch any bad guys yet?" He chuckles, knowing the jab would take his pal's mind off his worries, at least temporarily.

Emotionally drained, exhausted and short-tempered, Rafe takes the bait.

"It's a real thing, Juice!" he huffs, tired of justifying his career move. "ViCLAS isn't just a game, you know. We do serious work there and—although you think it's just small-time connect-the-dots—police departments all over the country, and the world for that matter, appreciate our expertise," he asserts with pride.

"Yeah, right!" Juice scoffs.

"I've worked on all kinds of cases from homicides to human trafficking and everything in-between," Kellar maintains. "Just last month, I helped take down a serial in Manitoba no one else even knew was operating!" he cries out, slamming his fist on the dashboard as Juice bursts out in laughter.

"I'm just jerking your chain, man. Relax. You're way too easy to get started, you know. I heard all about your Teulon Torch case."

Rafe settles his temper and takes a calming breath.

"Not the name I came up with for that piece of shit," he says. "The young kid who got shot's the one who came up with that one."

Kellar stares silently into space as he recalls Constable White. Although he hadn't known him long, the young cop had made a lasting impression on him.

"Just made TST the month before. His first time out, and he was so pumped," he pauses another moment. "He and his wife were barely back from their honeymoon."

"I'm sorry, Arch," Juice says quietly.

"Yeah, well . . ." Rafe's voice trails off. He wanted to tell him how good it felt to put the cop-killer down with a single bullet to the head from his service weapon, but thinks better of boasting about taking another life, as much as he feels the dirtbag deserved it.

"Glad you put him out of his misery," Juice says for his friend, but oddly enough, it doesn't help. "You surprise the other guys with that shot?"

"Probably," he grins. "Like you, they were under the impression I was just some geeky computer nerd." He rarely talked about his former life as a commando in the Canadian Armed Forces Airborne Regiment, prior to its being disbanded after the Somalia Affair in 1995.

"If they only knew, right?" Juice grins. He knew.

They ride in silence and come to a stop at the traffic lights at Wellington and Metcalfe with the 'Hill' to their right. Rafe stares quietly at the flag blowing proudly in the wind atop the majestic Peace Tower of the Centre Block of the Parliament Complex.

March 2013

5

Vancouver, British Columbia - March 2013

The traffic light turns to green, but still he has to wait for the old Chinese couple waddling through the intersection at Main and Powell. The plumber revs the engine, and the cargo van roars angrily, but the unflinching elders carry on their way without hastening their stride.

"Hurry up!" he barks from inside the van. He would love to plow through the pair, but resists the temptation. Giving in to temptation is for the weak, and weak he certainly is not.

A few blocks north of Chinatown might not be anything like Mr. Roger's neighborhood, but he's convinced people would still notice a plumbing truck rolling over an elderly couple on the street, even in the glum and soggy daylight. Glancing across the intersection to the fire department, he figures that if no one else around him reacted, those two idiots washing their fire truck in the rain would probably raise a stink about it. He doesn't need any unnecessary attention, so he avoids even the horn.

"Hurry up!" he screams again instead.

His light turns to yellow as the seniors finally make it across the right side of his van and he quickly turns left onto

Powell, slowing to a stop in front of a parking meter adjacent to the pink-trimmed strip club.

He glances at the parking lot behind the establishment. Not much activity going on this early in the afternoon, just a white cube-van and its husky driver carting a delivery of beer kegs up the back stairs, but he doubts that the guy will even notice him. And even if he does, who cares?

He climbs out of the van and locks the doors, then makes his way to the parking meter. He runs his bony fingers through his shaggy red hair and then shoves his hand into his pockets while he studies the street in both directions. There's still no sign of trouble, so he feeds a couple of loonies in the meter and wonders if he should add more time. For good measure, he inserts another couple of bucks. There's no way of knowing how long he'll have to wait for her. No one would ever notice a legitimately-parked plumbing van in front of a strip joint for a couple of hours, but if the meter runs out, that could bring some of that unwanted attention he would much rather avoid.

Her stage name is Lacy J. He's done his homework. He knows she works here and that she's one of their headliners. He also knows that he will have absolutely no trouble getting her out of the club for a private party.

The music is loud, and the place is practically empty. From inside his neon-lit booth, the disk jockey screams through the speakers for the handful of party animals to make Cinnamon Cake feel welcome as the more experienced, dark-skinned dancer makes her way to the stage with as much dignity as she can muster.

The cellulite on her thighs wiggles with the flabby skin as she reaches for the pole and begins her gyrating performance to a small yet seemingly appreciative crowd. The drunken college students don't seem to care that she's probably as old as their own mothers. They whistle enthusiastically and wave their hands in her direction.

The plumber walks over to the bar and measures-up the man behind the counter retrieving beer mugs from the dishwasher. The guy is enormous. He could probably give a UFC championship contender a run for their money, but he doesn't scare him. Not even a little.

"Hey! Looks like you keep the good stuff for later on, eh?" he critiques, throwing his thumb back in the performer's direction.

"What can I get ya?" the bartender replies, ignoring the jab about one of his girls.

"Nothing. I'm just looking for someone," he answers.

"Two-drink minimum!" comes the gruff reply.

"I just paid ten bucks to get in," he protests.

The bartender flips the dishtowel over his shoulders and stares back at him, arms crossed, biceps bulging, and brows furrowed.

"Fine," he huffs, not wanting any trouble. He could take this ape out in less than three seconds, but what good would that do? "Give me two of whatever's on tap," he says with a smile. "Please?"

The bartender grabs two glasses and pours a couple of cold locally micro-brewed favorites.

"Thanks," he tells the big guy. "Keep the change," he adds, tossing a fifty on the counter.

The bartender smiles amicably.

"What time does Lacy J usually come into work?"

"She's here now," he says to his new favorite customer. "She's over there," he adds, nodding in the direction of a young, attractive blond in purple sweatpants and matching hoodie.

Not much to look at with those rags on her, he thinks to himself, but leaving his recently-purchased beverages on the counter, he slithers over to where she is seated at the back of the club eating a greasy cheeseburger and washing it down with a diet cola.

"Hi, I'm Tony," he lies and slides into the booth across the table from her. "I hear from a reliable source that you like to do a bit of . . . shall we say, freelance work?"

"Beat it, perv!" she says with contempt. "I'm not working yet."

"Hear me out," Tony replies defensively, his hands coming up. "I'm not just some jackass off the street looking to hassle you. I'm a legitimate businessman looking to entertain some very special friends of mine," he explains, as he pulls an envelope from inside his jacket and gently places it on the table. "There's twenty thousand in cash in that envelope. Take whatever you feel you deserve to make this happen," he grins, knowing she will never have an opportunity to spend a dime of it.

He watches with amusement as she slides out of the booth, stops then turns back to stare at him with the tell-tale signs of an internal struggle, as though appraising him and his thick envelope with a mix of skepticism and intrigue. He can see the wheels turning. She's probably wondering if he really *is* a business owner with a serious offer. He knows he doesn't look like one, but the cash on the table is very real. He shoots her a warm and friendly smile and her mood softens. He snickers as she takes her seat across from him again, lustfully staring at the envelope within her grasp. She's hooked.

"What sorta business you in?" she inquires nonchalantly, doing her best to appear uninterested.

"I'm a plumbing contractor," he replies. "I'm bidding on a big new project downtown and I could definitely use something as hot as you to sweeten the deal and land the contract, if ya know what I mean," he winks.

She always knows what they mean. A plumbing contractor does explain the work boots and jeans. She stares at the thick envelope on the table. For that kind of coin, she could easily look past his scrawny frame and nasally voice.

"There's twenty grand in that envelope?" she asks.

"Yep!"

"And I can take whatever I want from it?"

"That's how I work," he acknowledges.

She pauses for a moment, then reaches for the envelope and shoves the whole thing inside the pocket of her hoodie, just as he had expected.

"You think pretty highly of yourself," he snickers.

"I'm worth every penny," the young woman answers with confidence.

"You better be," he warns.

Cost is not a factor. What *is* a factor is that she agree to go with him. With a wad of cash that big as bait, none of the girls in her line of work would ever decline as generous an offer, regardless of their self-imposed limitations.

"I know you go by Lacy J, but what do your friends call you?"

"What makes you think we're friends now?" she scoffs.

"My twenty thousand other friends just told me."

"Fine. It's Madison," she shrugs.

"Madison," he repeats. "That's a pretty name. What made you decide on Lacy J?"

"That's who my mother used to listen to when I was growing up in Calgary, Lacy J Dalton. I figured if I dropped the Dalton, Lacy J was a pretty good stage name."

"Yeah, that's a pretty good stage name, I guess. I don't usually come to places like this and stuff, so I guess I really wouldn't know," he pretends, keeping her off her guard.

"When's the party?" she asks with her mouth full of food.

"As soon as you're finished your lunch."

She wads up the unfinished burger inside its wrapper and slides out of the booth. "Give me a minute," she says, swallowing, and disappears backstage. She returns a few moments later, shouldering her 'go-bag' as she nears him. "Hey, Brian!" she shouts to the bartender.

"S'up?" he replies.

"I'm calling in sick for tonight," she announces. "I'll see you tomorrow," she adds and beams a seductive smile in Tony's direction.

The big guy swears and complains, but Lacy J grabs her client by the arm and escorts him outside.

"Where's your ride?" she asks, squinting from the afternoon sun.

"Right this way," he says, taking the lead. "C'mon."

Together, they walk west along the sidewalk toward the back of the club and stop at his cargo van on the street.

"Looks like one of 'em 70's party trucks," she says, scrunching her nose. "There better not be any shag carpet on the walls, or I'm outta here," she warns, visibly perplexed.

"My truck's in the shop getting a new muffler today, so I'm stuck with this one, and no, there's no carpet on the walls."

"You not afraid that people might recognize you from this ginormous billboard on the side of this thing?"

"The advertising's good for business," he smiles.

"I suppose even old beer-drinking perverts need plumbers too."

If he were a real plumber, he would probably be offended. Ignoring her comment and the front of the van, he slides open the side door for her.

"Here. You'll have enough room back here to change into your party clothes," he suggests with a wink and helps her in, then follows her inside.

She drops the bag onto the tread plate floor and reaches for the zipper as he slides the door shut.

"You looking for a little pre-show peek-a-boo or something?" she asks, standing and staring contemptuously.

"Wouldn't dream of it," he replies, zapping her with a cattle prod and watching as her incapacitated body hits the floor. Then he slips into his plumber's coveralls for phase two of the plan.

VI

"You can't do this to our family, Helen," Stan Doyle pleads as his wife begins her climb up the stairs to pack a suitcase and fetch their daughter. He reaches and grabs her elbow, but she recoils violently.

"*I* can't do this to our family?" Helen fires back. "I'm not the one who had sex with a prostitute in my office, Stan!"

"Look, I tried to tell you we had problems in our marriage, but you wouldn't listen—"

"So now, this is somehow my fault?" she cuts in, moves down from the first step and glares up into his eyes. "I'm the one who gave up a career to raise our daughter; I'm the one who gets up at all hours of the night to change her diapers and feed her; I'm the one with the big ugly scar from the C-section; I'm the one with the deformed body and the bleeding nipples. You think all that gives you the right to run around behind my back—with a hooker?"

"It wasn't a hooker. It was an exotic dancer," he reaffirms irritably.

"She's a whore!" she fires back.

"It wasn't my fault, Helen. It's the guys at work."

"They brought a hooker into your office, ripped off your pants, and forced you to have sex with her on your desk next to the picture of your family, huh?" she scoffs.

"It wasn't like that, I swear," he pleads.

"That's pretty much how it looked on the Internet."

"I have no idea who could have sent you those pictures."

"That's your big concern right now? Who sent me the pictures?"

"That's not what I meant, dammit!" he cries out with both hands reaching for his temples. "Stop putting words in my mouth."

"You're telling me what not to put in your mouth? I don't even want to guess at what that filthy whore put in your mouth," she screams, her bottom lip trembling.

Stan lets out an exasperated breath and flops onto the couch, staring at her for a long, quiet moment. He'd loved her since the first time he laid eyes on her. He gave up his playboy lifestyle for her and even gave her his 'little black book' to burn as an engagement present right after she accepted his ring. The little black book was actually his PDA, which took her less than thirty seconds to turn into scrap metal and plastic fragments with a hammer. They've been married for nearly six years, and not once has he ever even entertained the notion of being unfaithful to her. Not that any of that matters right now, apparently.

"I know how stupid I was, and there's no excuse for what I've done, and I'm really, really sorry," he begins to say.

"Don't you dare think you can apologize your way out of this!" she fumes.

"Please," Stan mumbles, his eyes moist. "Just give me a chance to explain."

Her entire body shudders, and her cheeks are black from streaking mascara. She turns to walk away, but his voice stops her mid-stride.

"Please!" he sobs loudly.

Without a word, she turns to face him. Fidgeting in place with her arms crossed over her chest, she ponders her next move. She mentally concedes that he has never done anything as deceitful as this before. But, he really hurt her! What drives a man to want to betray his wife and family?

She wonders if somehow, she might have had a role to play in this, but quickly dismisses that idea completely. "I'm the victim here!" The words reverberate loudly in her mind. She wonders what her life would be like if she were to file for divorce. What about their daughter? What would the breakup be like on her? If push came to shove, would she be able to file for full custody and keep their daughter away from him? She casts away that thought just as quickly. She has no idea what to do or say anymore. Confused, she takes a seat on the loveseat opposite him.

"Thanks," he says.

She doesn't answer. She simply stares at him, her face devoid of emotion.

"I know I screwed up royally," he begins.

She purses her lips sarcastically.

"I know you've been exhausted lately because of the baby."

She rolls her eyes in annoyance.

"Look!" he says with an edge. "I'm not trying to lay blame on anyone else here other than me, but I need you to understand what happened."

"Fine!" she says curtly.

He groans and picks up from where he left off. "You've been moody and tired lately because of the baby, and we haven't even had a hint of sex in over eight months. Now, I know I shouldn't have said anything to Frank, but looking to vent out my frustration, I might have said something about it—and now, I know that I should've kept my mouth shut. That idiot thought he was helping me out by getting me drunk and hiring a stripper for the office Christmas party," he rationalizes, slumping further into the couch as he lets out another deep sigh.

"After all those drinks, it's almost as though someone else had control of my body. I knew what I was doing was wrong, but I felt powerless to stop it."

She knows Frank very well and knows how easily his powers of persuasion can get other people into trouble.

"I have no idea who took the pictures and even less about how that stuff ended up on the Internet."

The incriminating photographs had somehow ended up on VancouverConfessions.com, an anonymous tell-tale blog site. The headline was particularly hurtful and embarrassing to her: "Former High School Principal's Husband Has Very Little Principle."

An anonymous user had emailed him a link to the site twice, copying his wife with the second. As soon as Stan had followed the email thread and realized that Helen had been cc'd, he immediately raced to their home. Too late. Helen was already seated at the desk in the corner of their living room, her eyes staring at the photos in disbelief.

"There's no excuse for my behavior, Helen. I'm really sorry. Do you think you can ever forgive me?"

A small part of her wants to. Another part wants to strangle him, and that's the part that brings her to ask, "Why *did* you come home from work?"

He stares back at her blindly.

"Why are you here in the middle of the day? How did you even know that I was looking at this?" she asks and hurries to the computer and discovers that he, too, had been sent a link to the site.

"You knew I had received this e-mail today, didn't you?" she says, her voice growing angry. "You came home because you were afraid I would learn what you had done, didn't you? What were you going to do, delete it before I had a chance to see it and pretend the whole thing never happened?"

"Helen," he utters and stands.

"You son of a bitch!" she screams and throws the stapler at him as the doorbell chimes.

He ducks and moves quickly toward the door.

"Get back here!" she orders, but he's already pulling the door open to greet the stranger.

Stan drops to the floor without a word, and Helen doesn't have time to react. As her husband's body convulses, a wiry plumber with a cattle prod in one hand and carrying a toolbox in the other races toward her. She tries to scream, but her legs fail, and everything goes dark.

7

The thick report lands noisily on his desk and startles Chen Miao, who stares at his supervisor quizzically and whines, "Whaaaaat?"

"You figure out where all the water's going?" Mark Friedman asks, wasting no time on small talk.

"Nope. Still looking, though," Chen confirms without the slightest hint of his parent's thick Mandarin accent.

"Look, the mayor's gonna be crawling all over me in the next couple of days if we don't figure this out," Mark warns in his usual dramatic tone.

The mayor really doesn't care about such trivial matters unless they make him look bad in the media, but Mark just feels that the exaggerated drama helps motivate his crew much better than screaming like a frantic lunatic.

"This is March, not June! No one should be filling their swimming pools for at least another month or two. We're missing almost half a million liters of water, and we're going to find it if it's the last thing *you* do," he adds.

Vancouver's action plan to become the greenest city in the world by 2020 depends mainly on its infrastructure's cogs working congruently, and part of that infrastructure is its intricate pipes system that carries the municipality's 360 million liters of water to its clients daily. A large portion of the green plan ensures that every liter of it is accounted for. Scrutinizing the water consumption and maintaining the business and residential water meters falls under Mark Friedman and his team at the city's water and sewer division of the engineering department.

"I did discover an unusual meter reading in the Victoria-Fraserview area," Chen offers, as he slurps the last drops of his medium double-double and rolls-up the rim. "Finally!" he exclaims. "I won a sandwich!"

"Chen," Mark says impatiently. "The water?"

"Sorry. I was thinking that this screwy reading might be where the problem's originating. The only other thing I can think of that might cause that big a gap between the readings and the actual consumption is a busted water main or an unbolted fire hydrant, and neither's been reported."

"What are you still doing here?" he criticizes. "Go check it out!"

8

It's typically dull and rainy as it can be in Vancouver. What isn't typical is the discomforting number of emergency vehicles currently camped along Randall Street. As the late afternoon—already darkened by the clouds and unrelenting precipitation—turns into evening, an eerie sense of excitement sweeps the neighborhood while the small crowd of apprehensive bystanders watch as bright strobes of red–and–blue paint their street into an unnervingly morbid canvas.

"Why am I here?" Staff Sergeant Jerry Morgan complains to Detective Watkins as he reaches the yellow crime tape and ducks past it. "Can't you morons solve a crime without me?"

Darena Watkins is one of the eight detectives under his charge and probably the one who dislikes him the most.

A veteran cop with almost thirty-seven years on the job, Staff Sergeant Morgan is a cranky old jerk with a bad attitude and BO that follows him wherever he goes: a potpourri of cigarette smoke, stale coffee, sweaty armpits, and unwashed, greasy hair.

His lousy mood has only worsened as his retirement party draws closer. The out-of-shape, crusty, old widowed cop is not looking forward to his retirement in a month from today, mainly because it's not happening by choice.

Detective Watkins doesn't care much for people who talk down to her—superior or not. As though daring him to intimidate her, she frowns and doesn't budge, but he walks up to her and stares her down.

She curses herself under her breath. She hates that she continually allows him to get under her skin.

"This one's not like any I've seen before, and no one else is available, so yeah, I need your help," she says with difficulty, her pride taking another blow.

The old cop groans. "You can walk and talk at the same time, can't you?" he grumbles.

"Victims' bodies were found in the basement. Coroner says the cause of death was drowning."

"Drowning?" he snarls.

"Yes," Watkins confirms. "You'll have to see it for yourself," she adds wearily, shocked at some people's disregard for human life, then leads her supervisor inside the house.

"No signs of struggle except for that smashed coffee table over there. Nothing especially *weird* so far except for the wet floor," he points out sarcastically.

"Basement's this way," she motions. He follows reluctantly.

They cross the kitchen to the basement staircase and bypass a couple of crime lab techs carrying sump pumps and heavy-duty hoses along the way.

The smell of bloated, decomposing bodies was certainly not as bad as it could have been. The cold water has done a decent job of delaying the decomposition process, but the stench was nevertheless beginning to creep up and into the main level as they head for the basement.

"Once the city shut off the main valve at street-level, it took our techs over two hours with four of those pumps to clear out more than 150,000 liters of water from the basement. They sent whatever evidence they caught with their filters to the lab," the detective fills him in. "Here they are."

They touchdown on the basement floor, and Morgan examines the polyethylene plastic covering the entire floor and all the walls. He turns to inspect the severed water line jutting from the busted gypsum wallboard.

"He waterproofed the entire basement and cut the main line here to make sure he got the maximum flow rate."

"What do you make of the positioning of the bodies?" Watkins asks, shifting her supervisor's attention to the victims.

The lone male's remains are duct-taped to a chair. His pants and briefs are pooled at his ankles with a scantily clad young woman also secured in place with the gray tape and arranged in an unflattering position with her head tightly secured in his groin area.

The second woman's body, bound to a chair with the same restraints, is positioned as a spectator facing the pair. Her head, however, is angled toward the top of the stairs, and the fear in her eyes is genuine.

"This woman had things other than kinky sex on her mind when she died," the old cop concludes. "Any dead kids upstairs?"

"We found a baby in her room on the second floor. She was unconscious, but still alive when first responders got to her. Medics rushed her to the hospital, and she's being treated for dehydration. He didn't harm her otherwise," she affirms, then hesitates. "There's—something else you need to see upstairs in the baby's room."

Ignoring her, he carries on with his investigation in the basement while she rolls her eyes, mentally calling him an ignorant, chauvinistic piece of donkey shit.

"I'm *pretty sure* all three victims didn't live here," Morgan says facetiously. "Have we identified any of them yet?"

"Husband and wife are the home-owners—Stan and Helen Doyle," she confirms from her notes. "Third victim matches the description of an exotic dancer from Club Pink, Madison Taylor, a.k.a. Lacy J, reported missing by the owner of the club earlier today. She was apparently seen leaving the place with a male customer for a private party three days ago but hadn't surfaced since."

"Really, Watkins? Surfaced?"

She cringes. "Sorry. Not how I meant it."

"No one reported the couple missing?"

"No. He's an accountant who took a few days off work earlier this week, stating personal reasons, and she's a stay-at-home mom. I spoke with her parents, who live in Burnaby. They said it wasn't unusual for them to go weeks without hearing from her, so there was no need to suspect that anything was wrong."

"Neighbors didn't see anything?"

"No, the property is surrounded by several mature conifers, and the water running down the driveway, well, no one noticed it with all this damned rain."

"So, how were they discovered?"

"The water and sewer department," she says. "They sent a guy to investigate a faulty water meter reading. When he got here, he noticed water streaming all around the bottom of the house under the vinyl siding and immediately called 9-1-1. Apparently, the water had been running for over three days."

"We get a possible description from the guy at the club?"

"The owner said he was working the bar that day and confirmed his girl left with a skinny-looking guy, 'bout five-seven, five-eight with red hair. No one noticed what he was driving."

"What's the baby's name?" he asks gruffly.

"The wife's mother said her name is Katelyn," she answers, consulting her notes again. "The grandparents are at the hospital with her now."

Morgan nods, and they leave the bodies for the coroner's people and head up two flights of stairs to Katelyn's room.

They reach the second floor, and Jerry Morgan's jaw drops as they clear the bedroom threshold. "Ah, hell!" he utters.

Above the rainbow and teddy bear decals on the wall next to the crib where the infant had been found, the freak had left a message for them in what the old cop hoped was only red paint:

"By the waters of the flood, the Prophet washes away their sins. No longer will their offshoot be subjected to their wicked ways," followed by the Roman numerals, VI:XXIII.

April 2013

9

Ottawa, Ontario - April 2013

"Hey!" Rafe says in greeting as he waltzes through the aluminum storm door at the back into the kitchen and is welcomed by the familiar powerful pine-scented cleaner. "Looks like you still don't close and lock your doors around here."

"Well, look who decided to drop by for a visit," the old man says gruffly, his jar of instant coffee in one hand, a can of evaporated milk in the other, and Charlie Pride singing about snakes crawling at night from the ancient 8-track player in the living room.

"Nice to see you too, Dad," Kellar sighs. "I see you're still cranking out the hits."

His father shrugs and wobbles over to the stove where his pot of boiling water is waiting for him.

"Gout acting up again?" Rafe asks awkwardly.

"Nope. Arthritis this time," Mr. Kellar clarifies. "You want a cup?" he offers without looking.

"No, thanks. I'm good. Mom around?"

"Bingo night," his father replies casually.

Rafe gives the place a quick once-over. Same wobbly wooden table with the same vinyl tablecloth sitting on the same faded linoleum floor. With second thoughts about coming in the first place, he turns to leave and faces the door, but the old rotary dial phone on the wall catches his eye, and he chuckles to himself as he remembers the way he used to jot down messages on the wall next to the phone. He reaches up and runs his fingers over the numbers still there on the outdated floral wallpaper his mother had selected for their new house. He had initially planned on speaking with her, but supposes he can ask his father since he's already here and doesn't really want to have to make the trip again unless it's absolutely necessary.

"You still have a Bible here?" Kellar asks, hoping the question will not get the old man started.

His father stops stirring the coffee long enough to look at his son, then turns his attention back to the mug. "You change your mind about church all of a sudden?"

"No," he answers curtly, not looking to get sucked into the same old religious rabbit hole. "I just came across a case at the office that's really unusual. A guy in Vancouver wrote stuff on a wall at a crime scene that looks like it could have come from the Bible, and I was hoping to get some insight into what might be going on inside this suspect's head."

"What, don't you still have the Bible we gave you for your Confirmation?" his father scorns.

He knows he should have gone with his gut and at least tried to find one at the bookstore. Maybe they still *do* carry those things in stores, and he could have avoided beating this poor, dead horse all over again.

"No, I don't have it anymore. It was ruined when our basement flooded a couple of years ago," he lies.

"Why didn't you say something?" his father criticizes while taking a seat at the table. "We would have given you another one for Christmas or something."

"Can I borrow yours?" he ignores the comment.

"Wouldn't have to if you had one."

Rafe's impatience grows into frustration.

"You want something to eat?" the old man offers.

"No thanks—not hungry," Rafe snaps back, earning himself a stern look from his father.

"Your mom should be home in about half an hour. She'd be happy to see you."

"Look, Dad, I'm in a bit of a hurry. Can I borrow your Bible or not?"

Mr. Kellar leaves the kitchen for a moment, then returns with the thick book and hands it over to his son. Rafe reaches for it with a nod. The padded cover is well worn, and the artwork's colors have faded from many years of handling.

"Thanks," Kellar whispers and turns to leave. "I should be able to bring it back to you in a couple of days."

"Oh, by the way," the old man says, raising his hand and slowly nodding his head. "We were very sorry to hear about Jake."

Rattled by the affectionate tone, Rafe settles his irritation and takes a deep breath.

"Thanks," he says, genuinely touched.

He hadn't bothered telling them for fear that they might show up at the funeral and cause a scene, but now wishes that he had. "Yeah—it sure hasn't been easy these past few months," he admits, letting down his guard and about to open up about Annie leaving him.

"Shame the boy's going to spend eternity in Hell now for taking his own life that way," the old man says glumly.

Rafe explodes. "What? How can you be so insensitive?"

"I'm not being insensitive. It's in the Bible."

Kellar tosses the book onto the table, and it bounces across the surface before landing on the floor with a thud.

"Keep your damned Bible. If that's what it says, then no wonder the world's full of crazies!" he shouts furiously and leaves without another word.

"It's always the same with those two!" he bitterly huffs as he pulls out of the driveway and squeals away from his parents' house. "They say stuff like that and think they're good Catholics?" he fumes. Who were *they* to damn his son to Hell for all eternity?

"There has to be a Bible for sale somewhere," he mumbles. "I'll pick one up there and be done with it!"

Speeding through a yellow light, he turns and finally pulls into the parking lot of a large bookstore chain and into the slot closest to the door.

10

Vancouver, British Columbia

"Watkins!" SS Morgan barks from his office. "Get in here!"

Detective Watkins lets out a sigh of discontent and tosses the folders on top of the other ones already strewn across her desk. Once, just once, she'd like that jerk to stop treating her like a dog; but then again, she's seen him with his dog and must admit the dog gets treated much better than humans do.

"What?" she says, spiked with attitude, which merits a scowl from the cranky old investigator.

"Look, I know I'm done here at the end of the week, but I'm still in charge for the next three days," he gnarls. "So, you can take your pissy little attitude and go back to your desk and sit down for a minute. Then you're going to walk back into my office, sit down in that chair, but your attitude stays at your desk! Are we clear?"

She smoulders, rolls her eyes as she spins around, and returns to her desk. She would love to report his abusive behavior up the chain, but there's no discrimination going on around here—he's an ass to everyone. Thank heavens he's gone as of Friday. She secretly hopes his retirement party on Saturday is a bust.

"Hey, Watkins!" he growls again before she has a chance to go through the motion of sitting at her desk and returning as ordered. "Get in here!"

She cringes and balls up both fists before slowly making her way back to his office, putting on her pretend-happy-face as she steps through the door.

"Yes, Staff Sergeant?" she delivers as calmly as possible. "How can I assist you?"

"The basement drowning homicides from last month—you already put all that stuff in the national computer, didn't you?"

"*I* didn't," she replies. "But I *did* fill out the ViCLAS Booklet and sent it to Ottawa like we're supposed to whenever we come across a violent crime."

"Didn't I tell you not to waste your time in the first place? Get it back from them."

"What are you talking about? It's an open homicide investigation. We likely have a psycho on our hands. We need all the help we can get before he strikes again."

"Case closed," he answers casually. "We don't need any pinheads who think they know everything hanging around in our backyard. We have big-boy pants on and can take care of things on our own. Case closed! End of story!" he adds with a smug grin.

"Who closed it?" she asks, taking a seat across from the landfill he calls a desk. "Why wasn't I involved?"

"Keep your panties on," he snickers.

Now she just wants to kick him in the groin.

"We picked up another case we had no idea was connected to yours," he expounds. "Your suspect's dead."

"How do you know he's my suspect?"

"His dead body told us so."

"What?" she asks as she rises.

"You know that case Bobby was called to last week—the guy they found hung in the back of a plumbing shop?"

"Yeah."

"As it turns out, that was your killer. They ran his prints in the system, and voila, it was a match to the unidentified prints found all over the house and in the blood he used to write that crap on the kid's wall." He reaches under his desk and scratches himself. She wants to vomit.

"The dirt-bag even had a hand-written note in his pants confessing to all three murders and asking us to personally tell his parents before they saw anything on the news; oh, and that he was *really, really sorry*," the old cop mocks. "The parents checked out. They went to the morgue this morning and confirmed he was their son. Said he had schizophrenia, like it's some kinda hall-pass."

Detective Watkins is flabbergasted. "Just like that? Cases don't usually just solve themselves, especially weird ones like that. It had serial killer written all over it," she reiterates. "There has to be more to it than that."

"No, there doesn't!" Morgan insists. "Case closed! They even recovered the plumbing truck three blocks from where they found the guy. A few of the dead hooker's prints were found in the back. Call Ottawa and tell 'em to toss your little notebook in the trash."

"That's not how this stuff works, Sarge; you should know that," she argues unconvincingly.

He laughs. "You know if they put it in their computer database thingy yet?" he continues as though she hadn't said a word.

She shakes her head in disbelief. "I just got confirmation last week that it had been assigned to an analyst, so if he did his job correctly, I suppose it is in their database by now."

"Go back to your desk and call the guy and tell him that we already solved the case and for him not to waste any more of my hard-earned tax dollars to catch a two-bit suicidal loony who's already dead."

11

Moncton, New Brunswick

The pounding music's decibel levels surpass the acceptable levels of even the old, converted movie theatre on Main Street. The fire marshal would have shut it down hours ago if he had been aware the place was thronged to capacity with clubbers *still* filing in—most of whom, under-aged.

The place is called "E" as a reference to the drug, but to police and the general public, the owners deny any involvement with the narcotic other than the use of its name as a marketing tool; however, to their "special guests," they sing a different tune. Drug dealers, pimps, and others with questionable morals acquainted with them are offered their own secluded section of the club on the upper floor.

Tucked away in a dark corner of the VIP level overlooking the dance floor is one of these guests, a small-time entrepreneur with morals as rigid as cooked spaghetti who holds himself in high esteem. With a narrow head and close-cropped eyes, he goes by the name of Bruno, and he strains to hear what the attractive young woman next to him on the sofa is whispering.

"I hear you do favors for people in exchange for—you know, other favors."

He leans back and checks her out, somewhat caught off-guard by her statement.

"What are you getting at?" he asks suspiciously.

"You know, maybe the kind of specialty service other people in your line of work get squeamish about?" she smiles tantalizingly.

In *his* mind, his empire is large, but it's really nothing more than a couple of tattoo and piercing shops with drugs coming and going from the back. Although he has been known to discreetly offer specialized surgical procedures to a very select clientele, having once been charged but never convicted for these alleged procedures, he prefers to avoid the legal headaches and steers the conversation in another direction.

"I don't know what you heard, but I run a clean and legitimate business," he says, feigning indignation.

"But I'm exceptionally good at returning favors," she purrs insistently. "And you come highly recommended," she adds, running her fingers seductively through his thick, curly chest hair.

He shifts in his place, aroused by her touch.

"My girlfriend cheated on me with a guy, and I didn't like that very much," she confesses with pouting lips. "I have to put a stop to that."

"Look, I'm not complaining, but you don't seem to have a problem swimming in other waters yourself," he winks. "You looking for me to sew her shut or something?" he chuckles.

She hesitates, leans in closer and whispers into his ear with warm breath and flicks of moist tongue. "Pretty please?" she licks her upper lip teasingly. "I hear you're particularly good at female circumcision, and I . . . am *very* motivated. I'll even pay you in advance," she says, nibbling at his earlobe.

"Your source is dead wrong," he decides curtly and rises from his seat. "I'm not into that. Now I think I hear someone texting me to cut you loose," he says gruffly, adjusting his silk shirt, which he always wears unbuttoned down to his hairy navel. "Too bad, too. You look like someone who's built to stay up late and could've appreciated my sexual stamina," he adds and starts to leave.

She laughs tauntingly.

His over-inflated ego stops him. He turns and forces a smile. "Women *never* have a reason to laugh at Bruno."

She shrugs. "You probably don't even have what it takes to satisfy me anyway," she adds, poignantly assaulting his deeply-held masculinity.

He checks her out from head to toe. She has to be at least as tall as he is without her heels. Her head is cocked to the side. Her long, black silky hair dangles over her bare shoulders, and her bangs hang teasingly over her suggestive dark eyes. She glances away for an instant, and in this light, he takes note of her strong cheekbones and chiselled jaw for the first time. She turns and glares at him alluringly. Can't be a dude, can it? No way would a dude fit himself into something as sexy as that.

He considers the strapless, satiny black dress with the narrow leather belt enhancing her curves and the extremely low-cut front offering him an eyeful of possibilities. There's no way that's a dude!

Intrigued by the enigmatic and beautiful stranger, he settles himself close to her on the small couch again.

"Okay, you win," he declares loudly over the speakers hanging from the rafters above their heads. "I guess I could consider your offer, but you'll have to prove to me how serious you are about this."

She wets her upper lip provocatively then smiles, waiting for a reaction.

He smiles. He's hooked.

She takes his hand and seductively leads his middle finger up to her mouth, slipping it deep between her full lips, her sexual assertiveness driving him to near ecstasy.

"Come on. Let's get out of here," he grins like an idiot and takes his finger out of her mouth, then lowers his voice for privacy. "I'll show you my shop and where I do my best work. Whaddya say . . . ?" he hesitates, not recalling having been told her name.

"Jezzie," she says, extending her hand. "All my friends call me Jezzie."

12

A twenty-two-year veteran of the force, Inspector Patrice LaChute leads the evidence-gathering unit of the Codiac RCMP. The moment it has been determined that a major crime has taken place in the Greater Moncton area, no one but he has access to the scene until it has been thoroughly documented and all the evidence collected. With the unusual nature of this homicide, it took the first officers on the scene less than a second to call him in and start sealing-off the area.

The inclement weather meteorologists had threatened all morning has finally arrived, and with the wind now cranking it up a few notches, the mix of sleet and rain stings his fatted cheeks and blurs his rimless glasses. He labors his overweight body under and past the ominous yellow tape roping off the entrance to The Tribal Print tattoo and piercing shop on St. George Street with his cases tucked tightly against his body.

Inside, he places the cases gently on the parquet floor and unfastens them, then undoes his jacket and wipes the mist from his glasses with the front of his sweater. He slips on booties and latex gloves before placing his headset over his balding dome. He sighs as he visually assesses the surroundings.

Except for the body and coagulated blood in front of it, this is the tidiest crime scene he's seen in his lengthy career.

The pungent smell of antiseptic lingers in the air as he walks the room, placing yellow crime scene markers on the floor and snapping photographs from as many angles as possible for later investigative use.

Inching toward the body, Inspector LaChute activates his audio recording device and begins dictating the scene through his headset with only a slight trace of his local Francophone upbringing.

"Victim is male, Caucasian, appearing to be in his late thirties. He is stripped naked and seated in the second of three parlour chairs. His clothes are not visible anywhere in this room," he pauses and scans the vicinity to reconfirm.

"His wrists and ankles are bound with gray adhesive tape and—" he gulps. "The tip of his penis is missing." He cringes. "There is no sign of it anywhere in the immediate area." He hates to imagine what that could mean. "Autopsy will confirm, but judging by the significant amount of blood on the victim's lower extremities, the chair and the floor, I suspect the coroner will determine the cause of death to be exsanguination due to sharp force trauma to the victim's penis."

Stepping away from the body, yet unable to take his eyes off the victim, he feels a touch remorseful for only being slightly affected by this atrocity. Though he reminds himself that to survive in this profession for as long as he has, he needs to detach himself from his emotions. If his career as a forensic investigator has taught him anything, it's that there will always be another more disturbing scene tomorrow or next week or next year.

"There's an empty bottle of vodka on the counter," he resumes his observations. "No glasses visible, but there appears to be a red substance around the neck of the bottle. Lipstick?"

he wonders and swabs at the bottle for a sample to submit to the lab. "Girlfriend? Maybe a witness?" he speculates. It can't be the suspect, right? A woman wouldn't be capable of such a gruesome and violent act, could she? He hates to be cynical, but recalls Lorena Bobbitt and shrugs. "Hell hath no fury, right?" he mumbles, then retraces his steps to lean in for a closer look at the victim's genitalia.

"Hmm," he says, noticing a ring of color remarkably similar to the one on the bottle. He swabs to confirm. "Looked like blood at first glance, but upon closer inspection, it appears someone, presumably a female, might have performed fellatio on the victim at some point before his time of death. If it *is* lipstick on the bottle and the victim, the lab will test for DNA and determine if it belongs to the same individual. Maybe she's in the system," he hopes. "Witness or otherwise, someone's gonna want to speak with her."

Across the street, the Cathedral reminds him that it's noon with the ringing from its carillon.

He stares in the church's direction for a brief moment, frustrated by the annoying distraction, then, turning his attention back to the counter, takes a peek into the trash bin on the floor next to a metal filing cabinet. It's empty except for an unused condom with its torn wrapper and an empty erectile dysfunction drug foil sample pack.

"Doesn't look like the night went quite like you had hoped, eh?" he says to the victim. "Gonna leave it to the coroner to order a toxicology screen to see if he had this or any other pharmaceuticals in his system." He figures the little pills will explain how the victim could bleed out from his decapitated member.

With all the evidence in the first room meticulously recorded, he gathers his equipment and, careful not to disturb anything, slowly makes his way into the adjacent room which functions as a makeshift lunchroom, and that's where he sees it.

Prominently displayed on a dirty plate in the center of the cluttered table is the victim's severed glans. On the wall behind the table, written with smeared blood, are the chilling words:

"The world will recognize his tribe by the sign from the blood of circumcision at the hands of the Prophet," followed by the Roman Numerals, VI:XXIII.

13

Ottawa, Ontario

Alone at his cubicle in the dark and deserted office, Rafe Kellar lobs the recently-purchased Bible across his workspace, irritated at still not having found any substantial links between the Vancouver homicides and the story of Noah in the Book of Genesis. Removing his reading glasses and tossing them next to his desk lamp, he rubs his face with both hands and groans loudly out of frustration.

It makes precisely zero sense! In the Bible, every living being was wiped out by the flood except for one man, his wife, their three sons and their wives, plus two of every animal—one male and one female of each species. If he understands the story correctly, God was flipping the reset switch on this whole creation thing by saving the only humans *he* felt were worth saving. And their responsibility, along with each pair of animals, was to repopulate the world.

How does that even begin to gel with this twisted Vancouver tale? It doesn't, that's how! Exasperated, Kellar curses under his breath.

According to the police file, three victims were found murdered in the basement. Granted, they were drowned, but the baby in her crib was the only one left alive. How is she supposed to repopulate on her own? Is that the point? She'll grow up without her parents and have a better chance at life? It's not like she was being raised in a crack house after all.

The report states that the police had collected damaging photos from the husband's work computer and the PC the couple shared at home. The dead stripper was identified as the woman with whom the husband had had sexual relations. Stan Doyle had clearly cheated on his wife, no doubt about that. Maybe Mrs. Doyle was going to leave him over the indiscretion. Cheating *does* damage a marriage, he ponders, but quickly back-tracks from the thought.

"Who am I to judge anyone else's marriage?" he grumbles, briefly reflecting on his own failed matrimony. "Sure as hell wasn't the killer's place either!" he maintains, refocusing on the case. Infidelity does *not* warrant a death sentence, much less three.

The familiar ding of an arriving message in his inbox is hardly a welcomed distraction, but he sets the file aside to see what new shit show needs his attention.

"What the hell?" he sighs.

In her brief but to the point email, Detective Darena Watkins wishes to advise ViCLAS that the gruesome homicide case she had submitted last month had been solved and that their suspect had been discovered hanged in his brother's plumbing shop. With the signed confession and suicide note they found on his person, they had closed the case and had moved on to other matters.

"Fine by me," he exhales, throwing his arms in the air. He closes his files as well as the Bible and stacks everything in a pile on the corner of his desk to deal with tomorrow, then heads home for a hot shower and a stiff drink.

14

Albert County, New Brunswick

A rush! There simply isn't any other word to describe the feeling. An absolute rush. She had often imagined, dare she even admit *yearned* for the exhilaration of witnessing someone's life slip away from them, but had never fancied the possibility of she herself being the one taking that life with her own hands.

Her pulse races. The vivid images flashing in her mind draw a chilling smile to her face as she revisits each glorious moment, her senses heightened from the elevated levels of endorphins her brain was producing—as it had that night. It's as though she's actually there reliving the experience.

The foreplay and the way she had toyed with his sexuality, seductively securing his full cooperation until it was too late for him, had been a thrill. The way she had lured him back to his place like a pig to the slaughterhouse under the guise of sexual escapades was intoxicating beyond belief. He was even the one to suggest closing the blinds for additional privacy.

Her only regret, although a minor inconvenience, is that, had it been up to her, she would have picked someone a lot better looking—and smelling. She still has a migraine from that god-awful cologne he had bathed with. All things considered, it's not as though she actually had had sex with him. Well, at least not more than with her mouth. The instructions were for her to simply leave a bit of lipstick there for authorities to discover, but she teased the guy a bit longer than was necessary. She thought giving him a little taste of her abilities and stopping short of pleasuring him before following through as instructed had been a nice touch.

Getting him into the chair had been child's play. It's unbelievable what a little exposed skin from a woman can do to a man. One look at her bare breasts and he was stripped naked and on the chair with high expectations of a much happier ending.

Feeding him the ED tablets as demanded had only evoked minimal objection from the man. But she had insisted on the rules, even with his whining and pointing out that he clearly didn't need it. After losing the debate with the threat of her leaving, he had complied without another fuss, which set the stage for the next phase of the plan: Securing the willing participant's wrists and ankles to his own chair and gagging his mouth with her dress. It was almost disgustingly simple.

The look on his face will be etched in her memory forever. She will treasure it for as long as she lives. Like those people with money to burn who hang expensive works of art on their walls and admire them from time to time, so too will she revisit the look on his face when, from between his legs, she showed him the sharp tool.

His screams were loud but muffled by the makeshift gag and the loud music in the parlour, so she wasn't worried about random passersby alerting the authorities; not that anyone would raise an eyebrow at loud music in this part of town, regardless of the time of night.

When first reviewing the details and specifics, she was pretty skeptical of the outcome, but with the promise of a nice payday, who was she to argue?

She still can't believe the luck which had befallen her. Who does that? Who hires someone they don't even know and send them a bunch of money and a script with the mandate of killing some poor schmuck in such an unusual and deliberate way? Beats her, but who cares? Everything from the name she had to use to the dress and wig she wore had been provided. The way she had to act and talk, how to set the scene with that weird crap to write on the wall before she left, everything had been meticulously spelled out for her. Whoever goes through this much trouble isn't someone she particularly wants to piss off—especially one who goes around calling himself the Prophet, so she's going to have to be delicate when bringing up the subject of money with him. It seems it wasn't in her bank account after all . . . but that's for another day, she reminds herself, dismissing her last assignment and focusing on this new one. But still, she can't rid her giddiness as she steers the car she was provided along the winding, heavily wooded stretch of Route 114 in the darkness.

This time, all she has to do is pick up a stranded motorist and drop him off in Hillsborough, a mere ten kilometers down the road, where he'll become someone else's responsibility.

"How does he even know this stuff?" she marvels as she nears the precise location she was told she would find the man and slows her car. She doesn't know or particularly care how he knows everything about everyone, but she's in awe at the thorough planning this individual has displayed up to this point. "This could be the start of a beautiful relationship," she hopes aloud, before coming to a stop.

She rolls down her passenger window. "Hey!" she shouts with a nod and a friendly smile. "You look like you're freezing. Let me give you a ride somewhere."

The man straightens from under his hood and stares at her with a look of despair. He reminds her of a stick figure. He blows into his hands in a fruitless attempt at keeping warm. "I don't know what's wrong with it," he shrugs, rubs his tousled hair and adjusts his thick-framed glasses. "I just had it serviced yesterday."

"Where you off to in the middle of the night?" she inquires as per the script.

"I'm supposed to meet my wife and kids at Fundy for the weekend. I had to work late tonight, so they went on ahead earlier today," he explains. "They wanted to set up the cabin for my surprise fortieth birthday party," he says bashfully.

"Well, then. Happy birthday!" she smirks. "Get in. I'll take you there."

"I couldn't impose," he resists.

"Not an imposition," she maintains.

"I—I'm not sure," he replies, nervously scanning the area.

"Look, you're in the middle of nowhere. The closest town is probably a couple of hours on foot. Get in," she urges. "You afraid of little girls or what?"

"Okay," he finally agrees as he sits next to her and closes the door. "Aren't you afraid of picking up strangers at this late hour?" he quizzes as he buckles his seatbelt.

She watches him open the bag folded on his lap. "No," she replies with confidence. "I'm pretty sure I could take you," she adds with a grin. "My name's Jezzie," she says, going off-script.

"Wow," replies the stranded motorist. "That's not at all the name I told you to use this time."

"What?" she barely has time to say as the Prophet shoves the chloroform-laden rag into her face. She struggles fiercely against the attack for the five or so minutes it takes the chemical to take effect.

He pulls the rag from her face and stuffs it into the plastic bag that had fallen at his feet during the scuffle. He curses as he rubs the raw skin above his left eye where she had scratched him.

"You shouldn't have done that," he chides eerily. "I'm not too worried, though. They'll never be able to trace the DNA back to me anyway."

With her head tilted back, he begins the forensic countermeasure of administering tequila with a turkey baster down the back of her throat past the trachea, making sure the alcohol does not inadvertently go into her lungs and careful not to scrape the mucosa. She will have enough alcohol in her bloodstream by the time he's finished with her for officials to overlook foul play and conclude she was driving under the influence and died as a result of a car accident.

She had followed his instructions to the letter—picking up the car in the abandoned parking lot and meeting him at this location—enticed with the promise of another fistful of money.

He stares at her for a brief, satisfying moment, before taking two trips to transfer his things from his vehicle into the backseat of hers, leaving his car out of sight in the empty woodlot clearing off the main road. He climbs into the rear of his victim's car, fastens his seatbelt, then powers up his laptop and activates the hacking software which allows him to operate the vehicle from his position.

Now in control, he steers them back onto the road and navigates twelve kilometers east. He turns left onto a dirt road that leads to the Petitcodiac River and accelerates. They race through the sharp turn, leap over the bank and plunge deep into the muddy shoreline half a meter away from the trickling brown water, the impact propelling his latest victim's unconscious body into the windshield.

He unlatches his belt and quickly strips his clothes down to the dark neoprene suit he's already wearing and slips a full-face skullcap over his head, removing his non-prescription prop glasses in the process.

Reaching over the seat, he checks for a pulse with his latex-gloved hands and feels the faint sign of life flowing through the carotid artery. He's not worried. He knows the murky water will soon take care of this loose end for good. Unconscious women can't hold their breath underwater. The thought amuses him.

As dependable as the rising and setting of the sun, he can hear the roar of the Tidal Bore making its way toward them at thirteen kilometers per hour in the distance. Leaving no physical evidence behind, he stows everything into his backpack and slips it over his shoulders, then carries out a final inspection of the backseat, making absolutely sure he hasn't missed anything. From the rear, he tosses the lightweight bodyboard through the open driver's side window into the muddy stream, then climbs into the front and over the victim to propel himself into the frigid water after his board, heading upriver.

The two-and-a-half-foot wave crashes against the vehicle, nudging it slightly without dislodging it from the thick mud's vice-like grip. The rushing water quickly rises to the open window, flooding the car by the time the first wave reaches him. Within ten minutes, the vehicle is completely submerged, and he rides the surf in the moonless night up to Albert Creek, which branches off back to Route 114 and his waiting vehicle.

May 2013

15

Ottawa, Ontario - May 2013

"And this just happened last week?" Rafe asks as he tosses his gym bag to the floor in front of the locker, opens its metal door and begins to unbutton his shirt.

"Yeah, man. I've seen strange crime scenes in my day, but this one takes the cake," Juice confides.

"And it's already closed?" Kellar says with skepticism.

"By all accounts, it would appear to be the case," the big man confirms.

"So, let me see if I understand correctly. Your Moncton crime scene techs investigated two separate incidents roughly a week apart, linked the two together, and closed the book on the whole thing. Did I leave anything out?" he asks, running a hand through his sandy, receding hairline.

"Just that the homicide was the most disturbing thing I'd ever seen. I mean, it was like someone had recreated some sort of bad horror flick, but for keeps, Arch."

"And your people found some weird religious-like writing in blood on the wall?"

"Yeah. Written in the victim's own blood, with the victim's own severed— you know," he squirms, unable to utter the word.

"And the suspect turned out to be a woman, the same woman whose body was discovered inside her car in the river a week later?"

"Yep," Juice corroborates, lacing up his running shoes. "Her prints and her DNA were all over the crime scene."

Kellar rubs his temples. "I need to look at your case file," he says. "You remember what was written on the wall, exactly?"

"Here," Juice hands Kellar his phone and allows him to examine some photos. "I took these myself."

Kellar studies them attentively. His investigative instincts tell him that the similarities are much too close for the events to be unrelated, even if they had taken place at opposite ends of the country.

"This is different, but it's still the same," he murmurs.

"Same as what?" his friend probes.

"A couple of months ago, a triple from Vancouver came across my desk," Rafe explains. "Husband and wife and a stripper were found murdered in the couple's basement. They had been drowned."

"The suspect drowned them and moved the bodies down to the basement?" asks Juice.

"Nope. The victims were bound into position. The basement was waterproofed, and the main water line was cut. The room flooded, and all three drowned. The only survivor was the couple's baby. The guy left a calling card similar to this one on the wall above the kid's crib. Different words, but the same Roman numerals."

"How do you know it wasn't *her*?" Juice asks about the suspect from his case.

"Cause in *this* case, just like yours, there was plenty of evidence to link the murder to some demented bastard who stole his brother's plumbing truck, abducted the stripper from her work, drove her to the couple's house and finished all three of them," he reports. "Apparently hung himself a week later with a note in his pocket confessing to the entire thing."

"Wow," Juice whistles. "You thinking these two were part of a cult or something? Maybe they're guaranteed a one-way ticket to heaven like terrorists or something like that?"

"Don't know," Rafe admits. "But I'm going to have to find the connection between these two cases. Maybe the common denominator is a cult, like you're suggesting."

"They recruit these people and convince them to off themselves?"

"Possibly. Not sure, though, but it's worth considering."

"How come the media hasn't caught on to any of this?" Juice quizzes.

"No drama, no ratings," Kellar shrugs. "We haven't released the religious angle to the media. All they know is that there were homicides in their respective communities, and then—poof! —the killer's dead and the fire's out. Just like that," he adds, snapping his fingers. "There's nothing worth going national with."

Juice appears unconvinced.

"Look, we have two crime scenes at opposite ends of the country committed a month apart. By the time the Moncton events unfolded, the Vancouver news chasers had already reported that the killer's body had been discovered and moved on to the next big story. New Brunswick media outlets probably never even had time to catch wind of the story in the first place."

"So now what?" Juice asks.

"I do my job and re-open these two cases. Meet me at my office first thing tomorrow morning and bring everything you have on your Moncton case."

"I came here to visit with you, Arch, not to get roped into a serial case. I didn't bring anything except the pictures you just looked at on my phone."

"Then have your staff email all of it to me. I need to see everything and look at both cases as a whole now."

"I'll call them right now," Juice says, then nods towards the other side of the changing room. "Hey? You know that guy over there listening in on our conversation?" he asks in a hushed tone.

"No," Rafe replies, annoyed.

"I'll take care of this," Juice suggests. "Hey, Arch," he says loudly. "That dude there looks just like one of us."

"What?" Rafe says, puzzled. "He doesn't look anything like a cop. He's too small," he chuckles, taking his friend's lead.

"Nah, man. Not us as in *cops*," he giggles. "Me and my other Black brothers, man. Check him out. Even through those boxers I can tell the dude's hung like a horse!"

The embarrassed stranger turns his back and hurries into his fresh clothes, tosses his things into his bag and races out of the changing room without glancing over to the pair.

"And that's how it's done!" Juice exclaims, and Kellar laughs.

16

Father Jakub Fischer fidgets inside the reception area as he awaits the commissionaire's return to his post. According to the sign, Commissionaire Leighland will be back in five minutes. The lobby, he must admit, resembles nothing like the scene he pictured in his mind. He supposes that, as with most everything on television, the commotion inside a police department is undoubtedly exaggerated. He runs a hand over his buzzed-cut scalp and adjusts his round, wire-framed spectacles with his finger as he absently paces the length of the lobby.

"Can I help you?" asks the older gentleman through the intercom from behind the square, mesh-reinforced glass.

"Yes," the young priest replies. "I believe that I have important information that could help with an investigation you're conducting," he states with confidence. "A . . . homicide case," he adds with trepidation.

"Well, Father," the man hesitates. "This isn't a normal police station where people come to report a crime."

"Yes, I'm aware of the sensitive nature of this establishment," he replies. "I've done my research, and I am confident this is where I need to be. The RCMP's Behavioural Sciences Branch, correct?" he asks.

The older man nods his affirmation from behind the glass.

"Then I would like to speak with the officer in charge of investigating two homicides. I don't know his name, but I believe he's looking into two related cases from different parts of the country."

"Father, I'm not privy to any case-related information regarding ongoing investigations, but I'd be happy to pass on your information to the investigators," he suggests kindly.

"I'm afraid I must insist on meeting with the investigator in person to explain how all the events are related to one another," Father Jakub returns.

The commissionaire, a fifty-eight-year-old retired Chief Petty Officer who saw action aboard the HMCS Athabaskan during the Gulf War in 1990, stares back at the unyielding priest and admires his dogged determination.

"Okay," he relents. "I can't guarantee anything, but I'll go upstairs and see if anyone might be available to speak with you," he adds with a shrug.

"That's all I ask. Thank you," he replies.

"Please have a seat over there. I'll just be a moment." Commissionaire Leighland says and disappears.

Father Jakub turns to gaze through the large windows and watches the groundskeepers preparing the flower beds lining the walkway from the parking lot rather than take the seat he was offered.

He was initially troubled about what to do, but, after prayerful discernment, his mind had been made. He had to meet with the authorities and, at the very least, tell them what he knows. If they dismiss his information, well, that's on them. At least he will be at peace knowing that he had tried his best.

"Good morning," the plain-clothed police officer says, extending his hand. "I'm Inspector Rafe Kellar. I hear you have some information for us."

Father Jakub hadn't even noticed him approaching.

"Yes, that's correct," the startled priest responds and clasps Kellar's hand warmly. "I'm Father Jakub Fischer from the Archdiocese of Toronto. I'm in town for a few days visiting with a sick friend. Is there someplace private we can speak?"

"Father Fischer, this isn't exactly a coffee shop," he chuckles. "We can talk right here. What's on your mind?"

"Oh. Well . . .okay, then," the priest stammers. "I thought you folks had a boardroom or something of the sort, but here is fine, I suppose," he says wearily, then hushes his tone and leans into Kellar. "The string of murders you're investigating, the ones with the religious tones of the crimes, I believe there's one more that took place before these two. I also believe that there are more to come."

"That information was never made public!" Kellar exclaims, straightening his stance and speculating. Who's to say this guy is actually even a priest? "How would you even know about these homicides?"

"I—" Father starts, but Kellar interjects.

"Unless *you're* the one we're after," the cop alleges with an arched brow. "You come here to confess something to me? Maybe get something off your chest?" he continues. "How about I take you into *my* confessional. We could talk a little more privately in there."

"Are you serious?" Father Jakub fires back in disbelief. "Don't be absurd!" he barks, catching Rafe off guard. "I only learned of all this initially when we saw each other for the first time two days ago."

"I don't go to church," Kellar smirks. "We've never met."

"We didn't formally meet," the priest confides. "I overheard you and your police officer friend conversing about the cases the other day."

Rafe shrugs.

"The other day at the gym. Seems your friend thinks I'm . . ." he shifts uncomfortably. "Well—uhm—that I reminded him of a horse."

17

"Chief Superintendent Kamarre Toure, please meet Father Jakub Fischer," Rafe makes the introductions with a wide grin, "Chief Toure is known as Juice around here."

"You look familiar, Father," Juice says, offering his large hand.

"Of course he does," Kellar cuts in. "But the last time you saw him, he was practically naked."

Juice throws his friend a puzzled glance.

"At the gym," Rafe continues, his smile wider across his face. "This is the guy who was listening in on our conversation at the gym. You know, the guy you said was hung like a horse?"

Juice's jaw drops. "I am so, so sorry, Father," he says, clutching the younger man's hand with a firm but warm grip.

"That's quite alright, Chief Toure."

"Juice," he insists. "Please call me Juice."

"Very well—Juice. And please, don't worry about the gym incident. It's not like I was wearing my collar," he chuckles.

"So, what important information brings you here today, Father?" Kellar cuts to the chase, annoyed with the apparent chumminess developing between his friend and the clergyman.

"What's your religious background?" the priest starts without picking up on Kellar's displeasure.

"How is that even relevant?" he scowls with Juice wondering why the apparent hostility.

"Well—it doesn't, per se. I was just trying to establish how much Church teaching I would have to get into before getting to the relevant parts."

"No disrespect Father, but we don't have time for catechesis class today," Rafe says. "Just bottom-line it for us, please."

"Right, then," the priest concedes. "Would you gentlemen mind just elaborating on the two cases you're currently working on so as to confirm my suspicions then?"

Rafe's hand is up before the priest has a chance to complete his sentence. "Wait a minute," he growls. "A moment ago, you were positive you knew about a *supposed*, yet-to-be-reported homicide somewhere based on the information you have. And now, you want us to fill you in on our two current cases under investigation?"

"Well, it's not as though you spelled everything out for me," Father Jakub reasons. "I only heard bits and pieces and wanted to make sure, that's all."

"Look," Kellar says firmly. "You tell us how you feel these cases fit together, and then we'll take it from there, okay?"

"Very well," the priest yields. "If the crimes were perpetrated in a certain order, then I know I'm on the right track. If not, then I'll apologize for having wasted your time," he says with a shrug.

Kellar doesn't say a word, but Juice urges the priest to go on.

"Of your two cases, I suspect that the first event to take place was the one with the drowning victims, and I believe this represents the Great Flood—the story of Noah."

"That one we were able to figure out on our own," Rafe mumbles audibly.

"Come on, Arch," Juice advises softly. "Give him a chance, man. It took a lot of guts for him to come down here and meet with us after the way we treated him the other day."

"*We?*" Kellar responds with a smirk.

Juice ignores the shot. "Please go on, Father," he cordially encourages the priest, who nods and continues.

"The first case, the one with the water, seems to be an attempt at depicting God's *second* covenant with humanity," Father Fischer explains with the air of a professor. "The second case seems to point to circumcision and God's *third* covenant."

"So, if these are the second and third," Kellar picks up, "That means there is a first one somewhere we haven't heard about yet," he says, reluctantly filling in the blanks.

"That's what I fear," the priest sighs. "Although these crimes would suggest your perpetrator is familiar with covenant theology, the similarity between the crimes and Sacred Scripture ends there. He is basically mocking the Church."

Kellar lets out a sigh but doesn't believe it necessary to let him know the actual suspects are both dead. However, his suspicion that a malevolent entity of a sort is orchestrating this entire string of murders is now confirmed.

"So, if we're looking at two and three with a first one somewhere else," Juice probes, "how many more of these *covenants* are we talking about?"

"There are seven," Father Jakub announces.

"Seven?" Kellar gasps.

The priest nods and expounds, "Scripturally speaking, six have taken place with the seventh coming to fulfillment with Christ's Second Coming on the last day."

"Alright, then," Rafe says, taking out his notepad and pen. "What's the first one all about so we know what we're looking for?"

"God has established these covenants with humanity throughout Salvation History," the priest begins. "Each covenant has a mediator, a role, a form, and a sign."

"Father Fischer," Rafe interrupts. "Please simplify it for us here. We aren't in one of your theology seminars."

Father Jakub takes a breath.

"God sought to broaden the reach of his relationship with humanity with each covenant."

"Enough with the word *covenant*, already!" Rafe fumes.

"Arch," Juice intervenes delicately. "Let me see if I understand, Father," he says, turning to the priest. "A covenant. That's basically just a fancy word for a contract, right?"

"It's more than a contract," Father Jakub clarifies. "A contract is just a temporary agreement for the mutual benefit of all the parties involved. I do this, and you agree to give me that in return, and that's where the contract ends. A covenant, on the other hand, unites otherwise unrelated people into a familial bond meant to last forever."

"So, who's the mediator?" Rafe picks up. "The guy brokering the deal?"

"Yes, that's correct," the priest affirms with a smile. "The first covenant was with Adam as the mediator, and the role—Adam's job—was that of the husband. The form, that's to say what God established with this new kinship between himself and us, was the marriage between a man and a woman."

"Ah, yes! And there it is!" Kellar stands in a huff. "I knew you'd find a way to bring your poison into the conversation."

"I beg your pardon?" Father Jakub says, dumbfounded.

"You and your church are such homophobes!" he rants.

Juice finally understands where all this animosity is coming from.

"What is up with this war on love you guys are waging, anyways?" he asks. "What is so wrong with two people loving each other, no matter the gender?" Then, jabbing his finger in the priest's direction, Kellar continues the verbal assault. "Why you hate homosexuals and why you teach others to hate them too is beyond all comprehension!"

"Arch," Juice says, placing a soft hand on Rafe's shoulder.

Kellar recoils. "You stay out of this!"

"Inspector! Let's be clear here!" Father Jakub fires back with the same tone. "You know absolutely nothing about me!"

"Oh, I think I know enough, you homophobic hypocrite."

"I am not a hypocrite, nor do I hate homosexuals!" the priest states emphatically, then sighs deeply. "How did this even become a debate about this?"

"Because that's what's wrong with the world today. People forcing their religious hatred onto others, and then once in a while, some idiot kicks it up to a whole other level of insane by killing innocent people who don't fit neatly into a tidy little box!"

Father Jakub takes a breath and ponders his next words wisely. "A moment ago," he says calmly, "You said we were waging war on love. What is *your* definition of love, Inspector?"

"What?" Kellar says.

"Love, Inspector Kellar. What do you understand love to be?" Father Jakub asks again, but Rafe doesn't answer.

"By love, do you mean unconditional, life-giving, and self-sacrificing love?" he inquires. "Giving one's very life for the sake of another? If so, then the Catholic Church is *all* about love. If your definition resembles that of the world's where love is boiled down to mere sexual pleasures—homosexual *or* heterosexual—then *no*, that's not what we preach. Fundamentally speaking, love and sex are *not* synonymous."

"You can't have one without the other," Rafe challenges.

"I beg to differ," the young priest persists. "Rape is not an act of love."

"That's not sex!" Rafe objects. "That's about power and control."

"Yes, I'll grant you that, but it's still referred to as *sexual* assault," Father Jakub says firmly. "I'll give you another example. In your line of work, I'm sure you've encountered prostitution. How many of those men and women have sex with their clients out of love?"

"Okay, I think you've said enough. This meeting's over!" Kellar decides, stands and marches to the door. "We'll take it from here," he says, showing the priest the way out.

"But we're not finished discussing your case," Father Jakub protests.

"We're not, but *you* are," Kellar shuts him down. "Marty, please see Father Fischer out," he demands from the first of his colleagues to pass by the door.

"You sure it was such a good idea to talk to a priest that way?" Juice asks, alone in the room with his friend.

"What do you care? You're not even Catholic!"

"Just saying is all," Juice shrugs.

Rafe's eyes bore into Juice's. "I wasn't about to let him disrespect the memory of my son for a millisecond longer!"

18

Mississauga, Ontario

Seated behind the immaculately tidy desk behind the closed door, the Prophet peruses the extensive electronic file he has compiled of the hundreds of thousands of people he's been keeping tabs on over the last eight months. He knows their names, where they live and what they eat. He has their banking information, health history and even knows how often they have sex, where and with whom. Nothing is out of his virtual reach. Oblivious to the business outside his office, he searches for the next unwitting participants in his nefarious production.

His finger grazes over the scar on his cheek, and he fumes. Reaching inside the top drawer, he clasps the small compact mirror and examining his face. He exhales, thankful now the scab that stupid bitch had left in his cheek is barely recognizable. Snapping it shut, he slips the mirror back into the drawer and carries on with his critically important work.

Scanning through the list of possible candidates vaguely, he dismisses them all, knowing exactly who he wants to use for this next phase. It's almost too perfect. He needs a judge for this one anyway. Who better than that one?

His mind and heart have been at odds all morning; the first, logically evaluating the myriad of reasons why staying away from anyone remotely connected to his past would be advisable; the latter, hungry for the vengeance he had never been permitted to exact.

The Honourable Judge Philip Saunders, retired Justice of the Supreme Court of Canada, is anything but honorable. Thirty-three years ago, at the time, a presiding judge with the Ontario Court of Justice, the man had ordered the murderous ten-year-old out of the orphanage and into a hell-hole for boys, where the entire course of his life was altered forever. One reformatory guard was never better than the previous and the abuse—mental, physical *and* sexual—he experienced worsened as time progressed. After serving his brutal sentence, his spiralling life was discarded into an imperfect foster system.

To this day, despite the ensuing torture he had endured, the Prophet still believes he had delivered a fitting sentence to Tommy Strickland. That little bastard had gotten exactly what he deserved for violating Sister Mary Joseph and expecting to get away with it. You don't peek into a nun's private quarters through an old keyhole in the hopes of catching her naked. Reflecting on the events, he regrets not having done a better job of disposing of the other orphan's body. No one would have even discovered the body in the burned-down barn if it hadn't been for Father Léopold and his stupid water brigade. But he was young and inexperienced at the time. He has most assuredly perfected his craft since. The memory of his subsequent crimes brings a smile to his face, but it quickly evaporates with the thought of Sister Mary Joseph returning.

She had the face of an angel and the only woman to ever make him feel loved. He fondly remembers her mild manner and how she always told him he would make a good priest someday. To no avail, the sweet sister had tried to reason with Mother Superior, but that incident had been the final straw in a series of unacceptable behaviors from the seed of the devil himself. He had heard the argument. The other nuns had all wanted him gone, so the ten-year-old boy had been taken away by the police and placed in front of the judge like the deviant he was.

A tear streaks his cheek as Sister Mary Joseph's passing resurfaces. He wipes away the tear and shakes the memory, focusing on the bittersweet hell he survived after being taken away from the orphanage and growing angrier as the photo of the judge on his screen comes back into focus.

Heart one! Mind zero!

"The Dis-honourable Judge Philip Saunders," he giggles. "Come on down. You're the next contestant on 'You're About to Die!'"

With his next victim selected, the Prophet turns his attention to a secondary list, the one from which will be chosen the unfortunate soul responsible for doing his bidding.

"Tom?" he hears her shrill voice as the short redhead with the wide hips raps against his door and barges in without the courtesy of waiting for permission.

"Sue," he says bitterly, restraining the urge to punch her in the face. "I told you I'd be there in five minutes."

"That was an hour and a half ago, Tom. You need a new watch?" she asks sarcastically.

He glances at his wrist and lets out a breath, smiles and taps his chest with a closed fist in mock sincerity. "Mea culpa," he says with false humility. "I was so engrossed in my work, I completely lost track of time."

"Look. I don't care if you stay locked in your windowless room in the basement all day. Heaven only knows why you'd want to use this dungeon as an office anyway. I thought IT Directors were upper management. You're the only brass I ever heard of who doesn't want a corner office with a view and your own private washroom."

"Is this why you barged in here, Sue? To criticize my choice of office again?"

"Ha, you'd like that, wouldn't you?" she says. "No, this time, I'm here to complain about the tracking software you built for us. It's on the fritz again," she says, waving her finger for him to follow her. "We have clients looking to track their shipments, you know, and now they can't. I want you to take a look at it on my computer."

"Right behind you," he affirms, trailing behind her up the stairs and through the maze of partitioned cubicles.

"You know, I don't like to have to get angry with the brass," she says almost apologetically. "But I have a job to do and clients to keep happy. And if they're not happy, I'm not happy, and neither should you be."

He obediently follows her into her office, drowning out most of her dribbling until her question piques his ears.

"You think they'll ever find Mr. Donovan?"

"What?" he replies, genuinely surprised. "Where's that coming from?"

"Well, you know I'm in charge of the birthday committee, and I know his is coming up next week."

"I'm sure he'll turn up," he lies.

"I mean, how does a person just disappear without telling anyone beforehand? Who does that?"

"Some people just need their space."

"Yeah, but they usually show up again at some point. It's been over eight months now. You think maybe he was kidnapped?" she asks with a concerned look.

"Couldn't tell you, Sue," he sighs. "That was before my time. Why are you bringing this up with me anyway?"

"It's a good thing that *was* before your time," she submits. "I don't think you're the kind of person Mr. Donovan would have hired in the first place. You lucked out, I guess."

"I suppose I did, Sue. Other than the tracking software, is there anything else troubling you today?" he asks with an edge.

"You know, the level of complacency has increased since he's been gone," she hints casually, with her finger nudging the air in his general direction. "It's hard to be competent at your job when you have to depend on others to do theirs, and they don't."

"I can take it from here, Sue," he says annoyingly. "Just grab a coffee or something while I take a look."

"I'll do that," she says, spinning on her heels, then makes her way to the breakroom, leaving him to imagine how delightful it would be to dismember the fat cow.

19

Ottawa, Ontario

"Dammit!" Kellar curses, unsure whether discovering another set of homicides or that the priest was correct is what's actually bothering him the most.

After coming up empty with similar cases anywhere in the country over the past two days, Rafe had decided to expand the search criteria to include the FBI's Violent Criminal Apprehension Program, ViCAP for short, and got somewhat of a hit.

"Same MO," he mumbles. "Two male victims, both staged into position. Just about a month before the Vancouver case." Clicking the mouse with speed, he opens another file and finds evidence confirming his hunch. "Okay, and here's the ambiguous file on the suspect now. Looks like a slam dunk, just like the other ones."

After reviewing what little was available from both ViCAP files for nearly twenty minutes, Kellar picks up the phone and dials the FBI.

Working his way through the endless string of pre-recorded voice prompts, he finally reaches someone with a pulse and a voice identifying herself as Agent Martinez in greeting.

"Hello, Agent Martinez," he replies. "This is Inspector Rafe Kellar with the Behavioural Sciences Branch of the RCMP in Ottawa. I'm calling in the hope that you're able to shed some light about a set of homicides that happened in your neck of the woods earlier this year in February."

"Is this an active investigation?"

"No, I believe you people closed it."

"What's the case number?"

"763-SA-1259," he reads from the screen.

"Alright, let me bring it up."

Kellar tosses his reading glasses onto his cluttered desk and leans back in his chair.

"Yes, it's closed alright," Agent Martinez confirms.

"Yes, I know," Kellar grumbles, then eases his tone. "Look, can you confirm that the suspect is deceased."

"That appears to be the case," she affirms.

"Did he leave some strange writings on the wall?"

"I'm sorry, I'm afraid I don't have that information available. And as I've stated, this case is closed."

"Yes, so we've already established, but here's the thing," Kellar says. "Although your suspect is dead and you guys have all moved on, I believe there's something bigger at play here. We may have some sort of homicidal cult operating between our borders."

"What do you mean?"

"We've had two events take place here in Canada in as many months that follow the same pattern as your investigation in San Antonio: equally disturbing homicides, followed by the discovery of our suspects found dead in some strangely unrelated or unfortunate circumstance. I don't like coincidences."

"I see. Send us your files, and we'll take a look at 'em."

"Are you kidding? I'm calling *you* for information that you're holding onto like a dog with a bone, and now you want everything *we* have?"

"If it's being re-opened, it's our case."

"You've had your chance. Whatever is going on is now actively happening up here in Canada, and since neither of *my* two cases is closed," he stretches the truth, "I believe that gives *me* the lead. Now, I'm happy to share everything we have and let you guys investigate on your end, but again, this is my case, and it's critical that I get my hands on everything you have in order to wrap my head around this thing and stop it before someone else dies."

"Very well. I'll have Agent Pat Nickerson, who opened the file, get in touch with you in the next couple of days."

"I want a face-to-face!" Kellar insists.

"When?"

"I'm on the first plane down there tomorrow morning."

"That won't work for us. I believe Agent Nickerson might be out of town tomorrow," she says unconvincingly.

"Then I'll park myself at his desk until he's back in town."

"Fine," Agent Martinez replies. "But you might just be wasting your time."

"I'll take that gamble," he says and cradles the phone without giving Agent Martinez another chance to object.

Kellar stands and fidgets around the small area of his cubicle, then sits again and stares at the phone with contempt. Not happy with what he knows comes next, and diverging from his character, he delays the inevitable by rationalizing he operates more efficiently when caffeinated, so rises to grab a cup from the breakroom but doesn't get far. His professional impulse gets the better of him and he knows that, as unpleasant as it's going to be, it's unavoidable. With a deep sigh, he slowly seats himself at his desk and curses under his breath as he picks up the phone, dialling while he looks up the number from the sign-in sheet.

"Good afternoon, Saint Faustina Parish," the woman says courteously in greeting.

"Yes, hi," Kellar replies. "I'm looking for a Father Jakub Fischer, please. Is he in?"

"Yes, he is. Who may I say is calling?"

"Who's calling isn't important," he says gruffly.

"Very well," the receptionist harrumphs.

"Father Jakub Fischer here," the priest announces a moment later. "How may I help you?"

"This is Inspector Rafe Kellar," he states officially.

"Inspector Kellar," Father Jakub scolds. "You can be rude to me all you want. For what reason, though? I ignore it all as I've never done anything to deserve your wrath," Father says. "But to be rude to our receptionist, Paulina, is completely unacceptable."

Kellar silently considers this for a moment and recognizes that he's allowed his personal feelings to interfere with his work.

"You're right," he admits. "I've been very unprofessional with you and your receptionist, and for that, I sincerely apologize."

Taken aback, Father Fischer hesitates, "Well then—apology accepted, Inspector Kellar."

"Look, the reason for my call is that I do need your help after all."

"With what?"

"You were right," Rafe exhales dramatically. "There *was* another murder."

"I'm very sorry to hear that, Inspector," the priest replies somberly. "I'll keep the victims and their families in my prayers."

"Yeah, well, I'm afraid that I'm going to need more than just your prayers," he sighs. "I don't have anywhere else to turn to for help in making any sort of sense of this, so you're hired."

"Hired?" Father Jakub gasps. "To do what?"

"Consult on the case," Kellar replies matter-of-factly.

"Surely you can't be serious, Inspector."

"I'm very serious."

"I'm the pastor of a church, not a trained investigator," the priest debates.

"You don't need to be. I just need you to interpret the evidence. I'll be the one doing the investigating, not you. You won't be in any danger."

"I don't know," the priest hesitates.

"Please, Father."

Kellar takes the silence on the other end as a positive sign, so persists. "Look, Father Fischer. We've only met once, but I'm sure you already know me well enough to know that I wouldn't ask if I didn't think you could help me."

Father Jakub sighs. "Very well, I'll help in any way that I can," he finally agrees after a moment. "What do you need me to do?"

"I need you here in Ottawa to review the case files and point me in the right direction. I'll look after the rest."

"Could I not look at everything from here?"

"It's a little more complicated than that," Kellar admits, calling to mind the phone call he had just placed to the FBI.

"How long would I be needed in Ottawa?"

"As long as it takes."

"Inspector," the priest begins.

"Please, call me Rafe," Kellar interjects.

"Rafe," Father Jakub starts again, uneasy with the sudden departure from formality. "I have a full-time vocation running this parish here in Toronto. I can't just leave it behind to play detective."

"Father Fischer. People are dying," Kellar says glumly.

The priest sighs. "I will have to clear it with the Cardinal's office first," he finally agrees. "If he says no, then I'm afraid you'll have to find some other consultant."

"We don't have time," Rafe stresses.

There's another long pause as Father Jakub contemplates the urgency. "Well, I suppose we could use one of the visiting priests to cover for me for a little bit."

"Thanks for agreeing."

"When do we start?"

"Tomorrow morning. Is your passport up-to-date?"

"Passport? Yes, of course, but since when is a passport required to travel to Ottawa?"

"Well, I'm afraid we're going to have to make a small detour on our way to Ottawa," Kellar says casually. "The first set of homicides happened in San Antonio, Texas, and we have an appointment to meet with the FBI to review their case files. I'll meet you at Pearson's Terminal 1 for a 10:40 departure. I'll email you your boarding pass in the next couple of minutes."

20

Kingston, Ontario

The instructions may very well be self-explanatory, but he'll undoubtedly have to ask a lot of questions. The money has already been deposited into his account; he just checked for the third time in less than two minutes. Should he do it? How could he not? This is Percy's only chance, and Percy means so much to Clayton. He hopes he's still okay.

Percy had come into his life the very day his wife had left him. It's as though the stray dog had intuitively sought him out to offer its playful companionship in Clayton's time of grief. And now, after missing him for two entire days and being completely beside himself, Clayton's fortune had finally taken a turn for the better when the encrypted message's link had come in from his private chat group just moments ago.

Standing at six foot five and tipping the scale at over two hundred and forty pounds, Clayton Bannister should have had a long and illustrious career in professional hockey if he could have only managed his anger and kept his head in the game. He casts a large shadow, but his wake is all the more unsettling whenever the paranoid schizophrenic discontinues his neuroleptic drug. And his condition has only worsened since his estranged wife decided she could no longer take the mood swings.

The cursor blinks a steady rhythm on his monitor as Prophet6-23 awaits his reply.

Who could this person reaching out to him about Percy be? Can Prophet6-23 be trusted? Clayton has had severe trust issues all his life, even more so with strangers.

"Is that you, you punk-ass little thief?" he roars at his screen as though his next-door neighbor's kid is there with him.

Every single time Clayton has whole wheat bread in the house, he just knows the kid comes rummaging through his personal belongings when he's not at home; that's why he's gone without it for the last three months. Could the kid have done this to him? Did he take Percy away from him because he stopped buying whole wheat bread? His anger rises at the thought.

"Do you agree with the terms or not?" the words materialize on the screen and bring Clayton back to here and now.

"Is that you, Curtis?" he types back. "If you hurt Percy, I'll kill you!"

"This is not Curtis," the stranger types in response. "But I told you how to find your dog and that he's okay."

Clayton calms with the reassuring words.

"I need to know if you're in," the inquiry comes back.

"Why do I have to kill him?" Clayton asks.

"Because he stole something from me a long time ago."

"Then you kill him."

"I would love to, but I can't. If you do it, I'll have an alibi. The police will never be able to connect it back to me should they start sniffing around. Plus, I already deposited thirty thousand dollars into your bank account, *and* I told you I would reunite you with your dog."

Clayton takes a moment to reconsiders the deal before submitting his reply. He's desperate to find Percy, but isn't entirely satisfied with the terms.

"I don't want any money," he writes. "I just want Percy back and one more thing."

The cursor blinks for several seconds before the writer finally responds.

"What's the other thing?"

Clayton grins and nods as he taps the words with his keyboard.

"When this is done, you have to take care of the neighbor's kid for me so that I have an alibi too."

"Deal!"

21

Flight 8109

"I just want to say thanks again for agreeing to do this," Kellar says. "I wouldn't have blamed you for turning me down after the way I treated you last week at my office. You came in to help us and I let my personal feelings cloud my judgement. I'm sorry about that."

Father Jakub turns to him with a warm smile. "Yes, I suppose we both got off on the wrong foot. I also apologise for my outburst, Rafe," Father Jakub says with sincerity.

Kellar reflects on the man's words for a moment. "I guess we both have strong opinions and things got a little heated," he admits. "Let's just agree to disagree on certain topics and not revisit that one in particular ever again, shall we?"

The priest smiles his acknowledgement with a nod as the aircraft reaches its cruising altitude.

"I'm surprised that you people fly commercial," Father Jakub states his opinion after a few moments of silence.

"What do you mean?" Rafe asks, setting his laptop on the tray-table.

"Well, I would have expected the RCMP to have its own fleet of airplanes."

Kellar laughs. "You think we're like the guys on TV?" he chuckles. "We have our own shiny Gulfstream like they do on 'Criminal Minds?'"

Father Jakub frowns. "I've watched a couple of episodes of that show. Not my favorite. Much too violent for my taste, I'm afraid," he admits rolling up the sleeves of his clerical shirt. "I'm just surprised, that's all."

"Didn't take you for the TV-watching type," Kellar says.

"There are a lot of things you *think* you know about me, Rafe," the priest emphasizes.

"Whatever you say, Father."

"Please, call me Jakub," he says. "When it's just the two of us, there's no need to be so formal," he clarifies.

"Okay, then," Kellar nods, reaching for his briefcase and pulling out the case files. "If you think television is too violent, you're not going to like what I have to show you one bit, Jakub. These were taken in Vancouver," he adds, laying the file on the tray-table before the priest. "Just keep them out of sight of anyone who comes this way to use the washroom."

Father Jakub examines his surroundings nervously. Although the two of them share the last row of the small aircraft with the lavatory to their right, he's still somewhat uncomfortable reviewing such sensitive material in public.

"Are you sure it's good for us to discuss these cases here on the plane?" he worries. "Couldn't this wait until we get to the FBI Field Office?"

"I need your head in this case as soon as we get there so you can keep up with me. Look," he says with a wave. "We're practically the only ones on board. The closest passenger is seven rows up. If someone comes down to use the john, I'll let you know."

Father Jakub lifts the cover sheet with reservations. He gasps at the violence staring back at him and immediately reaches for the vomit bag in the seat pocket in front of him and makes full use of it.

"Yeah, they're a bit graphic," Rafe admits, handing the priest a facial tissue from his briefcase and waving off the worried flight attendant. He waits patiently and observes Father Jakub mentally working up the courage to re-open the file.

"If you're going to be of any help to me, I really need you to look at them," Kellar urges.

The priest glances throughout the cabin once more and takes a calming breath, then cracks open the file again. He cringes as he takes in the Vancouver crime scene photos one by one.

"You want another bag?" Kellar grins.

Father smiles weakly and shakes his head.

"These are the ones from Moncton," Kellar says after a few minutes, laying another file on the small table.

Father Jakub shoots Rafe a bewildered look as he closes the first and opens the second one.

"What do you see?" Kellar asks once the priest reaches the last photo.

Father Jakub concludes the viewing and stacks the files neatly on the tray table. Then, slipping off his glasses with one hand, he rubs his eyes with the other. Retuning his glasses to the bridge of his nose, he gently lays both hands on the stack of files and bows his head. His lips part as he offers a silent prayer for the victims and their families.

"Were these crimes perpetrated by the same individual?" he finally asks.

"No. In both cases, the suspects were found dead elsewhere not long after the murders," Kellar explains. "Cause of death appears to be suicide in one case and a motor vehicle accident in the other."

Father Jakub studies Rafe's intense expression. "And in San Antonio?" he ventures.

"Not sure yet," Kellar admits. "That's why we're going down there. We need to learn as much as we can about this whole thing. So far, all we know for sure about our cases here at home is that both suspects had histories of mental illness. Prime targets for cult recruiters."

"Is that what this is?" the priest asks. "A cult?"

"That's the working theory for now. Our cybercrimes division is combing through their online history to see if there's any connection with cults operating across our borders."

"You seem a bit skeptical," Father Jakub observes.

"Even though the cult angle is the only thing that appears to make any sense, for now, that's not how these people usually operate," Kellar explains. "Cults with violent tendencies are typically smaller groups and operate locally. Traditionally, they don't enjoy attracting a lot of attention their way. There are satanic cults all over the place, but they're not usually connected to each other, as this particular case seems to suggest."

Father Jakub nods his understanding.

"What do you make of the writing on the walls?" Rafe shifts the conversation. "Anything like that in the Bible?"

"The only writing on the wall in the Bible is in the Book of Daniel. The writing is a warning regarding the evil king's demise," he answers.

"Did the king die?" Kellar asks.

"Slain that very night," he confirms.

"Okay, so we know whoever's writing these warnings means business," Kellar says. "The warning isn't for the victims, though, because they're already dead. A warning for whoever finds them, or everyone in general?" he ponders. "What about the wording? The wording match anything in the Bible?"

"A few scattered words, of course, but the messages themselves have no scriptural significance."

"What about the Roman numerals, VI:XXIII?"

"Well, at first glance, nothing concrete comes to mind," Father Jakub sighs. "Two of the later popes of the last century were John the Twenty Third and Paul the Sixth, but that hardly seems to be what this would suggest. The numbers are reversed. It doesn't make sense."

"It's not the only thing that doesn't make sense," Rafe exhales. "What about the timing?"

"What about it?"

"These events took place pretty much a month apart," Kellar says. "San Antonio in February, Vancouver in March and Moncton in April. Are these covenants you keep referring to each a month apart?"

"No, I'm afraid not. Centuries and millennia,"

"So, they're making up their own timeline, and if they hold true to their cause, they're only going to be finished in August if we don't stop them first."

"July, perhaps," Father Jakub suggests. "If they're re-enacting the covenants, again, scripturally and historically speaking, the seventh one, the *fulfillment* of the last and eternal covenant, hasn't taken place yet."

"Okay, so depending on their level of delirium, July or August, then," Kellar agrees.

The flight attendant draws closer to their row with her snacks and beverage cart and offers them refreshments with a warm smile, which they politely decline.

"Wanna know what pisses me off the most?" Rafe picks up once the attendant has returned to the front of the cabin. "Is that we're no closer to putting an end to this, whatever *this* is. We're coming up empty with cult research."

They sit in silence for a while as the plane continues its flight, Rafe reviewing his notes, Father Jakub studying the photos.

Father suddenly elbows Kellar in the ribs. "I think I have it," he announces enthusiastically and clutches the Bible from his own briefcase under the seat in front of him, then thumbs through the pages of the New Testament excitedly. "I believe the numbers indicate the chapter and verse and that the Roman numerals could refer to St Paul's letter to the *Romans*," he shows his seatmate, pointing to the verse. "Romans, chapter six, verse twenty-three reads: For the wages of sin is death."

The cop and priest share a glance.

"So, what, these people know everyone's dirty little secrets and sentence our victims to death like some kind of morality enforcement squad?"

"This cult is very frightening!" Father admits soberly.

22

FBI Field Office - San Antonio, Texas

"Where the hell is this guy?" Rafe curses impatiently as he and Father Jakub sit in the spacious, modernly appointed conference room waiting on Agent Pat Nickerson for over an hour. "I bet he's making us wait out of spite."

"Inspector Rafe Kellar?" the tall, athletic blond woman asks, her FBI credentials dangling between her blazer's open lapels. "I hear you're waiting for Agent Pat Nickerson."

"Well, it's about time!" Kellar barks. "Where is he?"

"Sorry about the wait. Didn't mean to take that long in the little girl's room," she says with a grin as she extends a firm hand to Kellar. "Agent Patricia Nickerson."

Father Jakub giggles, and Rafe glares at him before shaking her hand awkwardly.

"I bet you were expecting a man, weren't you?" she grins. "That trick never gets old."

Rafe stands motionless as she grabs a chair at the head of the table.

"What?" she says in his direction. "You don't play well with girls, Inspector Rafe Kellar?"

"No." he squirms. "There's nothing wrong with female agents," he blushes. "It's just that this was such a last-minute trip, I—I didn't have time to properly research you," he reasons weakly.

"Okay," she smirks. "You know, I've never worked with a Canadian Mountie before. I'm kinda looking forward to the experience. Come on over and take a load off," she points to the chair next to hers. "Who's your priest friend here?"

"Uhm, this is Father Jakub," he replies, regaining his composure. "He's consulting on the case," he says, seating himself and inviting Father Jakub to do the same with a nod of the head.

"Nice to meet you," she smiles with a friendly wave. "Welcome to San Antonio, y'all," she adds with a playful southern drawl. "So, let's get down to business. How can the FBI be of assistance to Canada?"

"As you know, we're here about the double homicide from February that you folks closed with the apparent suicide of the suspect. As I've stated, we've caught two similar cases in our country and believe they're all related. Can you walk us through your crime scenes?" Rafe takes the lead. "Starting with the homicides and then the suspect's suicide."

"Alright, but you'll have to tell me all about your cases after, *eh?*" she pokes at her Canadian visitors. "You know, I show you mine, you show me yours?" she winks with a seductive grin.

Kellar smiles uncomfortably, his complexion reddening slightly again. "Of course."

"Well, okay, then," she continues with a northeastern accent not usual for parts this deep in the south. "Two male victims were discovered in one of our victim's house. Their naked bodies were found taped together, face-to-face on the bed of the master bedroom. Both victims were shot in the head with a small calibre weapon. The evidence showed they were executed right where they were found," She shifts uncomfortably. "This is where it gets a little dicey," she takes on a more serious tone. "Each victim had half of an apple jammed into his mouth. All things considered, that's the weirdest it got for the homeowner, but the same can't be said about his companion. His face was smeared with a thick, unflattering coat of makeup, and a discount store wig had been shoved on his head. He looked like a cheap hooker after a rough night."

"So, your suspect basically turned your second victim into a woman," Kellar says.

"Oh, no, Inspector Kellar. I'm afraid things got a whole lot darker for this man. He wasn't simply made to *look* like a woman. He quite literally was *transformed* into one. And not just with the wig and crappy makeup job, either. She emasculated him!" she shudders. "The victim's genitals were surgically removed and were *missing* from the scene," she says with air quotes for the added emphasis.

"Missing?" Kellar asks, leaning in.

"I'll get back to that one in a moment when we're done with this first scene if that's okay."

"Sure," Kellar concedes and shares a glum look with Father Jakub, then turns his gaze back to her. "Anything bizarre written on the wall?"

"You don't miss much, do ya?" she says.

Kellar shakes his head.

"Here's a shot of what we found there," the agent corroborates by sliding a photo between her guests.

Although they know what to expect, the images visibly shock Father Jakub. Kellar notices him wince, but try to hide it.

"His covenant was made between a man and a woman to fill the earth with life. With this sacrifice, the Prophet restores the covenant," Kellar reads aloud. "Same Roman numerals," he confirms in Father Jakub's direction.

They quietly examine the photos for several moments until Kellar breaks the silence.

"You said the victim's genitals were missing. Let's get back to that," he says, lifting his eyes to her.

"Well, for that, we now have to go to our suspect's suicide," Agent Nickerson announces, opening another file. "This whole thing started out as a hate-crime investigation. That's why the FBI was initially called in," she explains. "But when the body of the woman was discovered with a note confessing to the murders, we ruled out hate crime and established it a crime of passion. Turns out our killer was the homeowner's wife."

"They're *all* hate crimes," Father Jakub laments woefully. "Hatred is hatred, and that's all I've seen in any of the photos the two of you have shown me thus far."

Agent Nickerson gives him a moment, then continues. "Evidence on the woman's laptop suggests she was tipped about the illicit affair and that the pair of lovers would be home at that time. She shot them both to incapacitate them and then went psycho on them. When she was done there, she went over to her husband's male companion's apartment, where she got into the tub wearing her wedding dress and slit her wrists. Oh, and incidentally, that's where we found the missing genitals. She was holding them in her hands like a bouquet of flowers."

Father Jakub closes his eyes and massages his temples.

"Okay, a lot of questions going through my head right now," Kellar acknowledges. "You described the victim's genitals as being surgically removed. You just mean the woman cut them off, right?"

"Nope. Surgically as with a scalpel and a lot of skills."

"Then she would have needed—"

"A medical degree?" Nickerson interjects.

"Yeah," Kellar nods.

"She was a heart surgeon," the agent informs them. "Had lots of experience slicing and dicing. She was sued three years ago in a malpractice suit and went off the rails. Got addicted to the pain meds she'd write her own scripts for, et cetera, et cetera."

A lull settles inside the room again as her new colleagues digest the gruesome nature of the crime scenes until Agent Nickerson cuts the thickening silence with an attempt at lightening the mood.

"How about I grab us all some coffee, and you guys can fill me in on your cases now? Cops in Canada eat donuts, *eh?*" she teases. "I think we ran out of the maple ones, though. I hope that's okay," she snickers and takes leave of the Mountie and the priest.

XXIII

Gananoque, Ontario

A light breeze whispers through the bourgeoning trees that line the streets of the mostly-deserted little tourist destination. The throngs of visitors eager to navigate their way through the Thousand Islands that straddle the Canada/US border along the Saint Lawrence River are still a few months away, with restaurants and inns along the waterfront in full preparation-mode as each anticipates another lucrative summer.

Clayton Bannister parks his old Chevette along Stone Street, a block and a half down from St Paul's Catholic Church as specifically instructed, and walks past the scattering of parishioners making their way home for dinner after the Saturday evening Vigil Mass. He enters the old church and is immediately struck by its oddly serene welcome. He dips his finger in the font of holy water and awkwardly crosses himself as he had observed people do on television, then takes a seat in the second pew from the back—as instructed.

Unsure of what to do next, Clayton admires the intricate design of the wooden ceiling, the ornate stain-glass windows at the back of the sanctuary and the marble-like columns running the length of the church.

"Don't turn around, or you'll never see your dog again," the voice warns from behind.

He complies.

"You're right on time."

"I know," Clayton replies, anxious to turn and see just who he's dealing with.

"Here's what's going to happen," the stranger briefs. "When I'm finished talking, you're going to keep staring at the front of the church," the man's voice insists. "You'll count to fifty, and then you'll get up, leave the church and walk down to the marina on Bay Road. The gate's access code is 7359, got that?" he asks, and Clayton nods.

"Repeat it to make sure you remember these instructions."

"Wait here till you're gone, then walk to the marina. The number to get in is 7359. Then what?" Clayton demands.

The stranger chuckles. "Good. Then you're going to make your way to slip seventy-three, where you'll find a twenty-foot Tahoe 500 TF. Here's the key," the small metal object lands noisily on the wooden pew. "The rest of the instructions are inside the helm storage compartment. Don't let me down."

"I won't," Clayton assures him.

"Good. God bless you, my son," the sinister voice snickers.

"Where's Percy?" Clayton asks as the stranger rises to leave.

The man places a hand on Clayton's large shoulder. "Your dog isn't important right now. You have work to do."

"But you said—" Clayton starts.

"What I said is that I'd reunite you with your dog once your end of our deal was completed," he interrupts with a warning. "If you screw this up, you'll never see it again."

"I won't screw it up," the large man promises.

"Good. Now start counting."

"One, two, three," Clayton begins in a loud whisper as the Prophet slithers away.

24

San Antonio, Texas

"Look," Rafe sighs. "We've been at this for the better part of three hours, and we're still no closer to understanding the motives behind all these homicides. As unrelated as all our victims appear to be on the surface, they still have to have shared a connection of some sort," Kellar insists as he, Father Jakub and Agent Nickerson review the case files scattered across the conference table.

"If this criminal organization stretches across international borders, maybe the locations of the crimes isn't what's important, but rather, the situations the victims find themselves in that fit the overall objective as Father Jakub and I were discussing on the flight over. I think the key to understanding why these people—both victims and suspects—were selected, is in the victimology," Kellar turns to the priest. "Father Jakub, starting with the San Antonio victims, in your opinion, what did these people do that landed them on someone's twisted Biblical radar?"

"Well, the Bible tells us that God created man and gave him the woman as his partner," Father begins. "The second chapter of the Book of Genesis is where we find a more detailed account of creation. After spending the sixth day naming all the animals, Adam concluded and complained to God that he had yet to find a suitable mate of his own. So when Adam was asleep, God took a rib from his side, and from it, we're told, fashioned Eve."

"Sounds like a fairy tale to me," Agent Nickerson snickers, to Kellar's annoyance.

"Agent Nickerson, that's a very ignorant statement," the priest gently rebukes. "The Bible is a library, not a single book. Within its pages, you'll find a collection of written works, authored at different times and by various people who, although inspired by the Holy Spirit, maintained the autonomy to use their own literary styles in transcribing the message God wanted them to convey— namely, his plan for our salvation. There are lots of literary forms contained in the Bible. We find poetry, we find detailed historical accounts, we find symbolic visions, and we find recorded facts, just to name a few. Some were written in simple language, while others are more philosophical or prophetic."

"Okay, but even *you* have to admit that taking a rib from Adam and turning it into Eve is more than just a bit of a stretch."

"We're not here to debate this!" Kellar grumbles. "Let's stay focused!"

Nickerson raises a hand in mock surrender and gestures for the priest to go on.

"The story of creation was written to tell people of that time *who* created us and *why* in a language that would have been easy for them to understand. It was never meant as a scientific and historical account of what took place. You know, we didn't have carbon-dating in the days of Moses."

Kellar shoots him a fiery glance, and Father Jakub yields.

"You're right. Enough preaching," he admits refocusing on the case. "The point of this original crime scene, in my estimation, was to symbolize Adam and Eve's union as husband and wife and their fall from grace. Your victims were likely selected because of the husband's unfaithfulness and homosexual desires."

"Ain't that rich!" Agent Nickerson murmurs angrily.

"Someone obviously knew about the husband's indiscretions and alerted your suspect who went to great lengths to stage the scene to the point of surgically making the other male victim symbolically into *the woman*," Father Jakub says.

"But God didn't kill Adam and Eve," Kellar argues. "But then again, I suppose you can't stage something like that with living and willing participants," he acknowledges grimly, with the priest and the agent agreeing in silence.

"Okay, what about the Vancouver case?" Kellar shifts gears.

"According to the file, Mr. Doyle's father is an Evangelical minister while Mrs. Doyle's family records indicated no religious affiliation," Father Jakub recalls.

"So, what's that tell us?" asks Nickerson.

"The Bible tells us that God's people intermingled with those of no faith, which watered down *their* faith and caused them to stray. So, with only one righteous man and his family remaining, God started all over again with the flood. Mr. Doyle himself strayed by committing adultery, which could have made him stand out to those responsible for these atrocities."

"We can all agree that adultery isn't an uncommon occurrence, so I'm thinking that the Doyle's might have been targeted primarily because of the differences between his and her religious upbringings then," Kellar says.

"Yes, I suppose so," Father Jakub replies.

"So, what, the church teaches that if you don't share the same beliefs, you're useless and deserve to die?" Agent Nickerson reproaches.

"Not even close," Father Jakub assures her. "It's neither ours nor the church's place to judge others. That's God's responsibility alone. He knows each human heart intimately and calls us *all* to repentance *regardless* of our religious affiliations."

Her mood softens. "Alright, so what about Moncton?" the FBI agent asks.

"Well, to me, the obvious thing is that of the killer's brutal rendering of a circumcision. The shop owner might well have been selected based purely on the name of his establishment," the priest suggests. "With the third covenant, God established his *tribe* through Abraham, and that victim's tattoo parlour was called The Tribal Print, unfortunately. The manner by which this poor man died would point to male circumcision which God demanded of his people from that time on."

"Plus," Agent Nickerson piggybacks, "even though he was never convicted, let's not forget that the guy's rap sheet indicates he *had* been charged with female genital mutilation, a.k.a. female circumcision."

"Ah, yes, that's true," Father Jakub agrees glumly.

"You've given this a lot of thought, haven't you?" she observes, somewhat warming up to the priest.

"I'm afraid I've thought of little else since being dragged into this investigation," he admits.

"Well, that gives us an idea of why these victims were selected, but how does a cult get this kind of intel?" Agent Nickerson questions. "If we're looking at a cult of this magnitude, one with plenty of resources to uncover all sorts of secrets on its victims, why isn't it on any of our radars?"

"I might have another possibility," Kellar suggests. "We're assuming the architect of these crimes is some sort of murderous cult. What if it's just that? *An* architect?"

Father Jakub and Agent Nickerson stare at him blankly.

"Each message is written by a 'Prophet' followed by VI:XXIII, right?"

The two others agree with quiet nods.

"What if this *Prophet* is simply an individual orchestrating the homicides as well as the apparent suicides and the fatal car accident?"

"Like what? A puppet master recruiting our suspects to punish and kill on his behalf?" Agent Nickerson asks. "That still doesn't explain how this individual would know who to target and who to use to commit the homicides. How does he know the victims' backgrounds and their supposed sins, and what's their connection to their killers? Why these suspects in particular?" she asks. "In San Antonio, we have a pissed-off wife. That connection is easy to make, but we haven't uncovered any obvious links between the killers and their victims in Vancouver or Moncton. Who are these killers to their victims? Did they have previous contact with each other before the homicides? Did they shop at the same stores? Were they social media friends? How do they fit together?"

"You're right," Kellar agrees. "In Vancouver, the guy wasn't even a real plumber, so it's not as though he would have done any work for the Doyles and had an opportunity to snoop around the house, so why him? In Moncton, witnesses say they saw the tattoo shop owner with a lady that fit his killer's description at a club the night before his body was discovered, but we haven't found any connections to suggest they might have known each other prior to that night. Why her?" Kellar asks and scans the room, but no one can offer a suggestion.

"And how do the suspects end up conveniently dead?" Agent Nickerson wonders.

Kellar shrugs his shoulders. "Not sure on that either. Does he have someone else tie up these loose ends too, or does he handle that part on his own?" he speculates.

"So, on the one hand, we could be looking at a murderous cult; on the other, we could be looking for a highly motivated and highly organized religious zealot with intimate knowledge of his victims. One who uses other people to do his deeds, and then may or may not be cleaning up after himself," Agent Nickerson sums up with a sigh.

"Excuse me," Father Fischer says, rising. "Nature calls," he smiles and slips away from the meeting.

Kellar glances at his watch and imagines that, despite the one-hour time difference, his colleague is still at his desk in Ottawa. "I've got an idea," he says pulling his phone from inside his blazer and dials. "Hey, Marty," he says without giving his researcher a chance at the usual small-talk. "I need you to check every airline's databases, both public and private. Look for names that might show up within the days and weeks of every city where the homicides took place."

"Wow, that's not going to take any time at all, Rafe," Marty says sarcastically.

"If nothing shows up, expand the search to neighboring airports as well," he adds and terminates the call abruptly.

"I like your style," Agent Nickerson says, winking as she tucks a loose strand of hair behind her ear. "How about you ditch the priest when we're done here, and you and I get to know each other a little better?" she propositions with an alluring smile.

25

Little Rose Island, Ontario

Little Rose Island is a one-and-a-half acre tree-covered piece of land and rocky outcroppings that juts into the smooth flowing waters of the Saint Laurence River. Having once served as a lookout for rum runners from Whiskey Island during the Prohibition era, it sits barely two hundred meters from the north side of the peaceful border between Canada and the United States in the Thousand Islands archipelago and has been in the judge's family for nearly a century. Referred to as "the cottage" by the judge, the two-story, 2,300 square foot residence that faces the south-west and offers spectacular views of the sunset was refurbished by his father in the late '60s and left to him after his death.

From the small pleasure craft, Clayton Bannister can't discern any movement inside the house. He slows and slips the vessel up against the floating dock as the sun slowly dips into the Saint Lawrence behind Wolfe Island at his back. He steadies himself from the gentle rocking of his wake, then ties the line around the piling and climbs the ladder up onto the dock. Unconcerned with covertness, the large man marches onto dryland and dashes up the wooden stairs that zig-zag around the protruding rocks up to the large, walk-out sundeck at the base of the impressive floor-to-ceiling windows. Walking past the bubbling hot-tub and patio furniture, he hurries to the side of the building and kicks down the solid oak door with a single blow of his size thirteen work boot.

He breaches the entrance and appraises the dim kitchen.

"Who's down there!" the judge's voice demands from upstairs, but Clayton doesn't respond.

"Get out of my cottage, or I'll blow your head off!" he warns from the top of the stairs, dripping wet, his waist draped with a bath towel and a bolt-action .22 caliber rifle in his unsteady hands. "What are you doing here?" he demands as the intruder slowly scales the stairs toward him. The judge shifts nervously in his spot, but does not back down.

"I want my dog back!" Clayton shouts.

"Dog? I don't have your damned dog!" the judge spits. "Now, get out of my cottage before I fill your face with lead!"

"Someone stole my dog, and if I want it back, I have to kill you," Clayton announces nonchalantly, gradually inching his way closer to the judge.

"Stop right there!" the judge's voice wavers. "I mean it!"

"I want my dog back!" Clayton insists, reaching the middle of the staircase.

"I warned you!" the old man shouts as his trembling finger squeezes the trigger, and Clayton's dead body crumbles and topples to the bottom of the stairs.

26

"How do you know he wanted to kill you and wasn't just here to rob you, Mr. Saunders?" the young Detective with Gananoque Police Service asks, taking notes on a small pad.

"You may address me as Judge Saunders, or simply Judge if you need shortcuts," he scolds. "But do not *ever* call me Mr. Saunders again!"

"My apologies, Judge Saunders," he says contritely. "But, again, what makes you believe he was actually here to kill you?"

"Because he said so," the old man replies.

"Hey, D'Acosta," a fellow officer calls him over. "You gotta see this."

"I'll be right back, Judge," he excuses himself and joins his fellow investigator near the dead intruder's body.

"Check out what this guy had with him," he says, holding Clayton Bannister's canvas bag in his gloved hands. "What is all this stuff, anyway?" he says, retrieving an antique pair of sheers, an icepick, bandages, a few granite stones and a crumpled piece of paper from the bag. They both read the note and share a worried glance.

"I bet he was here to do more than kill the judge," the partner whispers.

D'Acosta examines the objects and returns to find Judge Saunders still seated at the kitchen table, arms folded and head hung low with a tumbler and a bottle of expensive scotch by his elbow.

"Judge Saunders," he says. "Did you know Clayton Bannister?"

"No," he replies and takes a sip.

"Ever see him around town? Maybe you bumped into him at the convenience store, perhaps the gas station, something like that?"

The judge slowly shakes his head without a word.

"Do you know of anyone who might hold a grudge against you? Maybe from one of your old cases?"

Judge Saunders offers another silent shake of the head.

"Are you in possession of anything an individual might want to obtain from you by any means necessary?"

His head shoots up. "What are you suggesting?" he demands.

"Sensitive information of any kind that someone might want to hurt you to get their hands on?"

"What, torture me?" he asks in astonishment.

"Yes."

"No!" Saunders responds emphatically. "Of course not. Why would you ask me such a stupid question?"

"Your dead intruder had articles in his possession that suggest he wasn't just here to kill you, but that he was going to torture you for reasons yet unknown."

The judge exhales and shakes his head. "I have no clue what that man wanted."

"Do you keep files from your old days on the bench here at your residence?"

"Of course not, you idiot!"

"Judge Saunders," the younger man says patiently, "we're just trying to get to the bottom of this. We're on your side. It would help us to know why he was here and what he was after tonight."

"Ask him," he says, pointing resentfully to the cadaver in the adjacent room.

Detective D'Acosta takes a breath and gives the judge a moment to settle his nerves.

"Could—" the policeman starts but the judge cuts in.

"Wait!" he cries out. "He was rambling on about a dog," he announces.

"A dog?"

"Yes, a dog."

"Anything more specific?"

"Look, I was pretty shaken," he admits. "I can't recall every single word that idiot spoke, but he said someone had stolen his dog and that he had to kill me to get it back."

"Okay, so that's interesting," the investigator ruminates. "Anything else?"

"No, that's all I'm able to recall."

"Well, that gives us something to work with. You've been very helpful, Judge Saunders."

The old man shrugs.

"Can we take you somewhere for the evening?" he proposes. "This is an active crime scene. You know the drill, right?"

Judge Saunders sighs reluctantly. "Yes, I do."

"Where would you like us to take you?"

"I'll take my boat into town. You can find me at the River's Edge Inn on Stone Street if you have any more questions for me," he says politely.

27

San Antonio, Texas

"If you don't mind my saying, you made the right call, Rafe," Father Jakub says.

Kellar shoots him a quizzical glance.

"I observed how Agent Nickerson was flirting with you earlier today," the priest reveals.

"Oh, you *observed*, did you?" Rafe replies with pursed lips.

"Yes, I gathered by her sour mood when I returned from the washroom that she may have taken advantage of my absence to make advances and that you had obviously turned her down. That was wise of you."

"First of all, my sex life isn't any of your concern," Kellar says bitterly. "Second of all, I didn't turn anything down. She invited me to dinner, and I declined. I can't afford to get distracted by anyone in the middle of an investigation like this. If she's still interested in me after we're done, then *I'll* make that call. Not you!" He is about to continue the tongue lashing when his phone interrupts. "Hello!" he barks.

A few seconds pass, and he fumes. "I can't hear a word you're saying, Juice. You're breaking up," he says annoyingly. "What?"

His frustration intensifies as the connection worsens.

"Call me back when you get to civilization!" he says, cutting the bad connection.

"That was Juice on the phone," he says to Father Jakub, only mildly less irritated with the priest. "He was trying to tell me something about a video or something that surfaced, but I couldn't understand very much."

"Was it about the case?" Father Jakub asks.

"Hard to say with him. For all I know, it was probably a video of a cat that got the snot scared out of it by a cucumber," Kellar chuckles. "He'll call back if it's case-related."

Both men remain quiet for several minutes.

Although slightly obstructed by the overhanging balcony, the early evening Texan sun's lingering warmth is still therapeutic as the light breeze from the ceiling fans above their table gently circulates its warm air around the outside dining area. The soothing effect is especially welcoming after the long, grueling day of dissecting three homicides in a windowless inner office.

Father Jakub slices into his center-cut beef tenderloin, and the juices deliciously spill out onto his plate. Drawing the fork to his mouth, he closes his eyes as the rich steak flavorfully erupts with each bite. He opens his eyes and turns to admire the scenic River Walk their table overlooks, as foot traffic picks up with tourists and locals enjoying each other's company strolling along the edge of the watery channel. A lazy boat streams past with cheerful passengers and, for a brief moment, he allows his mind to detach itself from its current worries. *If life on earth can be this enjoyable at times, how much greater will life in heaven be?* he ponders, but is brought back from the reverie as the waiter returns to top off their wine.

"My compliments to the chef! This has to be the best steak I've ever had the pleasure of eating," he says, cheerfully raising his glass.

"Well, thank you, Father," the tall, well-groomed waiter replies.

"And the garlic mashed potato!" he adds. "Wow! I was originally thinking Brussels sprouts, but, wow. I'm so happy I changed my mind at the last minute."

"Thank you for that. I'll be sure to tell the chef," the young man says with a friendly smile.

"You know he's gay, right?" Kellar says under his breath once the waiter is out of earshot.

"So?" Father Jakub replies. "I told him the food was great. I didn't ask him out on a date!"

Kellar shrugs. "Isn't it against your religion to be nice to gays and lesbians?"

"This again?" Father Jakub sighs. "You know, for a man who seems to believe he understands the Catholic faith, you don't know very much about it at all, do you, Rafe?"

"I knew enough to give it up as soon as I got out of my parent's house."

"Your parents are Catholic?"

"Yep! Judgemental, opinionated and homophobic too," he rattles off. "Everything you need to be a good Catholic."

"You're wrong if that's how you feel," Father Jakub gently rebukes.

"Are you suggesting my statement isn't based on personal experience?" Kellar fires back.

"Look, it's true that some people consider that to be what they're supposed to believe, but they're just as wrong as you are."

"Yeah? Well, tell that to my son," Kellar says.

"I'm sorry, I don't follow," Father replies blankly.

"He hung himself because he was gay and thought I hated him because of it," Kellar reveals.

Father Jakub's heart sinks as he sits quietly, waiting for Kellar to go on.

"My parents raised me to hate homosexuals because that's what they were taught in church."

"Rafe," Father begins. "That's not at all what the Church teaches. People only hear what they want to hear."

"Don't try to tell me that the church isn't against homosexuals!"

"Rafe," the priest says pointedly. "I'm going to tell you something deeply personal that I am not ashamed of," he opens up. "I have a homosexual brother."

Rafe stares back at him, stunned.

"According to your understanding of Church teaching, I'm supposed to reject him," Father Jakub continues. "I can't reject him. I love him. But just because I love him doesn't mean I have to agree with him. The list of things the Church prescribes we abstain from is long, but we can't spurn everyone who, for one reason or another, disagrees with the Church. We need to love them more."

"How can you say you love them in one breath and condemn them in another?"

"I'm not condemning anyone, and neither is the Church," he shakes his head. "Look, we can debate this at length when we have more time, but for right now, I'm more concerned with being present for a grieving father who recently lost his son," Father Jakub urges. "Please, tell me about him, Rafe."

Rafe's eyes moisten. "Maybe some other time," he declines in a whisper.

Kellar's phone interrupts them as Father Jakub is about to encourage him to go on.

"It's Juice again," he says in the priest's direction, rubbing the dampness from his eyes, and swipes the screen to connect with his friend. "You back at the office?" he says, clearing his throat.

"Yeah, I am," Juice confirms excitedly. "We just caught a huge break in the Moncton case, Arch. We have a video, not a great one cause it was shot in the dark from far away, but we have enough to see a shadowy figure diving from the car into the river and swimming away from the car not long after it crashed into the mud."

"Wait, how'd we come up with this video?"

"A local resident, a little way on the other side of the river, was trying out his night-vision video recorder and inadvertently caught it on tape," he responds.

"So, someone else was there?" Kellar whistles in astonishment.

"Yep. That lady was left to die, either by a passenger with no connection to the tattoo shop homicide or a co-conspirator doing some house cleaning."

"Send it to me and make sure the media doesn't catch wind of it."

"Too late. It's already on the local news."

"Dammit, they already linked it to our serial cases?"

"No, they still don't know this is related to the other sets of homicides. The only thing they're reporting is that a passenger traveling with our deceased female suspect fled the scene. They're asking for the public's help in identifying the individual who may or may not be her accomplice and promise to get to the bottom of it."

"Okay, let's be sure to keep the national and international connections to ourselves until it's time. We don't need a panic on our hands."

28

Halton Hills, Ontario

He seldom returns here anymore. He hasn't crossed the house's threshold in the nine months since initially conceiving the plan. The once-happy place where he had tended to her has little meaning to him, and he prefers avoiding it outright, keeping his distance from her memories as well as muting the voice who frequently demands too much of him. But the shrill reverberation of the voice signals him back for meditation and clarity when he isn't feeling quite himself.

Fraught with anxiety and despair over the Clayton Bannister debacle and his uncharacteristic lack of attention to details, the Prophet instinctively returned to the house with an eagerness to revisit the refuge and implore the voice's mercy for not having anticipated the judge's means to defend himself and having failed so miserably.

"I'm sorry," he sobs loudly in his candle-lit sanctuary. "I'm so very sorry. Please, don't be angry with me," he implores, prostrated before the full-length mirror. "I can still fulfill my mission."

The wind drives the spring rain and rattles the closed exterior shutters as the flame atop the beading wax flickers from the drafty, poorly-insulated windows.

He rises awkwardly to his knees and, with his usual flair for the dramatic, rips open his shirt with a desperate cry. His eyes are red and swollen, and his mouth still wet with bloody drool from the nervous cheek-biting. With his sleeve, he wipes the dribble from his trembling lips.

"I can make this right," he promises. "I *will* make this right!"

He takes several long and soothing breaths and slows his heart rate considerably.

The judge has to die. It's as simple as that. The man who killed the boy inside the man still *has* to die. In a moment of clarity, he recognizes a means by which to make this happen, and the thin-lipped smile returns to his ashen face.

The risk is significant but worth it, even if it means exposing himself to a number of dangers before it's time. The voice reassures him that nothing will happen to him until his work is accomplished.

With renewed exuberance, the Prophet stands and prances up the squeaky staircase to the master bedroom and collects two bolts of recently-purchased fabric from the antique wardrobe, then positions himself at the vintage treadle sewing machine. His bare feet rest on the foot pedal as he feeds the thread through the needle with a revised plan that will afford him the pleasure of dealing with the judge face-to-face.

29

Gananoque, Ontario

The wig is a bit hot and somewhat uncomfortable as usual, but entirely necessary, he fears. He checks himself in the rearview mirror and touches up his lipstick for good measure.

"You look simply ravishing, Delilah," he compliments his reflection and exits his vehicle at the marina as a petite and elegant woman dressed for a date with an important gentleman. He's done this so many times now that walking with four-inch heels is nearly as natural for him as breathing.

He shoulders his heavy purse and struts his way along Water Street, then across the bridge that overlooks the River's Edge Inn. He casts a scornful glance toward a pair of barely-concealed teenagers making out behind a minivan in the parking lot. They're too wrapped up in their lust to notice him, so he dismisses them as a threat and rounds the corner of the street and enters the Inn's impressive lobby. His excitement grows as he approaches the clerk at the desk. It's incredible how far people are willing to trust you for the right amount of financial incentive, especially when you're as prepared for a role as he is.

"Good evening," he says in falsetto. "I believe my friend is expecting me," he lies. "Mr. Douglas Jones' room, please?"

The clerk, only somewhat able to suppress a grin at the prominent Adam's apple in the woman's throat, greets him, "Absolutely. I'll ring his room, Ms. . . . ?"

"Names aren't important," he replies. "We both know that Mr. Douglas Jones' real name is Judge Philip Saunders," he says assertively. "His good friend, our retired Police Chief Willard, asked me to pay him a visit this evening," he adds, slipping the young man a folded hundred-dollar bill from his heavily padded bra with a wink. "But he's not supposed to know about it. My instructions are to collect the key from the handsome desk-clerk and simply walk into his room to surprise him."

"I—I'm not sure if that's allowed," he says, glancing between the bill and the cross-dresser in front of him.

"C'mon, Justin," he purrs the clerk's name, reading from his name tag. "No one's going to get in trouble," he assures him with another folded bill from his bra.

"Okay, fine," he concedes after a moment of mental deliberation, smiles and pockets the money while reaching for the room key.

"Here you go," he says pleasantly. "Enjoy your stay." He chuckles.

"Thank you so much," the Prophet replies with a charming smile and climbs the staircase in the foyer up to the Judge's floor.

30

"Yes, I'm sure!" Judge Saunders insists. "You don't need to babysit me. It's bad enough I can't get back into my cottage; you're not going to hold me hostage in my hotel room."

"Judge Saunders, it's for your own protection," Detective D'Acosta says without much luck in persuading the cranky old man.

"I said, no!"

"We still don't know who hired Bannister. What if this guy comes back to finish the job?"

"If he comes into my room, he'll get the same reception as the last guy!" the judge promises.

"Judge Saunders, please be reasonable," the policeman pleads.

"I *am* being reasonable," he maintains. "I'm paying close to $200 a night to be here while you people play detective on my island," he complains, oblivious to the door creaking open behind him or the killer dressed as a woman slipping into his room.

"When you get your crap together, call me to let me know that I can move back into my own residence," he growls and brings down the phone as the mechanical sound of the door latching behind him draws his attention.

"What the hell?" he gasps at the intruder while the phone slides into place on the base.

The Prophet blows a kiss in his direction. "Surprise!" he exclaims.

"Who the hell are you and what are you doing in my room?" he demands, but the Prophet pulls a can out from his purse and sprays its contents into the judge's face. He coughs, but staggers toward his assailant and manages to land a fist squarely on his jaw. The Prophet retaliates with a series of frantic punches and kicks, and the judge finally folds to the ground, succumbing to the aerosol drug he had inhaled.

The Prophet curses and cries out in anger, wiping the blood with his hand and kicking the old man in the ribs.

"That's for the hole you threw me into!" he screams with another blow to his groaning victim's side.

He settles his nerves, knowing he must work swiftly as other guests had to have heard the commotion. He quickly pulls the sheers from his handbag and hacks the older man's hair, giggling uncontrollably as the thick salt-and-pepper locks puddle onto the carpeted floor. So absorbed is he in his task that the blood dripping from his nose and onto his victim's face goes unnoticed. He would prefer more time with the old bastard, but knows that he's working on a tight schedule, so he blinds his victim, then immediately pulls a rock from his bag and smashes it hard against the judge's skull. Rising, he swipes the bloody puddle with his index finger and moves to the wall. From the open window, the faint sound of the approaching siren warns him to hurry.

"It's not ideal, but they'll still get the picture," he reasons and paints the familiar Roman numerals with Judge Saunders' blood. Turning to leave, he stops to reconsider and scrawls something more on the wall for the police before he slips away. As he hurries across the hall, an elderly couple from a few doors away witness him race down the stairwell that leads to the inn's side exit.

June 2013

31

Ottawa, Ontario - June 2013

"There was another one, Rafe," Marty Bloom exhales, tossing a file on Kellar's desk.

"Where? When? Gimme specifics, Marty!" he demands.

"The Thousand Islands region, on one of the islands, two and a half weeks ago," the researcher says. "A Judge Philip Saunders was the victim,"

"This latest victim was a judge?" Kellar says, astonished.

"A *retired* judge," Bloom clarifies. "This is where it gets interesting, though," he adds with a long pause.

Kellar gestures impatiently for him to go on.

"On the night of May twenty-seventh, it was business as usual for the retired judge. He took a shower and was toweling off when he heard noises coming from the main level. He grabbed his rifle and confronted the intruder, a six-foot-five giant named Clayton Bannister, who was coming toward him up the stairway," he narrates dramatically from memory. "The judge warned him not to get any closer or that he'd shoot him. The intruder responded that someone had stolen his dog and that if he ever wanted to see him again, he had to kill the judge, so the old man shot him in the face with the guy's next step."

"So how do we know this case is connected to our other ones?"

"Bannister had a couple of items with him in a bag when he broke into the judge's residence, among which was a note on a crumpled up piece of paper with the usual messed-up wording that Bannister was presumably supposed to write on the wall after staging the scene."

"Interesting indeed. Okay, so things didn't go exactly as planned this time around, eh?" Rafe concludes. "Let's go talk to the judge," he says excitedly.

"I'm not done yet," Bloom interjects glumly, and Rafe shoots his colleague a puzzled look. "The judge checked into a hotel under a pseudonym while his place was tied up for the investigation."

Rafe follows attentively.

"A couple of days later, a woman sweet-talked a room key from a pimple-faced kid behind the desk and made her way up to the judge's room. Luckily, the judge was on the phone with local law enforcement at the time, and they heard a heated exchange right before Saunders hung up. They rushed over but were too late. Witnesses say they saw a woman stagger out of the room and run away through a side exit."

"Another woman!" Rafe explodes. "Dammit! How does he keep recruiting these people?"

"Witnesses say she was dressed like a prostitute and was banged up pretty good, bleeding from the nose and mouth when they saw her fleeing the scene of the crime."

"The judge must have fought back. Maybe we get lucky, and he has some of her DNA on him," Rafe hopes out loud.

"She was in a hurry and didn't seem to care about witnesses or the trail of evidence she was leaving behind. A blood trail was discovered in the hallway and the stairwell that led outside and ended in a parking lot across the river. Unfortunately, except for the kid who let her in and the couple who saw her leave, no one saw her drive away, so we have no description of her vehicle."

"So, what *do* we have?" Kellar asks.

"This one was just as messed-up as the other ones, Rafe," Marty sighs. "The judge's hair was chopped off, his eyes were gouged, and he was bludgeoned to death with a rock. She might have been in a hurry and presumably didn't have enough time to stage the rest of the scene because the only thing that was on the wall this time were the words 'Boy Killer' and the usual Roman numerals—nothing more. Leaves me thinking she was interrupted."

"If this happened two-and-a-half weeks ago, why are we only hearing about this now?" Kellar fumes.

"Because of the victim's high profile, the locals wanted a crack at solving his murder on their own. Collected and catalogued every piece of evidence they found and shipped it all to our lab. We didn't make the connection until they realized they were way over their heads and reached out for assistance."

Kellar nods, pondering his next move.

"Hey, did you start looking for a possible connection between air travelers and the homicide locations like I asked?" he changes the subject.

"Yeah, but all my queries came up empty. I couldn't find a single name that overlaps the dates and locations of any of them."

"Private and public airfields?"

"Yep. Nothing."

"Chartered flights and private jest as well?" he grills.

"Nothing at all, and before you ask, I checked with trains and bus companies. I even contacted those ride-share guys," he affirms. "Nothing!"

Kellar grins at his thoroughness. "Okay. Thanks."

"You need me, you know where to find me," Bloom says, leaving Kellar alone at his desk.

"Hey, Jakub," Rafe says over the phone. "I need you back here ASAP."

"There's been another one?" the priest asks grimly.

"Yeah. I need you to interpret what I'm looking at again if you don't mind."

"Absolutely. Where are we going this time?" he replies.

"To Gananoque. I'll email you your boarding pass as usual," he says and cradles the receiver, then turns his attention to the computer monitor on his desk.

"Okay, so, no obvious names on any of the manifests, hmm?" he ponders. "But what about businesses?" he asks Bloom by email. "Are there any businesses that have offices in all of these locations?"

32

Gananoque, Ontario

"Weren't they supposed to leave the crime scene intact until the case was solved?" Father Jakub asks as he and Kellar enter the immaculately tidy hotel suite where the brutal homicide had recently taken place.

"No, unfortunately. This close to tourism season, the owners pressured the mayor, who then pressured the local police department to quickly wrap things up. Locals collected all the physical evidence, including DNA. Although the room's been sanitized, it's still available to us without any fuss."

"So what evidence are you hoping to find here?" Father Jakub asks.

"Nothing physical, but I can usually get a good sense of what happened and how by looking at the crime scene photos and reviewing the area where it was committed," he says, shuffling through the images and following the events inside the room.

"The judge was found here on the floor in a pool of his own blood and hair," Kellar narrates. "Autopsy confirmed the presence of an incapacitating agent in his lungs. The judge was old, but still in decent physical condition. There's evidence that he was at least able to throw a punch or two before losing consciousness."

He looks to the floor before moving on to the next photo.

"You know, our initial cult angle is getting weaker with every case," he admits. "We're likely dealing with one sick mother f—" he stops short, censoring his speech and throwing the priest a worried glance.

Father Jakub barely suppresses a smile. "Does this new homicide support this theory?"

"The coroner's report says our victim was severely beaten before he was killed, and the desk clerk confessed this morning to taking money from a guy dressed in drag. He said he didn't say anything sooner because he didn't want to tarnish the Judge's good name in a sex scandal. I believe that the suspect the witnesses all saw was our dirtbag disguised as a woman."

"How can you be sure?"

"A couple of things are nagging at me," he begins. "We know things didn't go as planned at the judge's cottage, and then this happened here just two days later. Think about it. In all the other cases, he had someone else do his wet work, and then these suspects eventually found themselves dead too. Bannister literally bit the bullet before he had time to complete his mission, so you think this guy has an army of lunatics just waiting to get in the game? This sort of thing has to take a lot of time and planning. I think he might have been forced to improvise and kill the judge himself."

Father Jakub shrugs. "That does sound plausible, I suppose."

"The coroner confirmed the cause of death was blunt force trauma," Kellar continues pointing to the judge's head wound in the photograph. "The hair thing aside, our victim was still alive when the killer blinded him and crushed his skull. Conscious or not, that takes a special kind of crazy."

The priest winces and nods his agreement.

"Cracked ribs, facial lacerations, hair chopped off, eyes gouged out and a rock to the side of the head. This remind you of anything from the Bible?"

The priest takes a breath and ponders. "Stoning *was* a form of punishment in ancient Israel," he muses unconvincingly.

"Here's a shot of what was found on the scrap of paper Bannister had on him at the judge's place," Rafe says, handing him the photo.

"The law has been handed down, and this judge was found unworthy of fulfilling his duties and thus must bear the full weight of the Prophet's wrathful judgement," the priest reads aloud. "This was also signed the same way as all the other messages," he adds.

"Now here's a shot of what was written here," Kellar redirects, handing the priest another photo and pointing to the wall.

"Definitely shorter," he observes.

"That's right. We suspect he barely had time to write anything before getting spooked," Kellar confirms. "But he still took the time to scribble a couple of words and his familiar Roman numerals so we'd know who we were dealing with."

"But the message isn't remotely similar to what was supposed to be written," the priest grumbles. "It makes no sense."

"I know, that's bugging me too. Why write anything down other than the numbers if you don't have time to write the entire message? Why a couple of words that didn't even show up in the original note? Why these words? What do they mean?" Kellar wonders. "What does he know about the judge that the rest of us don't?"

Father Jakub shrugs his shoulders.

"Walk me through what you see here."

"Okay, so chronologically speaking, we should be looking at the fourth covenant," Father begins. "The fourth covenant began with Moses and the liberation of God's people from Egypt. The Hebrews went from being the *Tribe* of Israel to the *Nation* of Israel, a nomadic nation, but a nation nevertheless, with God as their leader operating through Moses as witnessed by the handing down of the Ten Commandments," he summarizes. "Moses was the nation's first judge, but when it got to a point where all he did was rule over the people's petty grievances, he assigned Judges to oversee the *minor* dealings while he dealt with the more serious charges. These Judges ruled over the people until God's next covenant. The most notable of these Judges was Samson," Father Jakub says, looking at the photo and then to the spot where the judge had been found. "According to the Book of Judges, Samson was a mighty warrior with supernatural strength. We're told his strength came from his hair that had never been cut and that one day his wife Delilah betrayed him. As he slept in her arms, she called a servant over to cut off all his hair. With his strength gone, the Philistines were able to restrain him and gouged out his eyes. They kept him tied to pillars for a long time, but once his hair had grown back and his strength returned, he dislodged the pillars and toppled the structure. He died under the rubble along with many of his enemies."

"Well, then," Kellar whistles. "Here, I thought the Bible was boring. Too bad our suspect didn't die here like they did in your story."

Father Jakub adjusts his glasses. "Unless I'm misinterpreting the scene, the story of Samson appears to be what he wanted us to discover, but he wasn't beaten to death—unless the suspect meant for the judge's injuries to represent the ones Samson sustained from the collapsed structure which killed him."

"Not sure," Kellar hesitates. "Okay, there's lots to this fourth covenant, but if I'm following along correctly, this time it's about these "judges" you're referring to. So, Judge Saunders was likely selected because *he* was an actual judge," Kellar suggests, pausing momentarily. "Was Samson a bad guy?" he asks. "Did he kill children—boys specifically as the message here would suggest?"

"No. Absolutely not!" the young priest maintains passionately.

"So why him? What made Judge Saunders stand out more than any other judge?" he asks rhetorically. "And why was it necessary for this homicide to happen so openly at the risk of getting apprehended in the process? Is there a personal connection between the victim and our suspect? That's an interesting question, isn't it?"

33

Ottawa, Ontario

The boardroom is somewhat reminiscent of the Command Post Kellar recalls from his days serving in Operation Deliverance in Somalia while with the Canadian Armed Forces' Airborne Regiment, with files and maps scattered over the large table and crime scene photos sub-categorized by homicide adhered to mobile whiteboards. The smell of strong coffee and stale food from Chinese takeout containers and pizza boxes littering the credenza at the back of the room permeates the space.

On the large map of North America, Kellar stares intently at the four circled locations where the homicides had taken place as he cross-references the list of companies that have possible links to the sites themselves. With the cult angle dried up and the passenger manifests a dead-end, he and Marty Bloom had built an extensive list of corporations with offices or warehouses at or in close proximity to where each of the brutal crimes had been committed. Over the last few hours, without any other more promising leads, they had narrowed the list of possibilities to six; each company was now represented with a different colored tag on the various hand-drawn circles on the map. He plans to pay each of them a visit over the next few days, starting with the most promising ones headquartered in the Greater Toronto Area.

"You ready to go, Arch?" Juice says, ducking his head through the doorway. "Phew, man, you need to get out of here and let the cleaners in once in a while," he teases with his large hand fanning his nose.

"I thought you were only getting here at 5:30?" Kellar asks, surprised.

"I was," Juice confirms. "It's seven o'clock, man."

"What? Sorry. This case is consuming me."

"I know. C'mon, wrap it up and let's go watch the game. It'll take your mind off the case for a couple of hours. Whatcha got going on with your map there, anyways?" Juice asks out of curiosity.

"These are the locations where all the homicides happened. San Antonio, Vancouver, Moncton, and Gananoque being the latest one. Marty and I put together a list of companies that are close enough to all these areas for us to look into."

Juice nods. "What's your angle?"

"Anything at this point. Could be a sales manager of some sort, maybe the CEO or CFO, maybe the head of the HR department, the union rep or even a truck driver. Anyone who would have any business dealings with multiple locations and could easily travel to any of these places on the map without raising any suspicion is worth talking to."

"Any of these companies have an office in Gananoque?"

"No, but it's only a three-hour drive from Toronto."

"A bit thin, Arch, even for you."

"I didn't say this was a solid lead, Juice, but I think it's worth a few hours to drop in on them. You up for a road trip?"

"I'd love to go with you, but I've got that seminar for the next couple of days."

"That's fine," he dismisses. "I told Jakub I'd pick him up, and he could tag along."

"So now it's—*Jakub*?" Juice smirks with a raised brow and chuckles in Bloom's direction. "You guys pals now, eh?" he taunts his friend, with Marty enjoying the banter.

Kellar grins and flips his buddy the finger. "He's growing on me—for a priest," he confesses. "He's actually been pretty helpful."

"Sure," Juice laughs.

"No, I'm serious. It's true, he's pretty tight-assed when it comes to morality, and I don't agree with *most* of what he has to say on the matter, but for the case, he connected dots I would never have been able to on my own."

"Whatever you say, Arch," the big man laughs with a raised hand. "Now, let's get out of here, go to the bar, and forget about the degenerates we chase day in and day out. I know you're a Toronto fan, and you stopped watching hockey when they got knocked out of the playoffs, but you have to admit, watching Chicago demolish Boston in the finals should be pretty entertaining."

34

Saint Faustina Parish - Toronto, Ontario

Kellar has never set foot inside a rectory. He wasn't even quite sure what to expect, but looking at the living room furniture, although somewhat outdated, he supposes priest residences are probably just that—residences. An overweight orange tabby runs up to him and rubs itself against his pant leg with a deep, rumbling purr, but Kellar shoos it away with a gentle nudge of his foot, and the cat scatters.

"Here you are, Inspector Kellar," Paulina offers, placing a cup of coffee into Rafe's reaching hands.

"Thank you," he accepts, drawing the mug to his lips.

"Father Jakub will be right with you. You can wait for him here in his office," she says, ushering him inside and leaving him with his thoughts.

Kellar notes the bold headline on the newspaper's front page folded neatly on the priest's tidy desk. Seems that authorities have finally identified the skeletal remains of Sister Mary Joseph, a Catholic nun who had been missing for over twenty years. He slowly crosses to an adjacent bookshelf next to the stone fireplace and examines the books.

"Riveting choice of literature, Jakub," he chuckles under his breath, noting the enormous collection of theological volumes.

He takes another sip from the cup and gazes at an old framed photograph of a priest hanging on the wall above the mantle. He approaches for closer examination. It looks just like Father Jakub, but the photo has to have been taken years before Jakub was even born; no way could this be a picture of the young priest. A distant relative, maybe?

"Saint Maximilian Kolbe," Father Jakub beams as he joins Kellar.

"A relative of yours?" he asks.

"I wish," the priest says. "No, a saint I greatly admire."

"He could be your father. Or at least your grandfather. He looks just like you right down to the close-cropped hair and little round glasses."

Father Fischer smiles. "No. No family relation whatsoever," he admits. "But he's had a profound impact on our family nonetheless."

"How so?" Kellar quizzes.

"Maximilian Kolbe was a Franciscan priest from Poland," Father explains. "He lived quite an extraordinary life and traveled extensively. He met his untimely death in Auschwitz at the hands of the German Nazis."

"What was *he* doing there? Weren't all their prisoners Jewish?" Kellar asks. "This guy was a *Catholic* priest, wasn't he?"

"Yes, he was," Father Jakub acknowledges. "But Auschwitz housed Jews, the elderly, the handicapped, and anyone who opposed the Nazis, regardless of race or creed."

Kellar listens intently as the young priest describes the events.

"One night, three men disappeared from the camp, prompting the soldiers to gather ten men from among the other prisoners as punishment for the disobedience. These men were locked in an underground bunker to starve to death. One of the men whose fate had been sealed, a young father, cried out for mercy but was beaten for his insubordination. He was about to receive another blow when the voice of Father Kolbe boomed over the thundering rain," Father Jakub describes soberly as though reliving the fateful night himself. "Father Kolbe asked the guards to set the man free and take him instead. The man was released, and Father Kolbe was taken to the bunker in the man's place."

"I've never heard that story," Kellar admits.

"When the guards were making their way between the rows of nervous men from which they would arbitrarily select their victims, they would suddenly stop in front of one man, beat him to the ground and drag him to the front. When they had selected the ninth man, they slowed and glared into the eyes of a young man in the back row. They stood there, focusing on him for what seemed an eternity, and then suddenly turned and grabbed the poor man next to him. The young man they left in formation was my grandfather."

"Your grandfather?" Kellar gasps.

"Yes," the priest nods with a deep sigh. "You see, I am a Pole of Jewish descent."

"I thought your name was a little out of character for a Catholic priest," Kellar grins.

"Yes, you're not alone," Father Jakub admits with a smile. "After the war, my grandfather moved here to Canada, where he met my grandmother, and they wed. He credits Saint Maximilian Kolbe for his conversion to the Catholic Faith. He often said that only the power of God could move a man to give his life for another in the example of Jesus."

Rafe is silent.

"Well, then, Rafe," the priest says, his arm on Kellar's shoulder. "Shall we go solve your homicides now?" He chuckles and leads them both out to Kellar's rental, parked along Roncesvalles Avenue.

35

Mississauga, Ontario

"Thanks again for lunch, Rafe," Father Jakub says cheerfully as they climb into Kellar's car.

"No problem. It's on the taxpayers anyway," he grins. "So, I guess if you look at it, I should be thanking you."

"Sorry that first lead didn't pan out," the priest says. "I have to admit, long shot or not, I think it was a genius idea to follow up with companies that employ people who could reasonably have been in the same places where all the murders took place."

"Yeah, but there's no way anyone from that last place works out. They don't have anyone traveling to any of those places on business. Everything's done online. Even meetings are done remotely," he sighs as he exits the restaurant's parking lot. Turning left, they travel north on Hurontario to drop in on the next corporate headquarter on the list.

"Can I ask you something personal, Rafe?" the priest asks delicately.

"Look, we're getting along, Jakub," Kellar raises his guard. "Don't get all priesty on me now."

The younger man grins. "No, no. Nothing like that," he swears.

Kellar shoots him a warning glance. "Fine, but tread lightly."

"Why does Juice call you Arch?"

Kellar sighs, relieved that his passenger kept his word.

"I told you before that my parents are Catholics, right?" he says. "Well, they're more than your standard run-of-the-mill, go-to-church-Sunday-Catholics. I mean, not so much now, but when I was a kid, they bought into all that shi—that stuff," he says, only mildly concealing his contempt for religion from the priest, but drawing a chuckle from him nevertheless. "Anyways, they were hoping for a boy and that I'd become a doctor and named me Raphael after one of the archangels. I never liked my name, so I shorten it to Rafe. Juice is a large man and not intimidated by anything, but he wasn't always a big guy. When he was a kid, his neighbor was a bully and regularly gave him a beating simply because he could. The other kid was also named Rafe."

"Ah, I see," Father Jakub nods.

"He didn't care to call me by the same name as someone he still loathes to this day. Honoring my parents' original intent and respecting my feelings toward organized religion, he shortened 'archangel' to 'Arch.' He said he felt that it was more, how would you say, *secularized*," he grins.

"Secularized?" Father Fischer chuckles. "Look at you using churchy lingo."

Kellar laughs.

"Well, just so you know," Father says. "Raphael is a very fitting name for your line of work, you know."

"Is that right?" Kellar cocks his head and says.

"Absolutely. Your parents were correct that Raphael's name means 'God Heals,' and he's the archangel credited with healing the earth when it was defiled by the sins of the fallen angel. He also delivered Tobias's wife from her demon. There's a striking similarity to what you do every day."

"I just chase criminals, not demons; although, with some of the stuff we've seen from this guy, maybe I do," Kellar says, and sighs. "Here we are," he announces as he pulls into the parking lot of Synthesized Logistics.

The structure is massive, with no less than 300 parked transport trucks surrounding the entire 700,000 square foot warehouse section. Although smaller, in contrast, the annexed head office is quite considerable by office standards, with three stories of window glazing and finely manicured grounds leading up to the opulent entrance, which welcomes both staff and visitors alike.

"I'm a bit nervous," Father Jakub admits.

"Nothing to worry about," Kellar replies calmly. "Just like the last one. We're not here to kick down any doors; we're just here to ask a few questions."

The air-conditioned lobby does nothing to calm Father's jitters, but he follows Kellar to the reception desk as the investigator introduces them.

"Hi there, I'm Inspector Rafe Kellar with the RCMP," he identifies himself and shows the young lady his credentials. "This is Father Fischer who's riding with me today. May we please speak with whoever's in charge?"

"That would be Mr. Hendrickson, our President, but I'm afraid he's not available today."

"How about the vice-president?" Kellar suggests.

"I'm afraid she's gone too," the woman responds remorsefully. "In fact, there's really no one here since this is the week our executive team has its annual corporate retreat up in Muskoka. There's only middle management here, I'm afraid," she explains as a plump woman waddles herself into the conversation.

"Hello, officer. I'm Sue Lockhart," she says, extending a hand to Rafe and then to Father Jakub. "I'm the best you can hope for this week. I'm the Team Leader for our customer support group, and I couldn't help but overhear that you have questions pertaining to police matters of some sort for us."

"Yes, well, these are questions that are best suited for someone on your executive team," Kellar clarifies.

"Ms. Quang, please dial Mr. Strickland's line and ask him to come up here," she says dryly, visibly offended that the investigator doesn't consider her important enough to ask her his questions.

"But Mr. Strickland is away at the retreat this week," the receptionist reminds her.

"No, he isn't. He doesn't go to those things, and quite frankly, I wouldn't be surprised if he's the one the police are here for anyways," she huffs in the visitors' direction. "He's a little squirrely if you ask me," she sneers, turns on her heels and tramps away, disappearing behind the heavy glass doors leading back to her team.

"I'll call Mr. Strickland," young Ms. Quang says, picking up the phone and dialling.

36

"Please, have a seat," Thomas Strickland gestures with a wave to the thick padded leather chairs around the conference table as he leads them inside the spacious boardroom brightly lit by the wall of glass that overlooks the parking lot from the third floor.

Father Jakub pulls one of the high-back chairs from the large table and takes a seat as Rafe lingers, contemplating the photos of various corporate locations displayed along the wall behind the priest.

"What exactly does Synthesized Logistics do, Mr. Strickland?" Kellar asks.

"Many things, Officer. But we mainly look after the logistical needs of a variety of companies. Some small, some large—we don't discriminate," he chuckles. "These companies find it easier to outsource their transportation needs, much like some of them outsource their accounting or customer support departments. They don't want to tie up their money in a fleet of trucks, so they come to us. We also avail our IT expertise to them by providing them with our tracking software. We can design the interface with a seamless corporate feel so that the end-user doesn't even know they're tracking their shipments from a third party. It's brilliant if you actually think about it," he boasts.

"Well, that's very impressive, Mr. Strickland," Kellar admits. "So, what do *you* do here, specifically, Mr. Strickland?"

"I'm the IT director. I'm the one who keeps everything running smoothly," he brags. "Electronically speaking," he grins.

"You folks have quite the organization, I have to admit." Kellar compliments. "Offices across Canada and the U.S., I see. Vancouver, Moncton, here in Toronto, and look, down there in San Antonio, too," he says, pointing to each as he rattles off the names.

"Yes, we're very fortunate to have grown considerably over the years," he proudly admits. "I've only been here a few months, but it feels like forever. You know, it's like we're one big happy family," he beams.

Kellar doesn't like the scrawny little guy standing before him, and based on Team Leader Sue's earlier comment, he's not the only one. "Yeah, I picked up on that downstairs," he grins.

"So, how may I assist you, Officer Kellar?" he asks in Rafe's direction. Then, turning to Father Jakub, he adds, "And Father, how did you manage to get yourself tangled up in Officer Kellar's investigation?" He grins as he and Kellar seat themselves with the priest at the table.

"It's actually not Officer," Rafe corrects. "It's Inspector. I'm charged with analyzing various crimes and determining if they qualify as serial offenses. So you may call me Inspector, and this is Father Jakub Fischer, who's just around for the ride today. He's really not involved; he's just looking for material for his next homily," he says sarcastically.

Strickland grins.

Kellar takes note of the fading bruises around the man's eyes. "You appear to have recently been in a bit of a scuffle, Mr. Strickland. That looks like it was quite the shiner."

"Yes," he says, clutching his face with embarrassment. "Nothing glamorous, I'm afraid. I was working on a server downstairs a few weeks ago and, being a bit clumsy, got my face in the way of a falling keyboard. Nothing nefarious, but thank you for the concern." He chuckles.

"Don't mention it," Kellar says. "But I'm curious. As head of the IT department for a corporation of this magnitude, you must have an army of people working for you in your satellite locations, right? I mean, how does a solitary guy keep all this information technology business running smoothly all the time?" he probes, beginning to build a profile in his mind and wondering if he just might be looking at their prime suspect.

***

The Prophet picks up on the line of questions. Truth be told, the police's involvement will be necessary, but not this early in the plan. He's somewhat worried that they're already sniffing around him, but is drawn to the attention and decides to play along with them, rationalizing that, despite having the authorities already here in his place of business, he's still very much in control.

"No one else," he answers with confidence. "It's a one-man operation. Everything can be done from my office here downstairs as far as the software is concerned. Hardware installations occasionally take me off-site."

"Really?" Kellar asks. "You don't outsource that? You know, like other companies do with your trucks?" he suggests with a playful tone.

"No, we prefer to keep this work in-house," Strickland shrugs.

"How often would you say these installations take you out of town?"

"Oh, probably once a month," he smiles, playing with the cop who has had a steady diet of monthly homicides.

"Have you been out of the country lately? To one of your U.S. locations?" Kellar probes.

"Yes, as a matter of fact, I was just in San Antonio last month," he lies.

"Wow. San Antonio. I've never been there. I hear it's quite lovely this time of year. I wonder what winter's like there. Have you ever had to make the trip that time of year?"

Is this the best they could send here on a high-profile serial case like his, this incompetent idiot with the stupid questions? A cadet in training would have less conspicuous questions. *Come on, Kellar, you're making this way too easy*, he laughs to himself, wanting to stab the cop with his pencil. At least he had the wherewithal to involve a priest on the case; he'll at least have to give him a few marks for that bit of foresight.

"No, unfortunately, I've never been there in the winter," he sighs. "In January, I was in Moncton, and before you ask, I'm heading to Vancouver in just a couple of days—since that was one of the locations you mentioned earlier," he says, enjoying this little game. "You know, I'm actually very *blessed*," he smiles in the priest's direction for emphasis. "This job allows me to travel and see places I wouldn't otherwise have any reason to visit."

"Can you tell me if there's anyone else from inside your company who might have a reason to travel to your other offices on business? Perhaps the president or the head of accounting, sales, or maybe HR?"

"I really don't keep tabs on the others with my busy schedule, but you might want to check with Cecilia, who books all of our corporate travels. She'll have a record of everyone's comings and goings," he says, standing. "Now I'm afraid I really must get back to work. I have a vitally important program I'm writing downstairs that needs to be executed in the next couple of weeks if we're going to stay ahead of the competition." He winks.

Rafe and Father Jakub rise, and Kellar shakes the IT manager's hand. "Thank you for your time, Mr. Strickland. I'm happy to have met you," he says and turns to the priest. "You coming, Father?" He returns his glance to Strickland and laughs. "You know, I get a kick out of calling someone younger than me, Father."

They all share a forced laugh.

The Prophet reaches for the priest's hand. "Delighted to have met you, Father Fischer."

Father Jakub takes his hand and hesitates. "Have we met before?" he asks.

"I have an exceptional memory, Father, and I can say in all honesty that you and I have never met."

"I'm sure I've seen your face before," the priest insists. "This may sound strange, but have you ever had religious training?" he queries. "Were you ever in priestly formation or maybe in the Permanent Diaconate program at Saint Joseph's Seminary?"

The Prophet's face pales. "No, of course not," he replies with a nervous chuckle. "What makes you say that?"

"No reason, I guess. You just reminded me of someone from my old seminary days, I suppose."

"I have a familiar face and get that a lot," he replies unconvincingly. "Not the seminary part, of course," he adds. "Gentlemen, please excuse me. I'll let you see yourselves out," he says and quickly escapes.

Kellar gives Father Jakub a congratulatory nod. "Not bad, Padre! Not bad at all. Looks like you rattled him more than just a little."

37

He paces the length of his depressingly dark subterranean office hysterically.

"Who is that *priest*?" The Prophet laments bitterly as he settles himself at his desk. "Where does he get off asking me that?" he fumes, frantically stroking his keyboard and looking up Father Jakub Fischer on the internet. "He'll rue this day!" he swears, following the search engine's results and downloading the "About Us" information from the Saint Faustina Parish website.

With angry strokes, he composes the counterfeit email that will appear to originate from Valison, the provider of Catholic printed material for most dioceses in the country. With it, he'll entice the priest to install the company's latest shipment tracking application on his smartphone and grant the Prophet access to all of the poor unsuspecting soul's digital activities. He snickers and recalls how successful this intelligence-gathering tool has been for him in the past.

How could he have overlooked this possibility? He was not kidding when he said he remembers everything—he has an eidetic memory and knows without the shadow of a doubt that he has never seen that priest before, ever! So how could that guy be so confident they had met? He worries the voice will be angry with him again. Will he have to return to the house? He rationalizes that the voice doesn't really have to know . . . but the voice knows everything! With a few breathing exercises, he relaxes and returns his gaze to the priest's photo on the website. He's reasonably sure that he'll be able to fix this as soon as he's granted even more access to the investigation than he currently enjoys. Who knows, this may end up a happy coincidence in the end. The priest was never part of the original design. But with him reopening the painful, suppressed memories from his past—a past the Prophet has so desperately kept guarded—the man of the cloth has inserted himself into his maleficent plan. A plan the Prophet is absolutely sure the young cleric will not like one bit.

"There you go, Father Jakub," he says, firing off the email and leaning back in his chair with his hands clasped behind his head.

Once downloaded and installed, the undetectable malware will grant him access to the priest's private life. Everything the priest sees, hears and says will be his. It might take a bit of time before he installs it, though, so the Prophet takes advantage of the downtime to find the priest's social media account. Like most people, the idiot uploads much too much personal information on the platform, and he quickly discovers that the priest had begun his formation program the same year he himself had been dismissed.

The memory calls back to mind the painful events that had led him to the school in the first place and the darkness that ensued. All that's behind him, though. He just hopes he can fix this before the voice finds out.

38

Father Jakub stares out the window as they travel east, and his phone vibrates silently in his coat pocket. He retrieves it, unlocks it with a few swipes, then reads the email. He smiles and taps the screen to download the software.

"It's a new app from one of our suppliers," he announces with a smile.

"I would have never taken you for a techie," Kellar grins.

"Well, I've come to embrace technology," Father admits. "This new little app will help me track my orders whenever we place one."

"Doesn't take much to get you excited, does it?" Kellar observes light-heartedly. "So how do you remember this Strickland character, anyway," he asks on the drive back to Father Jakub's parish.

"I don't, really, I've never met him," the priest admits. "There was a student they released from the seminary my first month there. I can't remember his name, but it wasn't Thomas Strickland, that's for sure," he recalls. "Officially, they let him go because they felt he had no discernable vocation to the priesthood."

"But unofficially?" the investigator is curious to know.

"The seminary isn't that different from regular university life," Father begins, but Rafe cuts in.

"What, you guys had frat parties and orgies too?" he laughs.

"Very funny," Father Jakub frowns. "No, nothing like that, but you know, seminarians are still guys, and guys like to shoot the breeze and stretch the truth like you and your policeman friends. There was talk about a second-year seminarian who kept getting in trouble and breaking all the rules."

"Gimme a for-instance."

"Well, again, this is merely hearsay, but stuff like touching other seminarians inappropriately and walking around the dorm in the nude when modesty was strongly encouraged, despite the absence of women inside our living quarters."

"So, he was a bit of an exhibitionist, was he?" Kellar jokes.

"There was also a question about the murder of a prostitute not far from the seminary," Father Jakub says ominously. "The police had very little evidence, but they paid our Dean a visit with a sketch that somewhat matched that particular seminarian. They claimed another prostitute had seen a man fitting his likeness strangle her friend after having rough sex with her. Because he had an alibi and she was high at the time, they felt they didn't have enough to proceed."

"So why kick him out if there was no evidence?"

"Rumor floating around was that the episode had been the final straw. The Dean and the other administrative staff members unanimously chose to release him from the program."

"So, if you've never personally met him, how do you know that guy looked anything like Strickland?"

"I saw his picture. It's been a few years, but I know it's him," he maintains. "You know, when you first came to me with this case," he hesitates. "I was sick to my stomach with the thought that your suspect could be a priest," he admits wearily as Kellar navigates the QEW's usual heavy traffic and considers Father's statement.

"Why didn't you tell me you thought it might be a priest?"

"Look, clergy sexual abuse scandals are deplorable and alarmingly frequent in the media—and rightly so, don't get me wrong. Those acts are abominable, and those men need to be put away. But to have a homicidal priest in our midst, I couldn't bring myself to voice that concern until I was absolutely certain."

Kellar glares at him with furrowed brows. "That really wasn't your call."

"Look, it's just that when you and I met, you would have probably kicked down every rectory door in the diocese looking for a killer priest had I mentioned it."

Kellar shrugs. "Yeah, you're probably right," he admits.

"Another thing," he hesitates. "When I shook his hand upon meeting him, I felt what I can only describe as an electrical surge. I knew right away there was something evil about that man," he asserts. "The same thing when we left. It's at that moment the memory from my seminary days resurfaced," Father Jakub claims. "It would make sense that our killer has had *some* religious training, given the nature of these murders."

"You're just happy to see the blame shift away from one of your priest buddies, aren't you?" Kellar teases.

"Probably just as happy as you would be if the initial evidence pointed to a police officer," the priest fires back.

"Touché!" Rafe concedes.

Father Jakub nods and adjusts his glasses.

"Well, given what we've pieced together so far, whether or not he's our guy, he's now at the top of my list of suspects for sure," Kellar declares.

39

He snickers and marvels at his brilliance. "It's okay, Father Jakub. You're not the first ignorant casualty of my genius," he says, eavesdropping on the exchange between Kellar and Father Jakub since the priest had installed his sneaky little spyware. "You want to tell stories about our days at the seminary to the cops, well, be my guest! I'll deal with you later. It's good that you were here today. I know the pig wouldn't have downloaded my app on his government-issued smartphone."

"So, you really believe it's him?" the priest asks as the Prophet listens attentively.

"Yeah, especially now after hearing your story," Kellar admits. "I suppose I started suspecting him not long after we met him, though. When you're working a hunch, you have to follow the evidence wherever it takes you. You can't force the evidence to fit your hunch, so when we got there, I really wasn't expecting much more than a routine interview, but the evidence was quickly piling up. My gut started telling me the sketchy little character could be our suspect. I don't have a clear bead on his motives yet, but that'll come," he swears. "That story about the keyboard falling on his face? I call bullshit! That's the judge's fist. I've been on the wrong side of an angry fist too many times not to recognize what a face looks like after it meets it. He was toying with me too, with his smug responses, almost daring me to catch him in a lie. It's him," Kellar exhales. "I just can't prove it yet."

"Was the DNA at the hotel Strickland's?" asks the priest.

"Unfortunately, our lab hasn't linked the secondary DNA recovered from the scene to anyone yet," Rafe confirms with a sigh.

"And you never will," the Prophet promises confidently. "At least, not to me," he snickers.

"He might not be in the system, but I know he's our suspect," Kellar states emphatically. "We still don't have enough to get a warrant to check his home and office computers, and that might be the only way to figure out where he's going to strike next."

Kellar is silent for a moment.

"That's the worst part, you know?" he sighs.

"What's that?" Father asks.

"That we won't be able to catch him before someone else dies," Kellar sighs, but presses on. "Any of those other locations on the wall have any biblical significance? Calgary, Winnipeg, Montreal, Halifax? What about any of the American sites? There're at least a dozen possible locations down there for him to pick from."

Father Jakub ponders for a moment. "The next covenant was made with King David, and God's people went from being a *nation* to a *kingdom*. Is that any help?" he offers.

"So based on the possible locations, what's a likely kingdom? Who could be the king?"

"I have no idea, Rafe. I'm just a priest, not a detective."

"Although Canada is no longer under British rule, we still have a strong relationship with the old monarchy," Kellar considers.

"You think he might go after the Prime Minister?"

"Him, or maybe the Governor-General. The Prime Minister is elected, but the Governor-General is confirmed by the queen herself."

"Does Synthesized Logistics have an office in Ottawa?"

"Affirmative."

"You really think he's going to strike next in Ottawa?" the priest worries.

"He could, but that's just a guess," Kellar admits. "His first homicides were carefully planned and executed. This last one was a mess, so if he's forced to make modifications on the fly, it's going to get harder to predict his next move. There's no telling where that psycho's headed next."

"I AM NOT A PSYCHO!" the Prophet screeches in the quiet of his office.

There's a lull in the conversation, and Strickland toys with his audio settings, uncertain if the pause is the pair taking a break from their discussion or that he's experiencing technical difficulties, but breathes a sigh of relief when the dialogue resumes.

"The guy could be headed to Memphis for all we know," Kellar grumbles.

"Memphis?" asks Father Jakub puzzled.

"You know, the home of Elvis—the King of Rock and Roll?"

"But Elvis is already dead," the priest dismisses the thought.

"Could be headed to either Disney theme parks in California or Florida," Kellar puts forth the unthinkable. "Some pretty big castles there, you know."

The Prophet is intrigued at how much progress the police have already made, and their timing *is* somewhat of an inconvenience considering he still has one more covenant to re-create before the ultimate climax in July. Nevertheless, he's still confident in his exceptional abilities to keep himself several steps ahead of them, especially now.

He hates to admit it, but this ViCLAS Specialist, Inspector Rafe Kellar, is correct. Clayton Bannister *had* completely derailed his carefully laid plan and carelessly forced him out into the open. The voice had warned him not to use the judge, but the circumstances were much too juicy to pass up the opportunity. He really, *really* enjoyed killing the old goat. But he now wonders if he shouldn't have heeded the warning. Perhaps his selfishness had put the mission in jeopardy. Maybe he had allowed investigators to get too close to him with his thirty-three-year-old vendetta. But that's in the past. He's more intelligent than they are. Sometimes a storm steers your ship off course and forces you to take an alternate route to the same destination. Things didn't go as planned, as Rafe Kellar had insinuated; still, the Prophet *had* exacted his revenge, and, although he has to make a few modifications for the next two covenants because of Bannister and the authorities, his confidence has returned. He will soon regain control of the helm.

With Kellar and friends on his trail, he tightens his timeline and settles on a simpler, albeit more dangerous plan. *What happens to me is inconsequential. Complete the mission! That's the primary objective.* At terms with having to expose himself to more significant risks once again, he turns his attention to the next sacrificial victim. He consults his extensive database, desperate to find a suitable subject for his reconceived design.

"Not you. Not you. Not you," he fumes as time goes by and the list gets shorter. "I know you're out there," he sings. "I'm going to find you."

Frustrated and unable to find a fitting candidate from his list of degenerates, he turns his murderous attention to another file of benign individuals innocently netted by his spyware to see if any of these morons might be of assistance.

He inputs the biblical search parameters hoping that a few of them will be flagged by the algorithm.

"Samuel Nathanson," he whispers. "A seventeen-year-old Edmontonian who likes to go fishing and hunting with his friends. Samuel was known as the King-Maker, wasn't he?" the Prophet considers. "I can definitely work with that, but would prefer something closer to King David," he whines and sets the kid aside for the moment.

"Well, well, well, Inspector Rafe Kellar," he murmurs with a devious grin. "Seems your parents live at 333 Emperor Avenue in an Ottawa suburb. 333 times two is 666, the number of gold talons of Salomon's tax. Hmm," he contemplates rubbing his chin. "Wouldn't that be fun?" he cries out excitedly. The chance to personally involve Kellar is of near-orgasmic intensity, but the stimulating thought quickly vaporizes. His face radiates with joy. He can't believe it had taken him so long to find this outstanding connection. It's almost too perfect. It's as if the voice had directly intervened.

"David King of New Orleans, Louisiana," the Prophet articulates with a slow drawl. "How very nice it is to make your acquaintance. Prepare to meet the Prophet," he proclaims. "It's a shame you don't deserve to die like all the other misfits before you, but you, my friend, were divinely selected."

He rejoices in the blessing and anticipates formulating the fine points. Although no longer able to involve Rafe Kellar's parents in his plan, he still wants to make the cop's life miserable and knows precisely how to accomplish this.

"So, you think you're smart, do you, Inspector Kellar," he scorns. "Very well, you'll get the credit you deserve. The whole world will know just how effective an investigator you are. And as an added bonus, it's time I reward you with another juicy little surprise for your exceptional abilities."

40

Ottawa, Ontario

"Kellar, get in here!" ViCLAS Superintendent Rajat Madan's uncharacteristically angry voice resonates throughout the entire floor.

"What's going on?" Kellar asks as he enters his supervisor's office.

"Did you know about this?" he asks, pointing to the wall-mounted television next to Kellar's head.

"Officials have now confirmed that a serial killer is currently at large and responsible for nearly a dozen homicides here in Canada and the United States so far. The RCMP's Behavioural Sciences Branch has joined forces with the FBI and local law enforcement officers from multiple jurisdictions," the network's Chief Correspondent announces. "We've been told that the killer, calling himself *the Prophet*, has left victims in his deadly wake in San Antonio, Vancouver and Moncton. He is also most recently responsible for the death of retired Supreme Court Justice Philip Saunders, who was found brutally murdered in Gananoque last month. The lead investigator on the case, ViCLAS Specialist Inspector Raphael Kellar of the Behavioural Sciences Branch, has confirmed that the killer leaves a chilling calling card at each of his disturbing crime scenes—a series of unusual prophetic messages and the notation 6:23 in Roman numerals written in blood. These messages appear to be rooted in the Bible and are connected to what investigators are calling *covenant theology*."

As if the divorce papers he'd been served yesterday weren't enough of a distraction and a kick in the groin, these latest developments only exacerbate his frustration. "Raj, this wasn't me," Kellar fumes.

"Look, I know you didn't leak it, but could that priest you're working with have said anything to the media or to someone he knows who couldn't keep quiet?"

"I'll look into it, but as sure as I'm standing here, Jakub didn't talk. We may have our differences, but he's a stand-up guy."

"Well then, how did they find out about this case?" he shouts, his hands frantically gesturing toward the television.

"My guess? *He* probably told them," Kellar reflects. "We're getting too close. He's feeling the heat and wants to distract us so we don't collar him before he's finished."

A file photo of Kellar and an image of Father Jakub grabbed from the internet appear on the screen as the popular commentator's recognizable voice continues his glum monologue.

"Inspector Raphael Kellar confirmed by telephone that he's been working with a priest from the Catholic Archdiocese of Toronto, a Father Jakub Fischer, who's been invited to join the investigation and serve in a consulting capacity to help law enforcement discern the significance of the messages and the killings themselves," he reports gravely. "Based on Father Fischer's assurance that the next killing will take place to reenact the reign of King David from the Old Testament,

Inspector Kellar also confirmed that task force efforts would be focusing on two separate locations he feels could be the Prophet's next targets: the Disney theme parks in Orlando and Anaheim."

"Holy shit, Rafe!"

"He's that good, Raj," Kellar swears. "You know it wasn't me they talked to. We need to have Gerry and his people trace where that call came from," he recommends, wondering how Strickland could have even known he and Jakub had discussed these as possible locations.

"We're about to show you some of the graphic images we've received from officials, but we have to warn you that these crime scene photos could be disturbing, especially to small children. Viewer discretion is *strongly* advised," the commentator warns as images from multiple crime scenes transition on television for the world to see.

"We hadn't even been there yet," Kellar remarks.

"What?" the Superintendent huffs.

"Look, "Kellar says, pointing at the screen. "These photos weren't taken by any evidence gathering team; they were taken by him or his puppets. Do you see any of the usual crime scene markers anywhere?"

"Yeah, you're right," Madan concurs.

"Will you be joining Inspector Kellar in Orlando or Anaheim, Agent Nickerson?" a female reporter asks, shoving a microphone in the FBI agent's face as the report cuts to an American affiliate.

"We have nothing to say on this matter. If the RCMP wants to plaster our case all over the news, that's entirely their business. The FBI never has and never will comment on any on-going investigation," she adds, brushing the microphone away with her hand and walking away.

"Pack your bags, Kellar," Superintendent Madan instructs. "You're taking a trip."

"To where?" Rafe grumbles. "Where do you want me to go, Anaheim or Orlando?"

"I don't care, just go!"

"You can't be serious, Raj," Kellar moans incredulously. "This is smoke and mirrors. He's trying to distract us while he's ending some poor bastard somewhere else."

"So where is he going?" his supervisor requests.

"I still don't know that."

"Then reach out to Agent Nickerson and find out where the FBI is mobilizing and get your ass on the next plane down there!" Madan instructs forcefully.

"Stay with us," the news anchor returns and advises. "We'll keep you posted on any further developments, but for now, here's our Religious Correspondent, Stephanie Lewis, and prominent Catholic theologian, Dr. Hans Scott, joining her by telephone to discuss the Catholic Church's understanding of covenant theology."

41

Montreal, Quebec

Circulation is down to a dribble along Autoroute 40 and takes its toll on her already frayed nerves. Annie St-Laurent is desperate to reach her parents. The text message from her sister was short but to the point. Their father had suffered a massive heart attack and has been taken to l'Hôpital du Sacré-Coeur de Montreal.

Frantically, she redials her sister's number, desperate for information, but as usual, the line goes directly to voice mail. She tosses the phone angrily into the backseat with a curse quite common in Québécois parlance. The phone bounces and lands under her seat as she slips her SUV in and out of traffic, narrowly missing a slow-moving dump truck.

From the safety of his hotel room in New Orleans, the Prophet follows her progress through the hacked onboard navigation system. He snickers as she nears the Boulevard Métropolitain off-ramp, where he remotely disables the power to her electronically controlled steering wheel before she's able to make it onto Autoroute 15 Nord.

Annie misses the turn and slams hard into the concrete Jersey barriers. The airbag deploys, its force violently propelling her head backwards. As she lay motionless against the seat with a broken nose, facial lacerations and a possible neck injury, she hears the bickering exchanges of angry bystanders as they debate whose cell phone to use to call emergency services.

42

New Orleans, Louisiana

The Prophet's GPS application on the tablet's screen goes blank, confirming the successful execution of the most amusing part of his plan. Even for someone as intelligent as he, he marvels at how quickly information technology advances. He's ecstatic with this new technological development and wishes he'd had it a few months earlier for disposing of "Jezebel" in the muddy waters of the Petitcodiac River. It would have made his life a lot easier and less risky—but hey, that's water under the bridge. Whether this woman lives or dies is irrelevant to him. He just needs his point to come across loud and clear.

With this enjoyable task carried out, he opens his next victim's digital file and reviews the details one final time before powering down and gathering his electronics. These he'll ship to himself before leaving the hotel. He dons the courier uniform and puts a fresh change of clothes inside a parcel he'll use as his prop for the job.

St. Louis Street is overflowing with tourists outside the hotel, and he's not sure which he hates the most: the sweltering humidity, the throngs of people, or the spicy aromas wafting from the open restaurant windows he passes along the way.

He makes a right at Bourbon Street as a drunken crowd staggers out of a popular drinking establishment and bumps him unapologetically into the crowded street, where he drops his package into a fresh puddle of vomit. Retrieving the dripping box, he wipes the alcoholic slime on the pant leg of a comatose wino propped against the front of the bar and mumbles unsavory curses in his assailants' direction. Reluctantly, he dismisses the inebriated encounter and carries on with the mission rather than gutting them for being intoxicated this early in the afternoon. Drawing undue attention is not an option, not that a public altercation would raise much concern with their common occurrences in the French Quarter. Still, he reconsiders and blends into the crowd until he reaches St. Ann Street, where he makes a left, passing a homeless beggar camped on the sidewalk under one of the city's many landmark balconies.

The crowds have thinned considerably as he proceeds up the much quieter St. Ann Street and then turns right onto the deserted Dauphine, stopping in front of the three-story, red-brick apartment building.

He accesses the rear staircase and quickly climbs his way up to the top floor. The ashtray smell combined with curry and fish is nauseating in the dingy hallway, and the whaling screams from a crying infant distract him, but he hurries his stride to the last unit at the end of the corridor where David King's door was left ajar, the jamb damaged from an apparent break-in.

"Hello?" he calls out and slips cautiously inside. "I have a delivery for you."

The rumbling hum from the window-mounted air conditioning unit in the kitchen is deafening and overpowers

Ella Fitzgerald on the turntable in the living room. He slowly edges his way into the hallway toward the bedrooms and hears the faint whimpering of a child, then finds the small boy slumped over the corpse of David King as he steps through the doorway.

"What the hell!" he exclaims.

The small black child stares up at him then turns his attention back to his father.

"He's dead," he snivels.

What's going on here! the voice inside his head demands.

"I don't know," the Prophet replies nervously.

"Some men came and killed my daddy," the young boy sobs. "I was playing in my room and heard a loud noise. Then some men started yelling at him. They said he owed them some money, and when he said he didn't have any, I heard a louder noise like on TV and then I couldn't hear anything anymore. I waited in my room a long time. Then I came here and found my daddy right here."

Kill the kid instead! the voice commands insistently. *I want blood! I don't care where it comes from!*

"No," the Prophet mutters weakly. "No!"

Do it! the voice stands firm.

"Mister, can you help my daddy?" the child pleads.

"I—I can't help him," he falters. "What are you even doing home at this time? You're supposed to be at your grandmother's house today," he whines, recalling the email thread between the kid's father and the grandmother he had so carefully committed to memory.

Kill the boy! the voice demands more forcefully.

"No!" he fires back. "That's not the deal!"

"Are you talking to the police on an earphone or something?" the boy asks.

"What?" he replies, confused.

"You look like you're talking to someone," he observes.

"No! Mind your own business!" he barks at the kid.

His heart races and his forehead beads with sweat. The voice is unrelenting in its demand for blood. The room spins, and he reaches for the wall as he loses his balance.

"You'll get your blood!" he swears and staggers away from the child and his dead father. "Stay here!" he orders the boy, and leaves the room.

Clutching the parcel firmly to his chest, he marches out into the hallway and pounds on the door immediately across the smelly corridor.

"Yes?" an elderly woman in her mid-eighties answers.

"Hi, I have a delivery for you," he says bitterly.

"I'm not expecting anything," the senior replies.

"Well, I guess this is your lucky day!" he insists, forcing himself into her apartment.

"Help!" she screams.

"Shut up!" he warns, brandishing a knife with an eight-inch blade. "No one heard the bastards kill your neighbour. So, who do you think is going to come to rescue you from me?"

"Who are you?" she begs.

"I am the Prophet, and I'm here to offer you as a sacrifice to the voice."

"Please," she moans her last word before the killer ends her life, and her body collapses to the floor.

His breathing slows. His heart rate stabilizes as he takes in a deep, calming breath and squats. He runs his long, thin finger through his victim's blood and traces the familiar Roman numerals on the floor next to her.

The noise from the door behind him startles him, and he turns to see the young neighbor from across the hall staring back at him, frozen in place and standing in a puddle of urine.

The killer glares at him, and the young child runs off to the safety of his apartment.

"Are you happy now?" the Prophet asks the invisible spirit only he can communicate with. He rises and wipes the blood from his hands and face with the old woman's dishcloth, then strips off his courier uniform and tears open the parcel to retrieve his change of clothes. With the bloody courier outfit in a bag, he exits the woman's apartment wearing a pair of shorts, sandals, a tank top, a pair of sunglasses and a ball cap. He closes the door behind him and drapes a string of festive beads around his neck.

43

Anaheim, California

The afternoon sun is hot, but the shade from the canopy of palm trees dotting the green space that spans the area between the hotel and the convention center offers a welcoming relief from the heat. A steady stream of hyperactive high schoolers ebbs and flows between the two massive structures as the Annual National High School Volleyball Championships held at the convention center heat up.

"We've been here for two days, and still no sign of our suspect," Agent Nickerson complains, shredding her salad into thin, manageable pieces with her plastic cutlery. "We might just be wasting valuable time here."

Kellar exhales and seats himself opposite her at the table, admiring the vividness of her newly-colored auburn hair in the sunlight.

"I *know* we are," he affirms and sips at his coffee. "That's what I told my boss."

"Yeah, but the intel that led us here was pretty convincing."

"He's probably not even in this state, let alone this country."

"You're convinced it's him, aren't you?" Nickerson asks. "Strickland?"

"I don't have anything in my back pocket that would stand up in court, but I know he's the guy we're chasing," he maintains. "The man works as an IT director for a large corporation with branches in every one of the locations where the homicides took place."

"Circumstantial at best," she argues.

"My boss tends to agree with that sentiment. He says the best he can do is authorize people to sit on the place and observe from a distance, despite the fact that these guys have at least five executives who have made trips to some or all the locations in the last six months— including Strickland."

"Come on, Kellar, there's gotta be a thousand other companies that fit that bill; besides, you said that none of their trips overlap our homicides," she argues.

"You telling me he couldn't get into the company's database and mess with his travel itineraries?" he says, fascinated with the way she picks at her food, one tiny green shred at a time.

"What about military personnel?" she suggests, not entirely sold on the Strickland angle. "Have we considered that possibility?"

"Military only fits if all the homicides happened in either one of our jurisdictions," he replies. "We haven't had any joint military training exercises anywhere recently. It's Strickland. I just can't prove it yet."

Nickerson shrugs and Kellar sips at his coffee, wondering how much of Father Jakub's story he should share with her.

"You're right," he makes up his mind. "There *are* plenty of other companies that fit the bill, but what no other company has, is Strickland," he says, easing in. "We were able to establish a connection between Strickland and his past as a failed seminarian, which suggests a functional knowledge of theology."

She cocks her head. "Really?"

Rafe nods.

"So, if you know it's him, and you know the connection between this place and the next covenant, what makes you so sure he *isn't* striking here next?" she asks.

"My gut," he affirms. "He's toying with us. He's a psychopathic narcissist who believes he's smarter than we are, but his next performance isn't happening here at Disneyland. He wants us as far away as possible from him where and when it happens."

She takes in her surroundings and wipes her puffy lips with a napkin while pushing the plastic food tray away from her. "Well, whatever's supposed to happen better happen soon," she exhales. "I like California as much as the next girl, but I've got other important things that need my attention," then adds, tucking her hair back behind her ear with her piercing green eyes boring into his. "Good thing the company's kinda cute."

Taken aback by her bluntness, Kellar blushes.

The attractive agent's face lights up.

Kellar chuckles. "Agent Nickerson, are you flirting with me?"

"I might be," she says playfully.

"You know Father Jakub wouldn't approve," he jokes.

"He's not *my* father," she winks, her hand brushing against his leg under the table.

Kellar's phone interrupts the sexually-charged exchange. "Saved by the bell," he grins. "What's up, Marty?" he answers on the first ring, rising to pace, like he typically does to concentrate on a call, as Agent Nickerson's phone comes to life as well.

"There's been another one," Kellar's researcher announces.

"Where?" Rafe sighs. "When?"

"New Orleans," he announces. "Just happened a few hours ago."

"New Orleans? That makes no sense."

"Victim was an elderly woman," he says and pauses for a second. "Huerta Chávez, age eighty-two. Her throat was cut."

"What's her possible connection to the fifth covenant?" Rafe wants to know.

"We suspect her neighbor."

"Why?"

"Neighbour's name was David King—" Bloom doesn't have time to finish before Kellar interrupts.

"King David!" he cries out, drawing more attention from passersby than intended. "So why not kill *him*?"

"King was already dead when he got there,"

"What?"

"Locals think it might have been gang-related," Bloom explains. "He was a counselor working with at-risk youths, convincing them that being upright members of society was more rewarding than being used by the local gangs to distribute their drugs and put their lives at risk. The NOPD believes he was making a difference with a lot of the kids and was putting a dent in their business. He was likely killed for being a good guy."

"So, how does the neighbor fit into this?" Kellar inquires.

"King's five-year-old son said he was kneeling by his dad when a courier arrived with a package. He said he was mumbling weird stuff like he was talking to someone else and then left in a hurry. The kid heard a commotion across the hall and went in to take a look. He said he saw the old lady on the floor and the courier drawing something next to her with his fingers. When the guy turned and looked at him, he ran back into his home and barricaded the door with a chair. The chair wouldn't have stopped anyone, though, so we believe the suspect fled the scene."

"Kid got lucky," Kellar says. "Was he able to give the locals a description of the guy?"

"Not much more than he was dressed like a courier—you know, brown shorts, brown shirt, and hat with a yellow logo on it."

"Does he remember if the guy had long hair, a beard, was wearing glasses? Anything?"

"No, just what I told you," Bloom confirms. "Anyway, NOPD reached out to the FBI because of the ritualistic nature of the evidence at the scene, and they looped us in. The locals are investigating the King homicide on their end, but have sealed off our victim's apartment for the FBI and us to deal with."

"Thanks, Marty," Kellar says, disconnects, and turns to Agent Nickerson. "You get the same call?" he asks, rejoining her at their table.

"Yeah," she admits glumly. "Looks like we're headed to New Orleans. Our ride will be here in twenty minutes to take us to the airport."

"What about Jakub?" Kellar asks.

"Where did you say he went?"

"He's visiting some big glass church. Something about it being a new Catholic Cathedral he wanted to check out. I don't know; I was only half-listening to him to tell you the truth."

"Text him that we'll send a car his way to pick him up. He can detour here to pick up his things, check out, then join us at the airport in time for our flight."

44

LAX, Los Angeles, California

Borrowing Dylan's timeless lyrics, Adel's velvety voice oozes through the ceiling speakers inside the private terminal at LAX while Kellar watches a plane take off in the distance. He turns to Agent Nickerson sitting next to him on one of the lounge's leather loveseat they share as they wait to board one of the Department of Justice's private jets.

"He's devolving even more," Kellar states. "He's gone from having people do the killings to doing them himself. His first kills went without a hitch. Then his minion got shot before he could kill the judge, and he had to finish that one on his own, and now, in New Orleans, his victim was already dead, forcing him to just pick some random replacement on the fly."

"Why not King's son?" Nickerson asks. "I wouldn't expect him to leave a witness behind. I mean, he sorta did with the clerk and the couple who saw him in the hallway at the hotel where the judge was staying, but it's not like he was dressed like a woman this time."

"Don't know. Maybe he's got limitations of some sort?"

"You mean he didn't *want* to kill the boy or couldn't bring himself to do it?"

They share an inquisitive stare.

"Maybe he saw himself in the kid and wanted to protect him as though protecting himself as a kid?" she supposes.

"Maybe," Kellar considers. "Maybe he's just too focussed on getting to the finish line; he just doesn't care anymore. Just one more to go now."

"New Orleans was number five, not six." Nickerson corrects. "I thought Father Jakub said there were seven of these covenants of his."

"Yeah, that was a bit confusing for me too," Rafe admits. "As I understand it, between number five and six is where the prophets come into play. Jakub says these guys were the glue that kept the Jewish faith alive as best they could throughout the Babylonian exile, hence the reason we believe he calls himself the Prophet."

Agent Nickerson nods her understanding.

"The sixth covenant is Jesus's death. So, to paraphrase Jakub, the seventh one hasn't taken place yet, scripturally speaking, so I'm working with the assumption that this next one will be the last chapter of his delusional agenda and will probably involve his own death."

"He's not planning to get caught, just shot," she chuckles. "So, six and seven at the same time, like he's supposed to be what, the Second Coming?" she asks.

"I guess?" Kellar shrugs. "Although we still don't have a bead on what his next target will be."

"So, in keeping with his twisted mind, if his grand finale is where the line ends for him, it makes sense that it will be all the more unpredictable and spectacular, making him all the more dangerous," Nickerson submits.

"That's right. There's no telling just how grand a finale he's planning."

"I'm not religious in any way, but don't Christians believe Christ will come to collect all believers at the end of time?" she asks. "What if he's planning to take out as many people as possible for this next spectacle? Someplace where a lot of people might gather to pray?"

"Okay, that makes sense," Kellar grants. "What if this next victim is supposed to be a proxy for Christ? Like a priest or a bishop?"

"He could be planning to take out an entire church?" Nickerson replies anxiously.

"Wait!" Rafe cuts in. "Jakub's been rambling on about World Youth Day in Rio next month."

"Yeah, I heard about that on the news," she reflects.

"Millions of people will be gathered to catch a glimpse of the new pope," he says. "It makes sense that he's his next target. We have to get down there before Strickland does."

"Not before we check out the New Orleans crime scene," she objects. "I want to talk to that kid. Let him work with a sketch artist. We might get lucky and get a glimpse of who we're chasing."

"I told you, it's Strickland."

"Let's just make sure," she says. "Anyone ever tell you, you smell good?" Nickerson asks playfully, drawing near to him and sniffing near his neck.

"Sorry I'm late," Father Jakub calls out as he enters the private lounge. "I hope I haven't kept you waiting too long. Traffic was terrible," he adds nervously, slightly uncomfortable that he might have interrupted a moment between his colleagues on the small couch.

"No, just in time," Rafe says, flustered, rising awkwardly from his seat and Agent Nickerson's unmistakeable discontent.

She sighs, stands and heads toward the tarmac doors. "Okay, people. Let's get ourselves some chicory coffee and beignets."

45

New Orleans, Louisiana

Huerta Chávez's small apartment is stuffy and overcrowded with FBI crime technicians as the investigators take photographs and collect evidence samples behind the yellow tape barricading the doorway, while the local police department conducts its own investigation in the King residence across the hall.

"You gonna be okay?" Kellar asks Father Jakub with a worried look.

The priest nods, but his pasty face tells a different story.

"You look like you're gonna be sick," Rafe observes.

Again, the priest dismisses him, but immediately draws his hands to his mouth and quickly ducks past the tape, vomiting on the carpeted floor in the hallway.

Kellar joins him outside the door and lays a compassionate hand on his back.

"This is a lot to take in, especially the first one," he acknowledges in a whisper. "Why don't you go outside and get some air?"

"I have to clean this up," Father Jakub manages weakly as he assesses the mess at his feet.

"Don't worry about it. It's not like anyone's going to notice that on *this* carpet, but I'll make sure it's cleaned up before we leave," he insists, leading the priest toward the stairs and motioning for a patrolman to take him outside. "Please make sure he's taken care of."

"Rookie!" Agent Nickerson scoffs.

"Cut him some slack," Rafe chides. "He didn't ask to get his ass dragged into this craziness."

Agent Nickerson shrugs off the remark and saunters over to the NOPD officer guarding the King crime scene. The local cop outstretches his brawny arms and blocks her way as she reaches for the yellow tape.

"Can't let you in there," he says forcefully.

"You boys *do* know we can work together here, right?" she complains. "Let us talk with the kid to find out what he knows."

The cop shakes his head.

"Does the kid even know his dad was going to die either way today?" she shoots dryly. "You guys know who killed his father. Let us catch the bastard who was here to kill him, but butchered his neighbour instead."

"That's mighty uncouth of you, Agent Nickerson," The tall and lanky detective says, stepping out to assist his fellow officer at the door.

"Uncouth?" Nickerson sneers. "That's a pretty fancy word for you, don't you think?"

"We are cooperating with your investigation as much as we are able to," Detective Robichaud slowly drawls, unfazed by her contempt. "You're right, we *do* know who did this to the child's father, but I'm sure you're aware that unless we cross the t's and dot the i's, these punks are going to walk as usual.

The boy was here when his father was killed, but, fortunately for him, he did not witness the murder and cannot identify the suspects. When we have more information to share with y'all, we will."

"At least let us speak with the kid," she insists. "We know for a fact that he *did* see *our* suspect."

"The child's not speaking with anyone tonight," Robichaud announces calmly. "He's currently with Social Services and awaiting his aunt to fly in from Houston. Together, his aunt and the social worker will decide when the time's right for us to speak with him, not you. Now please, just concentrate on Mrs. Chávez's apartment and let us do our job in here," he adds with a stern frown toward the FBI agent and the Canadian cop before ducking back into his crime scene.

"Fine!" Agent Nickerson lets out a frustrated breath and crosses the hall back over to their respective investigation. "You coming?" Nickerson asks over her shoulder.

"No," Kellar replies.

She shoots him a quizzical glance and folds her arms across her chest.

"There's nothing in there for us to find. Strickland might be playing a delusional game, but he's not the kind of lunatic who's leaving clues behind just to taunt us. I already told you who we're chasing and where he's going next. We can't waste time here. We need to work out a strategy to intercept him in Rio next month. That's who we're chasing. That's his next target!"

She considers this for a moment and grins. Kellar looks so sexy, all intense and wound up. She knows he's convinced this Strickland character is their suspect, but without any real evidence, they might as well be chasing a ghost—something she feels they've been doing ever since Kellar had initially reached out to her. She hopes the King boy will be able to shed some light on the suspect's identity, but knows how unreliable eyewitnesses can be. She peers into Mrs. Chávez's apartment then turns back to Kellar. She's been crushing on the Mountie for the paste few days and figures now is as good a time to get to know him better—and who knows, maybe into bed if they're lucky.

"You're right," she concedes. "Let's let the techs finish up in here, and you and I can relax over dinner and a few drinks."

Rafe contemplates the suggestion. "I'll see if Jakub's up to it."

She rolls her eyes and slumps her shoulders. "Give him some time to process this and put himself back together. We can meet up at the restaurant at the hotel, and he can join us after if he feels up to it."

"Sure. Okay," Rafe hesitantly agrees.

46

The food was satisfying, but the bourbon was exceptional. Kellar couldn't believe the selection he had to choose from and was happy to sample several whiskies he had never even heard of.

"Looks like you enjoyed that burger," Pat remarks as Rafe wipes his mouth.

"And you've hardly touched that rabbit food," he kids.

"I like to watch my figure," she winks. "You know, you're pretty laid back when you want to be," she snickers.

"Bourbon's helping," he says, raising a hand to draw the server's attention.

"You ordering another burger?"

"No, another round of bourbon," he grins like a child.

With the case weighing on him for months, Kellar hadn't allowed himself the pleasure of many distractions. Although his work has him investigating a variety of serial cases, homicide and child sex trafficking rings are the ones that weigh him down the most, and no other investigation has taken its toll on him quite like this one. He feels sorry for the young boy who just lost his father, but reflects on how much worse it could have gone for the child. Strickland had let him live; maybe that's something—but probably not. As he preaches to anyone who'll listen, Strickland *is* their suspect, and he's going to strike next month in Rio. They have plenty of time to gather intelligence, plan a strategy, assemble a task force and catch the bastard. But tonight, with Father Jakub resting in their room and Strickland's days numbered, he allows himself a brief respite from the madness and longs for another round of the smooth, burning whiskey. And for the touch of the free-spirited beauty across the table.

"You want another one too?" he asks as the server draws near, and she accepts with a playful smile.

The server nods in Kellar's direction. "I'll be right back with your order," he says, retreating to the bar area.

She frowns seductively. "Why, Rafe Kellar, if I didn't know any better, I'd think you were trying to get me drunk and take me back to your room."

He chuckles. "Not my room. I'm sharing one with a priest."

She laughs and reaches under the table, and her eyes grow wide. "Someone's packing serious heat," she smiles.

He chuckles awkwardly and straightens himself in the chair.

"I'm sorry," he says sheepishly. "I'm a little out of practice here," he admits nervously. "Juice keeps telling me to get back in the game, but, you know, it's tough to balance a normal personal life with the crap we see every day."

"Hey, who says we have to make this personal?" she says mischievously. "We're both adults. What's wrong with a couple of law enforcement officers taking a break from the freaks of society and letting off a bit of no-strings-attached steam?"

He cocks his head and smiles. "Are you like this with all the cops?" he jokes.

"Just the cute Canadian ones," she replies.

"Good thing Father Jakub isn't here," he smirks, taking the wind out of her sail.

She sits upright as the waiter arrives with their drinks.

"What is it with you and that priest, anyways?" Nickerson asks dryly, grabbing the drink from the waiter's hand and lifting it to her lips.

"What do you mean?" Kellar answers.

"Well, every time we start making some sort of connection, you always bring him up in conversation. It's like you're using him as an excuse to keep me at a distance."

"What? That's not true," Rafe exclaims unconvincingly.

"Yes, it is," she insists.

Kellar stares back at her, speechless. She's correct. In his mind, he replays all the advances she's made, and each time, he's brought up the priest and immediately extinguished whatever spark she had attempted to ignite.

"You're right," he sighs after a moment. "I'm sorry," he says honestly.

"What is it with you, you don't like American women?" she teases, laying on a thick helping of guilt.

"No—it's not you, it's—"

"Don't you dare finish that sentence," she cuts in. "What are you, in junior high? I know damned well it's you and not me, so why don't you just grow a pair and tell me what's really going on inside your head?" she demands.

He nervously rubs the nape of his neck, pondering his response.

"Look, it's not like I'm some sort of wild bachelor. I haven't been single all that long," he explains, which she acknowledges with a nod. "The circumstances that ended my marriage were pretty bad," he admits, remembering the last time he saw his wife at his son's funeral. "You know—yeah, I definitely feel that there's some sort of chemistry between the two of us, but . . . I'm just not ready for any type of relationship."

"Holy shit, Kellar!" she cries out, much to his dismay, as other guests stare at them. "You really have been out of the game for a long time. Who said anything about a relationship? Sometimes sex is nothing more than sex!"

His mind races. This woman is obviously out of his league. She's fourteen years younger, but clearly more experienced than he. He recalls fantasizing about girls like this in high school, but he was always too shy to even talk to them. If they'd been as forward as this in his days, he would have spent a hell of a lot less time thumbing through porn magazines in the privacy of his bedroom under his parents' roof.

He dismisses the memory and swallows his drink in a single gulp. "You wanna get out of here?" he suggests with a crooked smile.

"It's about time," she says, tossing a wad of cash on the table and grabbing him by the arm. "Let's go. My treat."

Kellar willingly follows, thinking to himself how right she was about the treat part.

Pushing their way through the drunken crowd on the street, the two quickly make their way back to their hotel a block around the corner from the Den of Bourbon. A band of noisy sailors on leave fall out into the street as they approach the main entrance. Kellar's pulse races as they hop into the elevator and the doors slide shut. He reaches for the button as Agent Nickerson's hungry mouth finds his, and they stumble against the elevator wall.

Almost as though scripted, Father Jakub reaches for the call button as the doors split open, and he comes face-to-face with the pair.

"Rafe," Father Jakub says with an alarming look of concern.

"Ah, shit!" Kellar grumbles, stepping into the hallway to meet the young priest. "What?" he barks. "You don't approve?"

The priest stares at him, dumbfounded.

"I told you to stay out of my personal life," Kellar spits.

"Rafe, that's not it," he says delicately. "I just got a call from Juice. He's—he's been trying to reach you . . . uhm," Father Jakub falters.

"Spit it out!" Kellar says bitterly.

"It's Annie," he sighs. "She's been in a terrible car accident, Rafe."

Kellar's face pales. "What?"

"Juice said that he's been trying to get a hold of you since he got word earlier this afternoon, but that you never answered your phone."

Kellar checks his phone and curses as he discovers it had been on silent with several missed calls on the display.

"I gotta go," he says, and, leaving the priest with the bewildered FBI agent in the hallway, disappears quickly down the stairs.

"Rafe!" Agent Nickerson cries out, but the heavy door slams shut behind him without as much as a nod from him in her direction.

"What the hell?" she fumes. "Who's Annie?"
"Rafe's wife," Father Jakub replies.

47

Montreal, Quebec

The last twelve hours were a blur, but thanks to his persistence with everyone from airline ticketing agents to off-duty cab drivers, Kellar had managed to travel from New Orleans to Montreal in record time. Still wearing yesterday's clothes and sporting day-old stubble, he hops out of the cab in front of the hospital and sprints through the busy lobby's automatic doors. He pauses momentarily to locate the information kiosk and hurries over to it.

"Where can I find Annie Kellar!" he implores.

"We don't have no Annie Kellar here, Monsieur," the French receptionist answers apologetically as best she can in English, after consulting the hospital's patient database.

"I was told she was admitted here yesterday, at this hospital, specifically," he insists.

"I'm sorry. I checked that name twice, and there is no Annie Kellar here at all."

"She has to be," he fumes. "She was in a car accident."

The receptionist sighs and looks to the person behind him, hoping he'd get the hint and move out of the line.

"Dammit," he mutters, remembering the law in Quebec that requires women to use their maiden name. "St-Laurent," he cries out. "Annie St-Laurent."

"Ah, oui, bon," she smiles. "She's on the fifth floor in wing B," she says, writing down the room number on a slip of paper for Kellar.

"Thank you," he says, rushing off to the elevator bank.

A pair of nurses climb in ahead of him, and he jabs at the fifth-floor button erratically.

The nurses leave him on three, and he immediately presses the close door button several times before anyone else has a chance to board. The elevator inches its way up the shaft, and the doors finally unleash him. Consulting the overhead signs, he navigates his way to Annie's room with only a few wrong turns.

"Rafe," the familiar voice calls out from a waiting room doorway.

Kellar stops mid-stride and turns upon hearing his name. "Thanks for coming, Juice, but I can't talk right now. I have to get to Annie."

"Wait," his long-time friend and colleague urges, clutching his elbow.

Kellar's glaring eyes bore into his. "Juice. You better let go of me," he warns sternly.

"Arch, I just gotta give you a heads up about something before you go in there," he says delicately.

"What?"

"Look, as soon as Annie was admitted, the Sûreté du Québec swarmed in, and they've arrested her."

"Arrested her for what?" Rafe says heatedly.

"Apparently, the female DNA that was found at our Gananoque crime scene was a match to hers."

"Are you nuts?" Kellar screams.

"Our lab confirmed it, and an arrest warrant was issued yesterday. Sûreté du Québec received an anonymous tip that she was here, and they dispatched a couple of officers faster than you can imagine. They've even posted a rookie constable to guard her door," the words barely leave Juice's mouth before Kellar slips away and races off to Annie's room.

"Désolé, Monsieur, mais vous ne pouvez pas entrer," the Québec policeman says to him.

"Look," Kellar gnarls. "I don't speak much French, but I think you just told me I wasn't allowed in there." He holds his credentials three centimeters from the sentinel's nose. "But I'm going in there with or without your permission."

"Okay, I'm sorry, Inspector Kellar," the baby-faced cop stands-down with his best English. "I wasn't told to expect anyone else from the RCMP. Please go inside."

"Merci," Kellar growls sarcastically, then pushes his way inside the room.

His heart melts as he takes in her swollen and bruised eyes, her bandaged-wrapped head, the neck brace and the IV drip as she lay sleeping peacefully.

"Oh, Annie, I'm so sorry it took me this long to get here," he whispers as he approaches her side. Reaching for her delicate hand, he notes the metal cuff around her wrists tethering her to the bed rails, and his anger boils over. For her sake, he maintains his temper and leans in to kiss her forehead. With his blood pressure rising, Kellar straightens himself, turns toward the door and fumes as the local cop enters the room behind Juice's towering figure.

"Uncuff her!" he orders.

"I—I can't," the young cop stutters.

"There's been a mistake. My wife did *not* kill that judge. She was in a car accident and deserves more respect than what you guys have shown her," Rafe insists. "Now, uncuff her!"

"I'm sorry, I have my orders," the constable replies with difficulty.

With both fists, Kellar grabs him firmly by the collar and shoves the rookie cop violently against the wall. "Uncuff her now!" he demands.

48

New Orleans, Louisiana

"Is the sketch artist nearly finished with the kid?" Agent Nickerson impatiently asks one of the NOPD officers inside the squad room.

"Shouldn't be much longer now," he replies.

She lets out a loud, frustrated breath and returns to the boardroom, where Father Jakub patiently sips at his tea. She looks at him with a touch of disdain, still upset that Kellar had rushed off last night and ditched the priest in her lap.

"You guys always have to wear those uniforms everywhere?" she asks about his black shirt and white collar out of boredom more than curiosity.

Father smiles and looks up while adjusting his glasses. "No, we aren't required to, but I like to dress like this as often as I can. It's who I am. I am a priest and am proud of it," he affirms cheerfully.

"You're proud of being a priest?" she asks, surprised.

"Well, yes, of course. There's nothing I'd rather be," Father Jakub says, his answer not sitting entirely well with her in her current state.

"So, you enjoy judging people and telling them what they can and can't do?" she scoffs.

"Agent Nickerson, aren't you doing to me exactly what you're accusing me of doing to you?" he calmly turns the table. "You're judging me."

She shrugs away his response.

"You don't even know me, Agent Nickerson," Father Jakub says.

"Oh, really?" she challenges. "You've been getting between Rafe and me since the moment we met," she glares. "Your approval isn't something I'm especially interested in, just so we're clear."

"Agent Nickerson, my opinion is irrelevant. I have no power over you. You're entirely free to do whatever you choose."

"I know *I'm* free to do whatever I choose, but you have no problem preaching your sexual morality and threatening hell with fire and brimstone to anyone who disagrees with you, don't you?"

"Are you asking me for my opinion or merely stating yours?" he smiles.

She ignores the remark, crosses her arms and turns her back to him.

"You're right," he says. "The Church and I *do* believe that human sexuality has a greater purpose than simply its resulting physical pleasure and that it should be treated with respect."

"You see, that's the problem with you people!" she whirls and points angrily in his direction. "You guys stand there at your pulpits, and you dictate what's right and wrong and condemn anyone who disagrees with your long-expired beliefs. You're old fashioned, short-sighted, misogynistic and controlling."

Father Jakub reflects on her words and considers his next ones carefully.

"Agent Nickerson," he begins and adjusts his glasses. "The church can only teach truth, and sometimes, truth is difficult—even uncomfortable—but truth is truth, and as Flannery O'Connor once said, 'The truth does not change according to our ability to stomach it.' None of our teachings are intended to lord some sort of worldly power over people. They're meant to hand down moral teachings as the roadmap to happiness in this life in anticipation of the life to come. It's like an owner's manual for a new electronic component of some sort. The dos and don'ts listed are extensive, but they aren't published to suck the enjoyment out of the experience of using the product. The manufacturer wants you to get the most out of your purchase and since they're the ones who designed and built it, they know how you should care for it."

"Wake up!" she challenges. "We're not electronic devices, and morality is subjective. What's right for you isn't necessarily right for me."

"That argument lacks a certain depth, I'm afraid," he suggests.

She takes a chair opposite him at the table and glares.

"A couple was arguing one day. Facing each other in their driveway with a chalk drawing by their four-year-old daughter between them, the wife argued that their daughter had drawn a lovely number six while the father argued that it was a nine," she says. "From each other's perspective, they were both right. So, when they asked their little girl what she had drawn in chalk, she answered that it was the toboggan the family had used to go sledding the previous winter. So, you see, the father and mother were both correct according to where they were standing, illustrating that the truth of the matter was subjective."

"You're right, Agent Nickerson," he admits. "It would appear that way on the surface, but as you stated, the author of that drawing was the little girl. Both parents believed they were correct based on their *own* interpretations, but the objective reality of the drawing is what the author had intended when designing it. It was neither a six nor a nine, and just like that little girl, God authored us and knows what's best for our true happiness, regardless of our opinions or interpretations."

"So, what if the little girl told her parents they were free to believe whatever they wanted?" she argues.

"That *is* correct of the little girl. She could have easily said that looking to please both her parents, but God never told us we are free to interpret his truths on our own. You have much more worth in God's eyes than a chalk drawing on the pavement by a little girl, Agent Nickerson."

She sighs and rolls her eyes.

He sees she's not convinced.

"Do you believe in science, Agent Nickerson?" Father Jakub asks.

"Of course, I believe in science," she answers bluntly. "My work as an investigator depends on it. I don't take my leads from a fairy-tale book like you, though. I follow evidence that's backed and confirmed by science."

"That's perfect!" Father exclaims. "Science and religion are not at odds. The Bible, as you so colorfully keep referring to as a fairy tale, tells us *what* God did for us and why, while science best explains *how* he did it."

"Wait, you actually believe in science?" she asks, surprised.

"Yes, of course," he smiles broadly. "The Big Bang was actually a concept first proposed by a Jesuit priest, Father George Lemaitre," he announces and continues enthusiastically. "Since sexuality brought us onto this topic, let's continue down this path, shall we?" he suggests, making the female agent noticeably uncomfortable discussing sex with a priest.

"Moments ago, you suggested that the Church is too old-fashioned when it comes to sexuality, but what we teach is that sex has two distinct natures: a procreative one and a unitive one."

Agent Nickerson's passion overtakes her discomfort. "Bullshit!" she blares. "I'm not a baby-maker, and there's absolutely nothing wrong with sex between two consenting adults who don't need complications in their lives."

The young priest takes a minute to gather his thoughts.

"As a professional investigator," he resumes. "I suspect you never base your judgement on opinions, but that you ascertain someone's guilt or innocence based on facts, is that correct?" he asks, and she begrudgingly nods her agreement. "Let's forget that I'm a priest. Let's consider the data we have available to us and, using an atheistic lens, even if one doesn't believe in God, one has to admit that we have certain parts of our bodies that are meant for certain functions. Ears are for hearing; eyes are for sight; the tongue is for speech; et cetera, do you agree?"

"So far," she concedes reluctantly.

"So, we both agree that these parts have a purpose, a reason for being."

She nods and follows.

"You know, throughout history, up to a generation or two ago before they were re-named sexual organs, they were called reproductive organs, Agent Nickerson," Father Jakub states. "But rebranding something only changes our perception of it, not its true nature. You mentioned pleasure a moment ago?" again, she nods. "Eating cheesecake is pleasing, isn't it?" he grins, and she returns a lukewarm smile. "But if you ate only that, you wouldn't be nourishing your body and would grow weak. The fact that eating gives pleasure as well as nourishes our bodies ensures our survival. The same is true with sex. If sex was painful and not at all enjoyable, I doubt very much humanity would have made it this far."

"But there's more to sex than pleasure," she argues.

"Yes, that's true. The flip side of sex is its unitive nature. During intercourse, chemicals are released in the brain. These neurochemicals strengthen the bond between the couple. When the bond is initiated and broken several times over with multiple partners, this naturally produced bonding agent becomes weaker and can lead to heartache, confusion, self-doubt and, oftentimes, self-loathing. We have empirical, biochemical evidence and many psychological case studies that support this—and that, Agent Nickerson, is science, not religion."

She reflects on his words and is about to comment when the NOPD sketch artist emerges from her office and enters the boardroom with the drawing.

"Here's your suspect," she announces, tossing a copy of the sketch on the conference table for the FBI agent and the priest to take in.

"Dear God!" Father Jakub gasps. "That *is* Strickland!"

"Get this out to everyone!" she instructs. "Make sure Kellar gets a copy of it as well."

49

Montreal, Quebec

"Whoa, Arch!" Juice steps in to defuse the escalation with a calm hand on Rafe's shoulder.

"Stay out of this, Kamarre!" he gnarls, recoiling from the touch and returning his outraged eyes on the trembling Québécois. "I told you to uncuff her!"

Nervously, the young man looks over to Juice cautiously assessing the situation from a close distance. As soon as the big man nods his approval, the policeman slowly reaches for the keys on his belt. Kellar releases him and the constable shuffles awkwardly to Annie's bedside with Rafe's eyes fixed on him. Fumbling with the keys, he manages to unlatch the handcuff from Annie's right wrist, nervously repeats the process on her left, then slowly backs away from her, his eyes never leaving Kellar's intense gaze.

"Now, you are going to sit yourself down in that chair and keep quiet!" Kellar insists.

"Okay, so now what?" Juice asks heatedly as Kellar runs his hands through his hair. "Tell me how this ends now."

"We figure out how the lab made a mistake, and we make sure Annie isn't bothered by these assholes again."

"Arch, you just assaulted a police officer," Juice reminds him.

"That's not how I saw it," Kellar shrugs and turns to the young cop in the chair. "How do you remember it?"

The distraught rookie officer doesn't respond.

"See, he can't even remember," Kellar chuckles.

"This isn't going away," Juice stresses. "The kid's going to tell his superiors. You're done, Arch! How the hell could you be so stupid?" he grumbles.

"You think she did this?" Rafe fires back.

"Of course I know she didn't do it!" he acknowledges. "But we're cops and have protocols to follow. You have to let this thing play out, Arch. Let us all do our job, and our job is to figure out the truth."

"So, let's get to work, then."

"I have been," Juice updates calmly. "I checked Annie's credit card activity. On the night of the judge's murder, she was having dinner in Old Montreal. Before you barged in here like a lunatic, I had this guy's boss send his people to check out the restaurant," he explains as the young officer's radio comes to life.

"Oui, Gingras," the static voice comes through. "Tu peux la déboucler. Tout est correct."

Kellar and Juice watch and listen as the Sûreté officer converses with his dispatch in French, understanding very little of the exchange.

"10-4," the young cop confirms in French. "Her alibi checked out. I just got my orders to release her," he picks up in English. "The restaurant's security footage has her there with another customer at the time of the homicide. She has a good alibi. She could not have done it. I'm very sorry about all of this."

Kellar lets out a long sigh, and Juice wraps an arm around his friend's shoulder before turning to the Sûreté du Québec officer.

"Look, there's no excuse for the way Inspector Kellar acted. What you have to understand, however, is that he *just* lost his son a few months ago," he says. "He's been chasing a serial killer for several months, and now, he just found out that his wife, who nearly died in a car accident a few days ago, is the prime suspect in the very serial case he's working. This just tipped him over the edge. Can we just keep this little incident between us? We're all on the same side here. He just got a little overzealous. Let's simply chalk this up to a bad call, and Arch will owe you a favor—*and* an apology. Anytime you need help on a tough case he wouldn't normally get involved with, give him a call. He has resources you don't have," he promises and turns to Kellar. "Tell him, Arch. Tell him, and apologize."

Kellar shakes his head in disbelief. "You're quite the negotiator, Juice," he chuckles and earns himself a stern look from his friend. "He's right. I do owe you an apology. My behavior was completely unacceptable and I'm sorry," he says in the rookie's direction.

The young man sighs. "I won't make an official report, but if anyone asks, I am not going to lie."

"Figures!" Kellar huffs.

"Enough out of you!" he warns. "Go take a walk."

"I'm not leaving!" Rafe contends.

"Then keep your mouth shut! I'm trying to save your career, here," he snaps and looks to the cop holding all the cards. "Sorry about that."

"What?" Kellar answers his phone.

"Rafe, you've been right all along!" Father Jakub announces excitedly. "It's him!"

"Who?" Kellar huffs.

"Strickland," the priest reveals. "The sketch artist drew him. It's him, Rafe, it's him, no doubt about it!"

"Son of a bitch!" he exhales. "The kid came through for us."

"Agent Nickerson is having the police department email you the sketch as we're speaking. You were right about him, Rafe. Strickland is the serial killer we've been after. What do we do now?"

"I'll be in touch," he says. "Good work down there," he adds and ends the connection.

"I was right," he says to Juice and the kid. "It's that bastard computer geek I interviewed last week. He's behind this whole mess. He's been messing with databases all along and somehow managed to swap Annie's DNA for his at the judge's crime scene. He's the reason you shackled my wife to her bed," he says in the Québec officer's direction, then turns to his friend.

"Juice, we have to send our best people to Synthesized Logistics right away, both crime scene techs as well as Cybercrimes. That guy was the head of their IT division and could have been using their computers for his personal projects. If we're lucky, he might have missed a few breadcrumbs that will help us confirm he's going to Rio next. Can I ask you to work on a search warrant?"

"I'm on it," Juice says and quickly leaves the room.

"You really think he swapped his DNA for your wife's?" the Sûreté officer asks.

"I guarantee it!" Kellar states emphatically. "He's afraid of me and took it out on her, thinking that's going to slow me down. He's dead wrong, and soon he'll just be *dead*!"

The two share a quiet moment.

"We're good, Inspector Kellar," the young policeman says, extending a hand. "You and I are good. Nothing happened here."

"Thanks, I appreciate that," Kellar says, clasping his hand, then watches as his new friend takes his leave.

"Rafe?" Annie's weak voice calls out.

"Annie," Kellar replies, hurrying to her side. "I'm so sorry you had to go through this."

"How did you know I was here?" she asks.

"Juice called me."

Annie swallows with difficulty. "You didn't have to come," she says. "Juice told me about the case you're working on," she closes her eyes. "I'm sorry I sent you those papers in the middle of all this mess. I had no idea."

"Shh," he whispers. "Of course I had to come. This case will still be there in a couple of days. I had to make sure you were all right. Don't worry about the papers for now. We'll deal with those after this nightmare is over. Just get better, okay?"

"Thank you," she murmurs as Kellar slides a chair next to her bedside, kisses her gently on the forehead and settles himself.

50

Mississauga, Ontario

"They're already here," Strickland seethes.

Seventy-three cameras surveil the grounds, the loading bays, all angles inside the massive storage facility and throughout the administrative office space, with every piece of equipment feeding into his own personal monitoring station affording him an unrestricted view outside his windowless office deep inside Synthesized Logistics' headquarters. His first order of business on day one was to redirect all the surveillance feeds to his desk. Without those, he'd be unable to watch the Tactical Response Team mobilize and cover all exits while the team of investigators march their way inside the main entrance.

He curses under his breath as he follows the army of officers and techs parading through the lobby flashing their serious-looking warrant to a seriously scared little girl behind the reception desk.

Rafe Kellar had carelessly communicated the raid to Father Jakub, and thanks to the priest's smartphone, he was able to anticipate their advance and is fully prepared, but would still have preferred to have been gone before their unavoidable arrival.

With a simple click of the mouse, he plants the code that will initiate the partial destruction of all his personal files as soon as the cops start snooping. They'll spend hours scouring his digital playground and congratulate themselves on recovering critical pieces of evidence, but in the end, all they'll have uncovered are the bits and pieces of lies he's left for them to find. He's thought of everything.

He appraises the room once more before slipping into the cleaning lady disguise he's kept in the closet, then exits his office, locking the door behind him and heads down the hallway toward one of the exits leading outside to the parking lot.

"Hey, you!" he hears the familiar nasal voice from behind.

He stops and turns. "Yes, can I help you, Miss Lockhart?" he asks the loathsome cow in his well-trained falsetto.

"Were you just in Strickland's office?" she demands.

"No, I wasn't. Why do you ask?" he answers, adjusting his skirt.

"I just saw you at the door." Sue challenges.

"I was just checking to see if it was locked," he lies. "My supervisor wanted me to check if Mr. Strickland had perhaps left his door open this time for us to clean and, as usual, it was locked."

"Figures!" she harrumphs.

"Why do you think that is, Miss Lockhart? I mean, our master keys work on all the other doors in the building so we're able to access them and do our work, except for his. Do you think he's got something to hide?" he prods, having way too much fun under the current circumstances.

"No idea, but we're about to find out," she declares with confidence as the heavy footsteps from the approaching platoon of police officers heightens his excitement.

"It's here," Sue points at Strickland's door with authority.

"Who are you?" the lead investigator asks crisply.

"Just a hard-working cleaning lady at the end of her shift," he grins. How he wished it was Rafe Kellar standing before him. Imagining Kellar conversing with a cleaning lady, completely oblivious to the duplicity, is arousing. "I'll let you get on with your work," he says, then disappears into the stairwell, knowing a simple cleaning lady will get little to no harassment from the monkeys guarding the exit.

***

"My key doesn't work," she whines. "That cleaning lady was right. That's so strange."

"Please leave us. If we need anything else, we'll come find you."

"You don't even have a key," she reminds them.

"Don't need one," he replies, pointing to the battering ram in his colleague's hands.

"But there might be something in there that's not pertinent to your investigation," she protests. "Proprietary client information and such. I need to make sure you don't seize anything that you don't need."

"Ma'am, this is a very serious criminal investigation. I don't want to hear another word. Now, please leave and let us conduct our investigation."

"Well!" she huffs as the locked door crashes open. "The nerve!"

"Murphy, you take the office and these computers," he orders, moving into Strickland's office, then directs another inside the darkened, temperature-controlled room behind the wall of glass next to the desk. "Lim, you get into that data center and start checking it out."

"I've seen lots of server farms, but the size of this one seems like overkill," Lim observes. "There's enough power here to run the government," Sue manages to hear before being rudely ushered away by the short-tempered lead investigator.

51

Montreal, Quebec

"Call me as soon as you find anything!" Kellar instructs over the phone as he absently wanders the long, congested corridor outside Annie's hospital room.

"Absolutely," Gerry Mullins acknowledges from Thomas Strickland's office.

A computer science engineer, Gerry Mullins served in the military in the early days of the information age and attracted attention from many high-tech firms with lucrative offers upon his honorable discharge, but a big paycheck and fancy lifestyle was never a consideration for a life outside the Service. To the chagrin of his wife, the pursuit of justice and a modest salary in digital law enforcement was where he ultimately settled, where his intellect, determination and unquestionable work ethic quickly earned him the rank of head of the RCMP's National Cybercrime Coordination Unit eight years ago. Gerry had never met Kellar prior to his arrival at ViCLAS, but had quickly grown to like and admire the man.

"Hey, Rafe!" he says.

"Yeah?"

"We're going to catch him," he swears.

"I know," Kellar acknowledges. "Thanks for all you're doing. I know you could have sent your people instead of going there yourself."

"I know how important this case is," Mullin dismisses and wraps up the call.

"You want some coffee?" Annie's sister offers quietly from behind as he pockets the phone.

"Hey, Val. I didn't see you there," Rafe says as a group of interns walks past them. "Thanks, but I think I've already had my quota for the day."

Valerie St-Laurent slumps against the wall with a worried look on her face.

"Annie's going to be fine, Val, don't worry," he reassures her with a compassionate hand on her shoulders. They may have had their differences in the recent past, but Rafe has always been fond of his sister-in-law.

"That's not it, Rafe."

"What's going on?" Kellar asks.

"Can we sit?" she hesitates, clearly distraught.

"Of course," he agrees and leads her to an empty chair inside the unoccupied waiting room nearby. "Talk to me," he instinctively encourages as he seats himself across from her.

"Rafe, I don't know what's going on, but I think someone tried to kill Annie," she blurts hysterically. "I don't know how, and I certainly can't imagine why, but something just isn't adding up."

"Like what?" he probes, wondering what might have brought her to draw this conclusion as he readjusts himself in his seat.

"Annie said that I sent her a text that Dad had had a heart attack. I didn't!" Val weeps. "That's why she was on her way here. But I didn't send her that text, Rafe!" she insists. "And the police said she slammed her car into that concrete divider. I asked her about that earlier, and she said that it was as though the car had come to life and had steered itself off the road. As hard as she had tried to force the steering wheel, it wouldn't budge," she says passionately. "Rafe, I know I sound beside myself—and for the life of me, I can't imagine who would want to—but could someone have hacked into our phones to make it look as though that text came from me? Could that same person somehow have taken over her steering?" she asks desperately. "Could someone have purposely lured her to that location and caused her to have an accident?"

Rafe rubs his chin, reflecting on how Annie's DNA had been miraculously matched to the judge's killer's. Strickland displayed the skills to breach a government database and alter DNA records and had snookered authorities into going to California while the bastard butchered an innocent elderly woman in New Orleans, so it's not a stretch to think he would also have the savvy to replicate a text from Annie's sister's phone or hack the vehicle's navigation computer and deliberately cause her accident. Strickland had declared war on him with this vicious act of cowardice, and he'll pay dearly for it. He also knows that if anyone can uncover Strickland's digital footprint, it's Gerry Mullins, but how much of it will they actually be able to trust? He sighs, determined to nail the bastard but recognizing how far they are from catching their elusive suspect.

"Val, I'm really sorry Annie was dragged into this mess," he admits. "You're right. Someone did do this to her. I don't know how yet, but I *do* know who," he affirms and rises quickly from his chair. "And I'm going to find him and make him wish he'd never heard of me."

"Where're you going?" she asks.

"Back to Annie's room to check in on her before I leave," he answers, leaving Valerie alone and confused in the tiny, depressing waiting room.

"Hey Gerry, did you guys find anything yet?" he asks over the phone as he maneuvers the hospital traffic through the corridor back to Annie's room.

"As soon as we started tinkering with his system, a self-destruct virus was executed, but we still managed to recover several files," he says.

"What sort of files?" Kellar asks, slowing his stride.

"We haven't gone through everything yet, but there was a pretty large one on you," he says, confirming Kellar's suspicions.

"We also believe we know how he selected his victims. He developed a cloning software that he distributed to his company's customers. As soon as they downloaded the malware, they opened a back door to their system, granting him full access to their entire digital history, which he copied onto his database. He had access to everything they did up to that point, and anything new was replicated on his servers. Makes our surveillance equipment look like toys," he grumbles. "Anyway, from there, algorithms would comb the network for his victims. He simply keyed in the parameters, and a list of possible victims or suspects that best matched his little role-playing game would come up."

Kellar hears him exhale deeply. "Rafe, he could have cloned computers from hundreds of thousands of people or more."

"You said he would send out a virus disguised as innocuous tracking software, right?"

"That's correct," he affirms.

"Jakub said he was emailed a new tracking app from one of his distributors. This was, like, minutes after we left Strickland's office. If that was one of his, could he have hijacked Jakub's phone and have the ability to listen in on any of our conversations, maybe use the microphone to record whatever it picked up even when he wasn't on the phone?"

"From what we've discovered, absolutely."

"Dammit! I wondered how he had picked Disney out of his ass to leak to the press. He was listening to us in the car."

"Rafe, we were able to follow his tracks into the database where he swapped out Annie's DNA."

"That only confirms what I already know, Gerry," Kellar replies. "Was there anything there to suggest he could hack into a vehicle and override it?"

"Haven't found anything like that yet, but we're still looking. It's certainly possible," he grants. "You think he used something like that on Annie?"

"I know he did," Kellar insists.

"There was very little personal information we could find on him, though," Mullins reports woefully.

"I'm not surprised," Kellar admits. "I'll bet you a steak dinner you guys only found what he wanted you to find. Digitally speaking, this guy hasn't made any wrong turns yet. I doubt he'd take any chances leaving anything other than the garbage we already know or stuff to steer us away from him. We're really close, and he's almost finished. His next move is already in motion, and you won't find any trace of it there. He doesn't need anything from that office anymore. It's all in his head."

"There *is* one other thing we found, Rafe. This one actually looks legit," he states.

"Yeah? Probably just something else from his endless bag of tricks," Kellar doubts.

"It's an electronic airline ticket purchased a few months ago for a Jude S. Cariot to Rio de Janeiro next month. That mean anything to you?"

Kellar chuckles. "Yeah, it's where the Pope's going to be in a few weeks for World Youth Day."

"You think he's going to try to kill the Pope?"

"I did a few days ago, but no. Now I believe he just wants us to *think* he's going to kill the Pope."

"You don't think we need to send our people there?"

"I never said that, Gerry. It's a credible threat given the past few months, and it certainly fits with his MO. But I still remember the Anaheim dog and pony show."

"This will be in my report, Rafe."

"As it should be, Gerry," Kellar settles. "Good work!"

"Thanks, Rafe.

"Hey. Gerry," Kellar shouts, hoping to catch his colleague before losing him.

"Yeah?"

"Can you do me a favour before you head back to Ottawa," he asks.

"Anything!" Mullins confirms.

"Can you pick up a new phone for Jakub and deliver it to him personally?"

"Yeah, for sure. You want to take away our suspect's ability to listen in on your conversations? Good plan!"

"You got it!"

"No problem. I'll even install some of our security software on it as well."

"Thanks, Gerry. Oh, and take his old phone from him and drive over it with your truck while you're at it," he scowls and disconnects as he reaches Annie's room.

He enters and quietly makes his way to her bedside, careful not to wake her.

"I'm going to catch him, Annie. He's going to pay for hurting you," he promises softly, pecks her forehead, and slips out of the room.

52

Ottawa, Ontario

"You were right, Rafe. There wasn't anything there we could find that we didn't already know," Gerry Mullins confirms as he excitedly joins Kellar at his desk the moment he steps in.

"I told you. He's a slippery bastard, this one, but I'm gonna put an end to his reign of terror," he promises with confidence.

"Inspector Kellar, I believe you know Agent Nickerson of the FBI?" Superintendent Rajat Madan says, walking into his cubicle with the agent trailing behind.

"Agent Nickerson," Rafe stands and offers his hand, but the FBI agent ignores it, with Madan not picking up on the sexual vibe.

"Agent Nickerson was just filling me in on the latest developments of our case. Seems the FBI has assumed the lead," he announces. "Agent Nickerson here will be heading a task force comprised of international law enforcement agencies to Rio in two weeks to intercept Strickland before he makes his move on the Pope."

Kellar whistles. "Congratulations on the promotion, Agent Nickerson," he says with a nod. "A new job to go with the new hairdo," he pokes about her freshly-colored brown locks.

"Well, you know how easily I get bored," she responds with a shrug.

"What's next, pink?"

"Nah, I'm leaning more towards purple," she says with a grin.

Madan dismisses the banter. "Agent Nickerson specifically requested you on her team," he announces. "I declined!"

Rafe heckles. "You're benching me?" he says incredulously. "This is my case," he argues.

"In my office, right now!" Madan orders curtly, and Kellar follows with a smirk, motioning to Nickerson with a finger that he'll be right back.

"You want to act like a damned idiot, Rafe, you're damned right I'm benching you!" he slams his office door and bellows, his rising blood pressure clearly visible by his reddening face.

"Why?" Kellar asks, already knowing the answer.

"Because you assaulted a fellow officer of the law, you jackass, that's why!" he spits.

"I knew I couldn't trust that guy not to talk."

"So, you're not even going to try to deny it?" his supervisor asks, not entirely surprised.

"He said he wasn't going to say anything," Rafe mumbles in his defence.

"He's not the one who told me this."

"Don't tell me Juice ratted me out!" Kellar exclaims.

"No, it wasn't Juice either," Madan sighs. "A nurse saw you through the window and told her husband, who's a lawyer, and he mentioned it to his father-in-law whose next-door neighbor happens to be a judge who routinely plays golf with the Chief and Director General of Sûreté du Québec, who wasn't impressed to learn that two of his officers were involved in a fistfight in a hospital room. When he started asking questions, no one would confirm the incident, but they did tell him that one of the two individuals involved in the alleged incident might have been one of our people who happened to be related to the patient in the very hospital room where the horse playing had been witnessed, so it only took a few more minutes for him to reach me and tell me to control my horse's ass ViCLAS Specialist," the superintendent rants.

"Wow!" Rafe exclaims. "That's pretty good detective work, there."

"Kellar," he says, now mildly composed. "I know this suspect is getting to you and made things insanely personal. Now, there's no official report about this incident, but you can't go around acting as mentally unstable as the people we hunt every day."

"You're right," Kellar admits apologetically, reflecting that this conversation could have taken an entirely different turn. "It won't happen again; you have my word."

"Good, but you're still not going to Rio," Madan asserts.

"Good," Kellar smiles.

"Good?" his supervisor asks, stupefied.

"He won't be there anyway."

"That's not what our intel suggests."

"Yeah? And you know where that spoon-fed intel came from," Kellar contends.

"You think we're wasting our time going to Rio? I know you're not religious, Rafe, but I can't imagine even *you* would want something to happen to the Pope."

"The Pope's going to be just fine, I'm telling you," he insists.

Madan doesn't share his confidence.

"Look, let them go. If it makes Agent Nickerson happy to lead her team to Brazil, let her have it. Me, I'm happy being sidelined and allowed to work my own angle—besides, two teams working two different angles are better than one," he reasons.

"Fine," he concedes and takes a seat at his desk. "Get out of my office!" he grumbles.

"You get a good ass chewing?" Agent Nickerson chuckles as Kellar joins her and Gerry back at his cubicle. "You mind giving us a minute, Gerry?" she requests.

He looks to Rafe, who nods his approval.

"Don't go far, though; I still need to speak with you," Kellar hollers as Mullins leaves, then shifts his attention back to Agent Nickerson.

"I was really hoping you could join us in Rio, and you know, maybe pick up where we left off," she says seductively with the two of them alone at his cubicle.

"Yeah, well, me too," he exhales.

"What the hell happened, Kellar?"

"Things got a little heated in Montreal," he replies, perplexed by the question. "I thought Madan told you all about that little incident."

"No, I mean in New Orleans," she corrects him. "You told me your marriage was over. I mean, not that it bothers me," she confesses, cocking her head and shooting him a teasing glance. "What's up with you, though?"

"Ahh, that's a little more complicated, Pat," he dances.

"It's really not, Rafe, you're either into hooking up, or you're not," she blurts without shame. "I don't need complications in my life right now, and you were pretty clear on your intentions as well."

"I'm sorry," Kellar musters.

"That's it? You're just sorry?"

"I don't know what to tell you. I'm sorry for leading you on. My life is complicated too, and this case is messing with my head," Rafe huffs.

"So? A little distraction from all the craziness is good for the soul," she proposes.

"Look, that night in New Orleans, as good as it would have been, would have been a mistake."

"Seriously? No one's ever accused me of being a mistake," she sulks.

"Don't take this the wrong way. You're a beautiful woman, and any man would be lucky to have you, but I've realized over the last couple of days that I'm not entirely over my wife."

"Whatever!"

"Whatever?" Kellar hisses. "What are you, twelve?"

She sneers at him and flips him off.

"You know, for an FBI Agent leading an international manhunt to Brazil after a serial killer who will probably be disguised as one pilgrim among millions, you sure are childish," Kellar seethes. "I'm chasing down a sick son of a bitch who doesn't like being chased and who, by the way, thought it would be fun to involve my wife by nearly killing her and making people believe she was the one we were chasing, so I'm sorry if I hurt your feelings, but that's all I have to offer you right now."

"Fine!" she scorns.

"Are we done?" he says impatiently. "I believe you have a task force to lead and a serial killer to catch."

She makes no attempt at suppressing a smile. "That really bothers you, doesn't it?"

"What?"

"You set this whole thing in motion and get benched as things are just about to get real," she grins, rubbing it in.

"Whatever helps you sleep at night, Agent Nickerson," he responds. "Please keep me updated on your progress. Maybe send me a postcard from Rio. Please let yourself out!" he adds, walking away from her and rejoining Gerry Mullins waiting for him just outside the bullpen doorway.

53

"Gerry, when you and your people searched Strickland's computers and servers at his work, were you able to find anything at all on Judge Saunders?"

"Tons, like all his other victims," Mullins replies. "But nothing that you wouldn't be able to google."

"There has to be a connection there that we're still not making," he confides as they take the stairs down one flight to Cybercrimes.

"What's sort of connection?" Gerry quizzes.

"A personal one."

"Not following, Rafe."

"Strickland personally involved himself in that one," Kellar reminds him.

"He did that in New Orleans as well, though."

"Yeah, but New Orleans was different," Kellar argues. "He was playing the long game there. He knew he had all the time in the world with our focus on the other side of the country, far enough away from him."

"Alright, you said yourself that he had to improvise with the judge to make sure that that covenant was wrapped up before he could move on to the next," Mullins maintains.

"Yeah, I know. But it's the message he left at that crime scene that keeps me coming back to the same conclusion that he really wanted *that* specific judge dead. Why that one? That question keeps me up at night. He also involved Annie in that particular case. That crime scene has to have some sort of special meaning to him."

Mullins shrugs his shoulders.

"We know from Strickland's computers how both the victims and the suspects were selected. Strickland was able to access thousands of terabytes of personal data from hundreds of thousands of people and use their indiscretions or mental illnesses against them."

Mullins nods quietly.

"Let's dissect everything we know," Kellar lists with his fingers. "First, in San Antonio, the suspect he selects is a washed-up surgeon with severe anxiety and depression. It's easy for him to use her husband's covert homosexual life to get her over the edge and do his bidding. Her victims, we discover, are her unfaithful husband and his lover. Second, in Vancouver, he finds the down-on-his-luck suicidal brother of a plumber he enlists with the promise of a better life and *his* victims are a cheating husband, his wife, and the hooker he had sex with."

Gerry follows intently without interruption.

"Third, in Moncton, he recruits a woman who had recently fled a group-home for recovering drug addicts, and *that* victim is a first-class dirtbag mutilator who got what he deserved."

"You almost sound like you admire that one," Gerry jokes.

"No!" Kellar replies quickly. "I just think *that* particular victim got what he deserved."

"Poetic justice?" Mullins asks.

"Something like that, I guess." Rafe acknowledges and continues. "And finally, we find ourselves in Gananoque, where we meet Bannister, the schizophrenic ex-hockey player with the missing dog and *his* victim, our Judge Saunders."

"That's accurate by my count," Mullins confirms. "But what about New Orleans?"

"That's different," Kellar suggests. "He heard the conversation Jakub and I were having in the car and figured he needed to modify his plans to confuse us and throw us off his trail."

Gerry bobs at the satisfactory explanation.

"You and your team were able to recover and decrypt every digital scrap of communication between Strickland and his unfortunate puppets as well as the financial transactions into their bank accounts, which mysteriously vanished days after their deaths. You were also able to find all their victims' dirty little secrets that Strickland had exhumed and meticulously curated," Kellar shrugs and raises his hands. "So, where's the dirt on the judge?"

"You have it with the rest of it."

"I've got the stuff you said I could just as easily find on the internet, but where's the evidence that tells us the judge was dirty? Where's the proof that he was ever bribed to throw a case, that he ever cheated anyone, drove over the speed limit, or even failed to recycle his pop cans?"

Mullins follows his colleague's logic. "You're right. He's squeaky clean."

Kellar stares at him intently. "Sometimes, the lack of evidence *is* the evidence. It's not what we know that's going to help us stop this dirtbag; it's what we don't know."

"Okay, so you think Strickland might have been keeping tabs of the judge for another reason?"

"Exactly!" Rafe concurs. "I'm sure there are plenty of other judges out there with skeletons in their closets. Why this one? I'll bet you it's because this one pissed Strickland off at some point in his miserable life. I think he knew the judge personally."

Mullins nods his head.

"I need you to dig up everything you can on the judge. Look at all his past cases and see if there's anything that might connect these two. Go back as far as you need to. Strickland could have been a kid when they crossed paths. I want you to work with Marty on this one. As good as you guys are at Cybercrimes, Marty's the best researcher in the business, and I don't think we can trust digital files anymore knowing what we know about Strickland. If he can swap out DNA results in a secured government database, nothing's off-limits to him—but he can't mess with hardcopies," Kellar believes. "Find something for Marty to work with. Report back on everything you guys find, as insignificant as you might think it is. I want to know about it as soon as you guys do."

"Roger that, Rafe," Gerry winks and hurries to his team to excavate the dead judge's life.

July 2013

54

Ottawa, Ontario - July 2013

"Figures!" Kellar grumbles with several F-bombs directed toward Pat Nickerson's image on the screen, who, at this very moment, is basking in the international limelight addressing the media on the live report streaming silently on his desktop monitor. She appears poised and confident, fielding questions by reporters from around the globe on the front steps of the Sercetario De Estado De Policia Civil in Rio. Although he can't hear her voice, in his mind, he can sense her pride swelling with each syllable he reads from the scrolling closed captions.

She can confirm that they have been in Rio for the past week and are working closely with the Brazilian Civil Police. Yes, she is confident that the serial killer known as the Prophet will be apprehended before any harm comes to the Holy Father. No, the Vatican denied their request to cancel the Holy Father's trip to Rio. No, the Canadians are not on this task force despite several of the homicides having taken place on Canadian soil. Yes, they were invited but opted to allow the FBI to take the lead with their considerable experience and superior resources. No, she is confident they do not need their help and that with the assistance of the Brazilian Civil Police, they can bring this criminal to justice. Yes, the National Security Forces have offered to help, but she is confident they will not need to make that call. How close are they to apprehending him? Unfortunately, she is not at liberty to comment on the specifics of the ongoing investigation, but is very appreciative of their questions and will continue to be forthcoming with any new developments she can share as soon as they become available.

55

Rio de Janeiro, Brazil

The beach is still relatively quiet compared to the massive crowds who hope to catch a glimpse of the new rock star Pontiff expected to converge on Copacabana Beach next week. The small international group of law enforcement agents, guided by Police Inspector Luis Oliviera of the Brazilian Civil Police, walks along the popular tourist attraction for a sense of the area and revisits their strategy for keeping everyone safe from the serial killer they're tracking.

"This is the new site for all the activities," the Brazilian waves. "The event was supposed to take place in the park, but the crowds they're now expecting forced the organizers to change the location," he explains, as several noisy construction crews set up the scaffolds that will support the twenty-six gigantic high-definition television screens along the four-kilometer stretch of sand.

"So, the recent political unrest in the area had nothing to do with the change of venue?" Agent Nickerson probes.

"None." The Brazilian insists.

"How many people are actually expected, Inspector," Agent Nickerson asks, only mildly satisfied with his answer.

"As of last week, more than 320,000 people had registered from around the world. Organizers suggest many more pilgrims will register upon arrival, and if past World Youth Days can serve as a benchmark, many more will participate without registering at all."

"Does this number include religious personnel as well?" she asks.

"No, more than 84,000 priests from all corners of the world have requested credentials, not to mention all the media covering the events throughout the week."

"So, what's the number?" Nickerson quizzes.

Inspector Oliviera shrugs.

"Just ballpark it," she nudges.

"We estimate two-and-a-half million," he sighs at the enormity of his responsibility and, for a moment, glances piously toward the majestic statue of Christ the Redeemer visible high above the city on its mountain, as he has with surprising frequency these last few weeks.

They walk past a group of ecstatic pilgrims snapping selfies with a well-executed sand-sculpture of Pope Francis, their flags suggesting they traveled from the Philippines to be here.

"He could be one of those people," Nickerson observes. Turning towards the shore to a lone nun splashing in the waves, she adds. "He could even be that nun over there," she muses.

"You want us to tail her?" Stan Roberts, one of her enthusiastic American colleagues, asks. "She looks kinda masculine, now that you mention it."

"We'll have plenty of leads to follow soon enough without tailing every hairy-legged nun on the beach," she dismisses, then turning to Juice, the last-minute addition on her international team, she smiles. "So, what's eating you today? Upset your pal Rafe isn't on the trip?"

"Why did you tell the media Canada isn't present?" he asks. "Last time I checked my passport, it says I'm from Canada."

"I didn't deliberately omit you guys," she argues. "I told them we were here with an international team of law enforcement agencies."

"Sure!" Juice scoffs.

"Relax, Juice," she coos. "We don't do our jobs for the glory. Well, maybe you guys do up north, but we do it for the public's safety."

He laughs at her and waves off the slight.

"Why are you even here?" she asks as she lights a cigarette.

"Someone's gotta wave the flag."

"No, not you as a Canadian; I kinda get that part. But why *you*?"

Juice stares back at her blankly.

"You're kind of a big deal as Commanding Officer of J Division. Isn't this grunt work a bit below your pay grade?"

"Putting criminals away is every cop's job."

"That's what you're going with?"

He takes a breath. "You're right, I'm not here in any official capacity," he admits. "I took some of my accumulated personal time to make the trip on my own dime to make sure Arch's efforts don't get hijacked by you."

She chuckles and gazes over to the shoreline for a moment gathering her thoughts while puffing on her cigarette. "Full disclosure?" she offers.

"Sure," he sighs. "That would be a nice change of pace."

They stop and allow the others to move ahead for more privacy.

"I did it for the optics," she confesses. "You know, when the FBI is portrayed in films and television, we usually come across as idiots who can't function cohesively as a group or collaborate with other agencies."

"Oh, you mean like how you told the world the RCMP had nothing to do with how you got here in the first place?" he says. "Bullshit!"

"You Canadians are way too sensitive."

56

Ottawa, Ontario

Seventy-two pounds overweight, Marty Bloom is a dangerously heavy breather, with the mere act of tying his boots winding him. His sneaking up on you isn't anyone's concern, especially when he gets excited and the heavy breathing turns into an alarming wheezing.

"You have to get that checked, Marty," Rafe suggest without taking his eyes off his computer screen.

"How'd you know I was even here?" Bloom whines in frustration, taking a puff on his inhaler.

"That's why they pay me the mediocre bucks, Marty. I have eyes at the back of the head," he jokes. "You've got something for me, don't you?" He swivels to face the smiling researcher clasping a thin file.

"I do," he beams with pride.

"Okay, fill me in."

"I finally found that connection you were looking for between the judge and Strickland."

"You think so, do you?"

"There's no doubt in my mind," Bloom assures him.

"Okay, you have my undivided attention, Marty."

"Judge Saunders held various positions in his long judicial career, but what raised a flag is his time at the Superior Court of Justice Family Courthouse in Hamilton. We know that sociopathic behavior doesn't just switch on suddenly, right? It evolves inside a young mind with the torturing or killing of small animals and then moving on to pets and eventually people. Well, Gerry and his people couldn't recover any more data on Strickland's hard drives but asked me to see what I could find elsewhere in the government archives. I pulled up a 1980 case over which our judge presided. The defendant was a young boy accused of setting an orphanage barn on fire, which resulted in the death of another boy in the institution's charge."

"We still had orphanages in 1980?"

"Just a handful across the country. Kids in the church's care were gradually placed into adoption homes, and the rest were sent into foster care as the provincial governments transitioned these minors from the church into the hands of social services."

"Go on," Kellar encourages.

"Because of his age, the boy was sent to a reformatory instead of prison, and then subsequently placed into the foster system upon his release."

"That happened to a lot of kids, Marty. They didn't all turn into serial killers."

"Sure, but then again, they're not all named—Thomas Strickland," he enunciates dramatically.

"Serious?"

"You heard me," he grins smugly. "Thomas Strickland was the kid responsible for the fire and accidental death of that other orphan and the one dumped into the system by Judge Saunders."

"And you have that in that file?"

"Not exactly," Marty hesitates. "Look, I know you said not to trust anything electronic, but that's all that's available," he insists, handing Rafe the thin folder. "Here, I printed everything I have for you. I could only collect bits and pieces of the file from family court's digital records. You know all the archives from the seventies haven't been digitized yet, right?"

"I know, so what about the hard copies?"

"Not a single sheet left. The City of Hamilton's archive vault where they keep old police files and court documents, well, that flooded about a decade ago, and most of the paper files were destroyed before they could ever be digitized. This is all we have, but that should still be enough to get you started. The place was owned and operated by an Augustinian order of priests called Mount Saint Vincent Orphanage. You should know that it was converted into a homeless shelter in the early '80s. I've included the street address in Hamilton and the priest's name who ran it, a Father Léopold Martin. You might also want to drop by the local paper. They might still have old newspaper editions available on microfilm."

"Okay, thanks, Marty," Rafe says. "I'm going to pay Father Léopold a visit and see what he remembers. Maybe they still have some of those old records, and then I'll head over to the paper."

Reaching for his phone and tuning-out the rest of whatever Marty is rambling on about, he texts Father Jakub requesting his assistance in an interview with a priest in Hamilton tomorrow morning.

Friday, July 26, 2013

57

Toronto, Ontario - Friday, July 26, 2013.

Kellar raps impatiently on the heavy wooden rectory door outside Saint Faustina Parish in Toronto for the fourth time in as many minutes, anxious about getting on the road with his priest sidekick to meet the people who ran the former orphanage in Hamilton.

"You looking for Father Jakub?" an elderly man walking his dog calls out over the clamour of the passing TTC Streetcar.

"Yeah," Kellar acknowledges.

"You'll find him at the church this time of day. He says Mass every weekday morning," the senior confirms.

Kellar looks at his watch irritably and sighs. "How long's that usually last, an hour?"

"No, he should be out at around 9:30 or so," the senior estimates. "As long as no one's there to see him after."

"Thanks," Kellar waves, surveys the busy street and ambles his way back to his parked rental to wait. Plenty of time for checking emails in the meantime.

He specifically said that he'd be there by nine o'clock sharp, and Jakub hadn't hinted at not being available. Maybe he should go on without him.

"Bad idea," he reflects. "Probably better to have him with me for this one."

He starts the car and turns on the satellite radio, tuning it to the '80s' channel and smiles as Sammy Hagar and Van Halen take him back to the 'Summer Nights' of his own youth while he scans through the few unread messages on his phone.

"About time!" he criticizes as the young priest hops into the car a half-hour later.

"I apologize, Rafe. I couldn't find anyone else to cover my Mass this morning," he explains.

"What, you can't even skip one day?" Rafe sighs. "It's not even Sunday."

This makes Father Fischer smile. "I'm here now."

Kellar pulls out onto Roncesvalles Avenue, and all is well until they reach the highway, and it turns into a parking lot moments later with the Gardiner reduced to two lanes ahead due to construction.

"I'm afraid it won't be any better as we approach Oakville," Father Jakub winces as he consults his map app. "Looks like there might be more of the same as we approach the Ford plant."

"I hate this place!" Kellar complains to Father Jakub's delight. "How long's this traffic jam?"

"We'll probably only lose about twenty minutes or so," the priest estimates, and the cop curses under his breath.

"Oh, just twenty minutes, eh?" he fires back sarcastically. "We just might get there by dinner if we're lucky."

Father Jakub chuckles and watches as traffic flows more fluidly in the other direction.

"That your new phone?" Kellar finally asks somewhat less abrasively as the Gardiner turns into the QEW.

"Yes, it is," Father replies excitedly. "Thank you. I like it a lot better than the one I had before, you know, the one you had your friend drive over," he chuckles.

"Don't be downloading any crap on this one," Kellar warns. "I don't need that asshole listening in on us again."

Inching their way west along the QEW with thousands of other impatient motorists, they finally make it past the construction site, and traffic lets out somewhat, allowing them to make better time for the rest of their ride into Hamilton.

"How's Annie?" Father Jakub asks, breaking the silence a few kilometers down the road.

"Physically, she's better," Rafe confirms. "Emotionally, she's a wreck, though. Thanks for asking. We've got people posted inside and outside of the house, but Strickland really did a number on her."

"I'm so sorry to hear that."

"She doesn't deserve any of it," Kellar sighs.

Father Jakub waits patiently for him to open up.

"When I was in the military, that time was hard on her, especially when I was deployed. I'd be gone for months at a time and usually not even able to tell her what part of the world I was in. All she knew was that I jumped out of airplanes and chased enemy combatants in some pretty shitty corners of the globe. Every once in a while, though, she'd get one of my letters and feel better . . . at least until she turned on the news."

"Were you often deployed?"

"Yeah, and for long stretches of time. You know, she basically raised our son on her own," he remorsefully admits, his heart heavy with the painful memory of his son's suicide.

"I can't imagine how losing a child must feel, Rafe. I am truly sorry for your loss. I know we spoke briefly about him in San Antonio before we were interrupted."

"He was a good kid, Jakub. He should have been able to come to me," he sniffles.

"I'm certain he knows how much you loved him."

"I didn't show it!" he grieves. "So much bigotry I inherited from my parents. I only realized the kind of person I'd become after it was too late. It only hit me after I lost my son."

They ride in awkward silence for a few moments, each contemplating how best to steer the conversation.

"Rafe," Father picks up cautiously. "I know a certain number of the Church's teachings are rather divisive, especially when it comes to human sexuality, but that's only because they're so grossly misunderstood. If you let me, I'd like to clear the air using a simple example to help explain what we *actually* teach."

Kellar exhales bitterly and rolls his eyes but offers no other resistance, so Father Jakub wades in delicately.

"When a person is anorexic, they look in the mirror and see an overweight person, even if a 90-pound stick figure is staring back at them. Something inside them misleads them to believe themselves to be obese. But they're not, and any loving family member or friend of that person would *never* encourage them to starve themselves or go to such lengths as undergo surgery for the sake of being true to themselves. When it comes to sexuality, though, all rational thought evaporates."

"Are you saying homosexuals have loose screws?" Kellar reproaches.

"No, of course not, and neither do people with eating disorders," Father Jakub argues.

"You *just* said that something's wrong in their heads."

"No, I suggested that their subconscious might be leading them to believe something that isn't true," he insists.

"You just made my point," Rafe persists, slapping the steering wheel, frustrated with this rabbit hole but wanting to get his point across. "They're born that way. You can't change them; live with it!"

"Sexuality does not define who we are. You can't label someone a particular way simply because they show certain characteristics early on in life. I used to hate opera, and now I listen to Bocelli and Domingo. I used to like grape Cool-aid, and now I can't stand it, but I *do* enjoy a nice, robust Zinfandel."

"Those are personal choices that change with age and maturity," Rafe shakes his head.

"Rafe," Father Jakub sighs. "I'm not a psychologist, and I don't pretend to have all the answers, but the Church does not preach the condemnation of homosexuals nor condone conversion therapy, and neither do I. What I struggle with, is our collective refusal as a society to examine or even *consider* the possibility that deep, suppressed emotional traumas could be at the heart of it. Why is the world so quick to label individuals as homosexuals instead of helping them discover who else they were *possibly* meant to be? Should we not want everyone to be the best version of themselves as God intended? Are they really gay? Maybe—maybe not, and the Church recognizes that this number is *not* negligible. I'm not advocating the need to find a cure for homosexuality; I'm merely asking if we adequately understand it scientifically speaking. Or even want to."

"So, what, you think I should have been able to therapy the gay out of my son rather than accept him for who he was?" Kellar growls sarcastically.

"No, Rafe. That's not what I said," Father insists patiently. "Shaming people or causing them physical or emotional harm to change them is barbaric and detrimental to their emotional and spiritual well-being. No, this isn't about sexuality at all. It's about healing the pain and suffering of anyone who suffered any kind of traumatic event in their lives. We humans are fragile, and inevitably experience hurt at some point, but everyone reacts differently to the trauma. Every single one of our actions is grounded in a desire for love and happiness. We're constantly chasing the high we get from worldly goods that bring us momentary joy to counteract the emptiness and darkness we feel when we're emotionally down. Some turn to sex, some to drugs or alcohol and some turn to food. All of these things are beneficial, even necessary, but we were made for things greater than what this world has to offers."

"Such as?"

"Heaven, Rafe. We're all made for heaven."

"But the Church, in its infinite wisdom, gets to decide who goes there and who doesn't, isn't that right?" Kellar asks gruffly.

"Not even close," Father Jakub asserts. "We as individuals are the only ones to decide our eternal fate. Not even God does that."

Kellar laughs. "If we can pick between heaven and hell, who's crazy enough to pick the smoking section for all of eternity?" he says mockingly.

"C.S. Lewis once said that the doors of hell are locked on the inside."

"Meaning?"

"Meaning that whoever goes there, freely goes there. It's their choice. They want nothing to do with God, so close themselves off from him forever; and he on his part, loves us so much that he respects our wishes. He doesn't force himself upon any of us in this life or the next. The fiery imagery we find in Dante's *Inferno* isn't an adequate representation of hell. Picture a parched individual suffering from an unimaginable thirst and yet unwilling to drink any water because water repulses them. That's what hell is like."

"Look," Kellar picks up, uncomfortable wading this deeply into theological thought. "I know we have differences of opinions, and I'm starting to like and respect you as an individual, so how about we just drop this conversation and agree to disagree on certain aspects of life, shall we?"

"I can respect that," Father Jakub agrees cheerfully.

"Good," Kellar sighs. "I think we're here," he announces, pulling over along King Street West.

He kills the engine and walks over to the sidewalk, and joins the young priest staring back at him quizzically.

Kellar scratches his sandy head of hair and studies the vacant lot where Marty Bloom had told him he would find the old building. He reaches for his phone and connects through the stored contact.

"Marty, did you give me the wrong address?" he grills.

"Is it already gone?" Bloom asks.

"What, you knew about this?"

"I told you that yesterday after I gave you the address. I said that the building might be gone as a demo permit was issued two months ago."

"No, you didn't," he flat out denies.

"Yes, I did," Bloom swears. "You were texting someone when I told you and probably didn't hear me."

Kellar recalls his mumbling something about some sort of permit yesterday at the office.

"You might be right, Marty. Sorry about that. I'll take it from here," he says, wrapping up the call and shifting his attention to the priest. "You know about this too?"

Father Jakub shrugs. "How should I know? We're not in my diocese."

"So, now what?"

"Let's go to the Chancery office. They're just down the street next to the Basilica. Maybe they can help us find your Father Léopold," he suggests as they climb into Rafe's rental and make their way to the administrative offices of the Diocese of Hamilton.

58

Hamilton, Ontario

"You sure this is it?" Kellar asks.

"That's what the receptionist at the Chancery office said," Father Jakub affirms.

"Not where I'd expect a retired priest to live," Kellar marvels, stepping out of the vehicle and moving quickly toward the converted 19th-century mansion, which overlooks the scenic Burlington Bay and once belonged to a wealthy politician as Father Jakub trails two steps behind.

"What's that supposed to mean?" he asks, catching up.

"Nothing, really," Rafe assures him. "I just pictured you guys all staying together in a more modest priest-like retirement home, I guess."

"Diocesan priests usually take up residency inside welcoming parishes and assist the pastor as their health allows once they retire from active ministry. Priests from religious orders, on the other hand, usually stay with their community until their deaths, but it's not unheard of for one to move into a retirement community," Father Jakub explains. "Perhaps a wealthy relative wanted him here—"

"You guys are way too complicated," Kellar cuts him off. "With all your rules and exceptions. Some priests are rich while some are poor; some priests are celibates while others are married. No wonder people are confused. You guys are always sending mixed signals."

"I understand how it might be hard to wrap one's head around the whole thing," Father concedes with a chuckle. "But it's not complicated at all if you take the time to understand. Much like you do in an investigation. You ask questions, and you seek answers."

Kellar dismisses the lesson with a grunt. "Okay, you're up," he says as they reach the entrance to the luxurious, castle-like retirement residence.

"Good afternoon," Father Jakub says pleasantly as the two approach the reception area. "We're looking for one of your residents, a Father Léopold Martin."

"Oh, yes, Father," the receptionist replies jovially. "You mean *Monsignor* Léopold, though. He's actually sitting outside with his morning tea. Just through those doors over there," she says, pointing to the lovely, treed gardens at the back.

"Thank you . . . Marjorie," Kellar says, reading her name from the tag pinned to her thick woollen sweater. *Too thick for this time of year*, he thinks to himself.

"How's a Monsignor different from a priest?" Kellar asks under his breath as they head toward the doors.

"He's still a priest," Jakub assures him. "It's just a title."

"So, the same, but different?" Rafe rolls his eyes.

"I'll explain later," the priest suggests.

"Don't bother!" Kellar grumbles.

With lush trees and fragrant flowers, the garden provides residents with an ideal place to sit and enjoy some fresh air beneath the dense foliage's shade. It's a place

Monsignor Léopold likes to frequent, to rest and appreciate the beauty of God's marvellous creation while sipping hot tea.

"Excuse us, Monsignor," the young priest says, crouching to eye-level with the elderly Reverend on the bench.

"Hello," he replies with a warm smile and an outstretched hand. "So good to see you again, Father."

Kellar and Father Jakub exchange a worried glance, and the young priest shrugs his shoulders then turns again to the old priest.

"I—I don't believe we've ever met, Monsignor," Father Jakub says hesitantly. "I'm Jakub Fisch—"

"Yes, I know who you are," the Monsignor interjects insistently. "You're Father Jakub Fischer of the Archdiocese of Toronto."

"How—how did you know that?" Father Jakub probes. "Did someone tell you we were coming?" he adds with a worried look in Kellar's direction.

Kellar's mind races, and wonders how Strickland could have already managed to intercept and derail his investigation once again by interfering with this old man. Could this actually *be* Strickland in disguise? His hand instinctively reaches for his sidearm as it does when the hairs at the back of his neck stand, but his misgivings weaken as he rationalizes the situation. Can't be . . . this guy's old. Makeup might be convincing on the big screen, but in real life? Nah, this guy even smells like an old man. But what did Strickland say to him? How and when did he get to this old priest? He's going to ask Marjorie for a look at the visitor's log on their way out.

"No," Monsignor Léopold appeases the pair. "I was at your ordination at St Michael's in May of 2003. I was teaching a semester at the seminary for a brother priest who had fallen ill at that time and thought it would be a wonderful idea to attend the ordination ceremony of the class."

"Wait, you remember Jakub from seeing him just once for maybe a few minutes over ten years ago?" Rafe asks, stunned.

"Yes, of course," he responds humbly.

"Your exceptional memory will be invaluable to our investigation," Kellar exhales in relief, with his posture relaxing considerably.

"And who might you be?" he smiles at Kellar. "I've met your friend here, but I can honestly say I've never had the pleasure of making your acquaintance," he adds.

"I'm Inspector Rafe Kellar of the Behavioural Unit of the RCMP in Ottawa," he rattles the familiar line. "May I take a seat?" he asks, pointing to the bench next to the Monsignor, who nods with a warm smile.

"Have you heard about the recent worry about the Pope being harmed at World Youth Days in Rio this week?" he inquires, taking a seat.

"Yes, that's very disturbing," the old man acknowledges.

"Well, the person we believe is responsible for this threat is a serial killer who has already murdered thirteen people on his way to whatever twisted conclusion he has in store for the Pope," Kellar highlights while omitting the part about the bastard psycho nearly killing his estranged wife. "Father Jakub and I have been working together in trying to identify the suspect and how to stop him."

Monsignor nods his understanding but is curious. "So how can I be of assistance from here?" he inquires, motioning his surroundings with a wave of his feeble hand.

Kellar continues. "We'd like to ask you about the Mount Saint Vincent Orphanage you ran in the early '80s, specifically about one of the boys in your care."

"Is this boy somehow connected to your investigation?"

"We're considering all possibilities. Do you remember a boy by the name of Thomas Strickland, by any chance?"

"Ah, yes, one of the children under Sister Mary Joseph's charge."

Rafe recognizes the name of the nun but cannot identify where he might have previously heard it. "Sister Mary Joseph. . . . Why does that name sound so familiar?"

"Perhaps you came across her name in the papers last month. She mysteriously disappeared twenty-two years ago. Her remains were discovered in August of last year, but were only identified last month. She was beloved by all," the priest reflects fondly.

"Yeah, now that you mention it, that's exactly where I remember her name from. Anyway, I'd like us to circle back to Thomas Strickland if that's okay."

"Ah, yes. Poor boy," the Monsignor sighs. "That was such a tragedy."

Kellar marvels at this wise old man's impressive memory.

"It *is* tragic that he killed another orphan."

The Monsignor chuckles. "Inspector, are you attempting to test my memory?"

"Not following, here, Monsignor," Kellar replies, rubbing his unshaven chin. "Thomas Strickland was sent to a reform school for burning down your barn which resulted in the death of a boy by the name of—" he consults his notes, "Brian Konacher."

"I'm afraid you're mistaken, Inspector. The police didn't give us much information when they brought Brian to us, just something about a family tragedy and that there were no other living relatives in the boy's life. Over the sixteen months he was in our care, Sister Mary Joseph was the only one able to connect with him. A most troubled soul, that boy was." He stares intently into Rafe's eyes. "Thomas Strickland died at the hands of Brian Konacher, Inspector Kellar, not the other way around."

59

Rio de Janeiro, Brazil

As reported by the media, the intelligence on the Prophet's possible whereabouts in Rio is considerable, and the FBI's analysts are doing an efficient job of deciphering the good from the bad as soon as it pours in. Over the last three days, the task force has chased down dozens of highly probable leads and has efficiently eliminated all but three thus far.

One of the remaining leads, this one on the verge of being eliminated, was called in by a bartender at the hotel where most of the foreign media had set up camp. The witness noticed a nun drinking alone in a darkened corner of the bar. When he approached to see if he could get her anything else, the bartender detected stubble on her cheeks, and his double-take alarmed the suspect, who darted out of the bar but was quickly tackled by the Brazilian authorities as he raced through the crowded lobby. An eager photographer wishing to infiltrate the Pope's inner-circle to score an award-winning shot of Peter's successor, he underestimated the event's tight security and is currently being detained until authorities can validate his story.

Brazilian Intelligence Agency began monitoring an individual whose passport was flagged as a possible ISIS militant yesterday. Although no one believes the Prophet to be working with terrorists, the Brazilian agency insisted they investigate this second lead personally in the spirit of National Security. And finally, Agent Pat Nickerson and her team follow up on the last remaining lead, the one that took them all the way to Rio in the first place: the airfare and accommodations booked under the name of Jude S. Cariot.

Hotel security had granted Agent Nickerson's task force unrestricted access to their surveillance, so while the other guests eat breakfast and reflect on the surprisingly peaceful gatherings around the city despite the large crowds, her team sips coffee and snacks on muffins in the privacy of their booth inside the hotel's restaurant, huddle around her laptop watching the live footage streaming from the security cameras.

"Was that Kellar?" Agent Nickerson asks Juice as he slides next to Inspector Oliviera into the bench opposite hers.

"Yeah," he admits. "He thinks he's a couple of steps closer to finding out who this guy really is."

The FBI agent rolls her eyes.

"The more we understand what makes him tick, the better prepared we'll be," Juice advocates.

"What's to know? He's a psycho killer that's holed-up here in a hotel room under the alias Jude S. Cariot, the same name he used to get here. We've been sitting on him since he checked in. Except for room service at his door three times a day, there's been absolutely no activity since his arrival two days ago."

"We're positive he hasn't left the room?"

"What? We look like beginners to you here?" Nickerson sneers. "Of course he hasn't left the room."

"How convenient for us," Juice comments sarcastically.

The FBI agent counters back. "Feel free to go back to Canada, *eh*, Juice?"

"No, I think I'm good."

She continues unfazed, unconsciously tucking a brown stand behind her ear. "We've had one of our agents pose as a hotel employee, and he's confirmed that it's our suspect."

"Confirmed visually?" Juice doubts.

"Yes, visually," she snaps. "We also have him on video when he checked in."

"Can I see that footage?"

Agent Nickerson huffs. "Fine. Here you go!" she says, replaying the transaction between a man and the desk clerk.

"It sorta looks like him," Juice concedes. "Same height and build, but it's obvious he's wearing a disguise. Strickland doesn't have a goatee or wear glasses."

"It's him, Juice," she insists, bringing the live feed back up on her screen. "We've got his room covered. It's not like he can slip out the back either. Balcony's on the twentieth floor. If he ever decides to leave, we'll have agents tailing him."

Juice rubs his temples and ponders if he should even bring it up. "Has the name Brian Konacher come up anywhere?" he hesitates.

"No, why?" she asks.

"Rafe didn't say," he replies casually. "Just asked if we came across this name since we've been here."

"Jimmy," Nickerson turns to her American colleague next to her. "We have any hits on the name Brian Konacher?"

"Can't say that we do, but as soon as we get upstairs, I'll check with the rest of the team," the junior agent confirms.

60

Hamilton, Ontario

"You still have microfilm here?" Kellar bellows at the young lady behind the welcome desk as he marches through the Hamilton Tribune doors with his RCMP credentials extended.

"Micro-what?" she replies, puzzled.

"How old's your manager?"

"Why?" she scorns.

"Because I need to speak with anyone born in the *last* millennium," he scoffs as Father Jakub squirms uncomfortably with Rafe's rude behavior.

"Jeannine?" she calls out over her shoulder. "Can you come out here for a sec?"

"How can I help you, gentlemen?" an older woman soon appears and asks.

"Do you still have microfilm here?" Kellar inquires, only slightly more pleasant.

"I haven't had anyone ask me about microfilm in, oh, at least twenty-five years," she chuckles. "Everything we have has been online for years, now."

"So, no to microfilm, then," Kellar exhales, casting a disappointed glance to Father Jakub.

"I didn't say that," the lady replies cheerfully. "You've never seen our microfilm machine, have you, Stacey?" she asks her younger colleague. "Come, follow me," she motions to the trio.

"Where are we going?" Stacey wants to know.

"To the bowels of the building," Jeannine laughs. "That's where we keep all the antiques."

61

Rio de Janeiro, Brazil

The Oceanic Prince Hotel is one of the tallest structures along Copacabana Beach, and although relatively narrow in balcony standards, theirs offer a breathtaking, panoramic view of the area to its guests.

Juice zips his windbreaker up to his chin against the chilly breeze and glances up at the cable car featured in 'Moonraker' making its ascent to the summit of Sugarloaf Mountain in the overcast distance.

"Cold?" Agent Nickerson grins, lighting a cigarette as she joins him outside.

"A little," he admits. "Though I shouldn't be surprised. It *is* winter down here after all," he grins. "Still a hell of a lot warmer than New Brunswick winters!"

"They say this cool temperature is a little unseasonal. At least there's no snow, right?" she smiles, but the loud and sudden cursing from inside the room interrupts the casual exchange. She drops the cigarette and stomps it out with her toe. "What's going on?" she demands anxiously as she slides into the executive suite's living room with Juice following close behind.

"Don't know how we missed this, Pat," Jimmy huffs in frustration.

"Am I going to have to shoot you?" the FBI agent chuckles.

"You just might," he acknowledges reluctantly. "That name you asked me to check out, Brian Konacher?"

"Yeah, what about it?" she replies with an edge.

"Well, he's not just registered here as a guest at this hotel," he reveals shamefully. "He's got the connecting room."

She processes this new intelligence as Juice, her people and Inspector Oliviera await the explosion.

"Connected to Strickland's, AKA Jude S. Cariot?" she gnarls, and Jimmy O'Neil nods, then turns to Oliviera. "Please send your people into those two rooms as house cleaning under the guise of taking in fresh towels. I want to know if that bastard's been coming and going right under our noses. And you!" she shifts her wrath toward Juice. "You guys couldn't provide us with this intel any sooner?"

"Hey, you got it as soon as we did! Hell," he smirks. "We're not even here, remember?"

"You know the search will be inadmissible at his trial if we go in there without a warrant," Inspector Oliviera warns.

"I don't give a rat's ass about that," she replies matter-of-factly.

"Agent Nickerson, let me remind you that you are only guests in our country," the Brazilian warns her. "I'll pretend I didn't hear that."

"I really don't care what you did or didn't hear as long as you get your people into those rooms," she shrugs him off.

Inspector Oliviera turns to one of his female agents and reluctantly barks his instructions in their native tongue.

"I knew I should have taken Spanish in high school," O'Neil complains.

"That's Portuguese, you idiot!" Nickerson chides. "I want you to review hotel security footage," she instructs. "Find Konacher. I want to know if he's actually Strickland with another name and another room. I want to know when he comes and when he goes. And when he goes, I want to know where he goes, how often, what he's wearing," she rattles. "I want a copy of his passport. I want a full background check on him. I want to know when he came into the country and where he flew in from. I want to know what he ate on the plane, and I even want to know how many times he got up from his seat to take a piss!"

"Juliana is nearly ready to go," Inspector Oliviera grumbles.

"The minute we have confirmation those two rooms are empty, I want us in there!" she tells her team.

62

Hamilton, Ontario

"What a brilliant idea you had to check the newspaper's archives, Rafe. Even if Strickland, or Konacher, or whatever his name is, has the knowledge to alter digital files, there's no way for him to alter this data." Father Jakub marvels over Kellar's shoulder.

"Well, I guess I can't take all the credit," Kellar admits. "Or any of it, actually," he corrects. "This was all Marty. He's the one who suggested we check out the local paper's microfilm library."

"Are you finding anything interesting?" he asks as Rafe speeds through the old news articles on the plastic scroll.

"I found the piece about the orphanage fire and that an unidentified minor had been taken into custody, but nothing more about that. It just confirmed what Marty already told us. Now I'm working my way backwards chronologically. I'm about to start looking through July 1979. Investigative work isn't always exhilarating, you know," he grins. "But it does help work up an appetite. Why don't you take the car and grab us some lunch?" he suggests, tossing the keys to the priest without taking his eyes off the viewer.

"What are you in the mood for?" Father Jakub asks.

"Food," Kellar replies.

"Fair enough," the young priest says, leaving the investigator alone with his research material.

"Okay!" Rafe cheers moments later. "Now we're getting somewhere."

The front-page article of the Hamilton Tribune for Tuesday, July 17th, 1979, was of an incident where Hamilton Police officers found a young boy named Brian Konacher on the front porch of his home, an apparent victim and lone survivor of a brutal home invasion. Police were looking for the landlord as a person of interest, but could offer no additional comments regarding his involvement while the investigation was ongoing. The boy's mother, Paula, and his younger brother, Peter, were both deceased, as well as the mother's live-in boyfriend. It had been a miracle that the child had survived.

"Miracle, my ass!" Kellar grumbles.

He scans the microfilm for several more minutes for anything the old priest might have missed but found nothing. Reasonably sure he had printed everything he needs, he makes his way back up to Jeannine and Stacey to wait for his lunch and his ride.

"Thank you," he says to them as he walks past the welcome desk and reaches for the door.

"Did you find everything you were looking for, Inspector?"

"Yes, I did. Thanks again."

"The photos, too?" Jeannine quizzes.

"What photos?" Kellar stops and stares.

"The crime scene photos," she clarifies.

"No, the files were all destroyed when the vault flooded years ago, so there aren't any."

"No, I mean ours, not the police's," Jeannine replies.

"How could you have your own set of crime scene photos?"

"Our crime reporter was new on the job and wanted to make a good impression. Let's just say he found a crafty way inside the house to take a few photos for the article. Oh, the managing editor didn't want them used in the article, of course, but we still have them here."

"Could you get them for me?"

"Yes, absolutely. It won't take more than a moment," she says, leaving him and young, awkward Stacey at her desk.

"Here you go, Rafe," Father Jakub says, returning from his errand, and hands him a cold cut wrap from a nearby deli. "I even blessed it," he adds with a chuckle.

"Thanks," Kellar says, raising a brow and pursing his lips while snatching the bag.

"Are you all set and ready to go?" he asks.

"I will be soon," Kellar confirms, nodding in Jeannine's direction as she approaches with the brown envelope she hands over to him with a smile.

"Here you go. These are just copies. We need to keep the originals here. I hope that's okay."

Kellar bobs his appreciation as he tears open the envelope and takes in the thirty-four-year-old crime scene photos, shaking his head with each new image.

"He's been at it for a long time," Kellar whispers to the priest as he pulls him out of the building by the elbow and leads him to the car. "Check this out," he says, handing him the last photo in the stack.

Father Jakub's jaw drops as he recognizes the familiar Roman numerals scrolled across the tattered, old wallpaper above the wrought iron headboard.

63

Rio de Janeiro, Brazil

"Brian Konacher doesn't look like an alias, Pat."

"Talk to me!"

"Home address is 40 East Street in Oakville, Ontario. Age 46. His most recent passport was issued three years ago. Works as an accountant for a small general contractor," O'Neil reads from his tablet. "Single. According to his various social media accounts, he frequently likes to travel abroad. Booked this trip nearly a year ago."

"Anything in his financial records to indicate he paid for the connecting room as well?" Agent Nickerson asks.

"That's the strange thing."

"What?"

"I can't trace how either room was paid for."

She stares back at her agent with a look of frustration.

"He checked in two days before Strickland did," O'Neil confirms.

"Go back and check security footage to when this guy checked in!" Nickerson orders.

"I did," he says, extending the tablet in her direction. "Looks like these two could very well be the same guy."

"Shit!" she growls, leaning in to take a look for herself with Juice squeezing in.

"Could be him," Juice acknowledges. "But he knows how to change his appearance and blend in. Hard to tell for sure from this."

"That's right," O'Neil agrees and brings up the last footage they have of Brian Konacher exiting the room. "The last time he left his room, his hair was red and a bit longer, and he had a beard. He was wearing little round glasses and was dressed like a priest."

"Pat, we're in," the static voice resounds over the radio. "The connecting door is open. We just checked out the other room, and it's empty as well."

"Son of a bitch has been playing us!" Nickerson fumes with rage. "First room was a decoy, and the second one allowed his movement without any of us the wiser. That's one for the bad guys, but we'll catch up quickly," she swears. "Alright. Go through both rooms with a fine-tooth comb and bring me anything that suggests what he's planning, where and when."

"Roger that!"

"You gonna call Rafe?" Juice asks.

"No, and neither will you."

"Why not?"

"This is *my* case, that's why," she huffs and turns to speak with her subordinates.

Juice shakes his head and pulls his phone from his back pocket, then slides out onto the balcony to text the latest developments to his friend.

64

"Here you are, Father," the waiter says loudly over the cacophony and places the small glass of beer on the table.

"That's it?" Konacher grimaces. "Looks kinda small for a beer."

"We serve this beer in a small glass because it's better cold," the waiter explains in his best English. "If you take too long to drink it, it gets warm, so it's better to drink it when it's very cold."

"Whatever you say," he dismisses the young man, then, remembering the importance of remaining in character, smiles at him and waves the sign of the cross in his direction. "Bless you, my son," he adds with a smile.

Seated at an open window inside the crowded boteco, he sips at the suds the waiter had recommended and savors the local favorite as the music, carried by the cool breeze from the beach two blocks to the south, reaches him. He chuckles as he watches the kids and their chaperones completely take over the narrow street. They sing and dance to the music as they process to the papal site with excitement and joy, shouldering their backpacks and carrying their cardboard mattresses under their arms, undeterred by the threat of another night under a cold and starless sky.

This is the most enjoyment he's had in a long time. He wishes his life could be as carefree as it appears to be for these kids in garbage bag ponchos, but alas, he knows his amusement is coming to an end. It won't be long before his mission is fulfilled and he is captured by authorities.

He takes another pull of his beer and swallows the rest of it in a gulp. Setting the empty glass on the table, he wipes his mouth with the sleeve of his other arm, but, failing to recall that his facial hair is merely adhered, it comes off on his sleeve. The glass shatters onto the concrete floor as he anxiously scrambles to retrieve the synthetic mustache and reapply it to his upper lip, the commotion drawing attention from his neighbors, but apparently none from the lone Brazilian police officer walking in.

He tosses enough cash on the table to cover his tab and blends into the crowd, hoping to avoid the policeman's gaze, then ducks into the kitchen and escapes through the rear into the courtyard. He hurries toward the alley, removes and discards his wig, mustache and glasses on the cobblestoned path, hops over the five-foot iron fence surrounding the building, then follows the crowd of pilgrims chanting and singing their praises to God.

65

"We just spotted an individual fitting our suspect's description at a boteco about two kilometers away," Inspector Oliviera reports pointing to the photo of 'Father Konacher' affixed to the whiteboard in the hotel suite's makeshift command post. "One of my officers noticed a, how would you say, a 'sketchy' looking priest a few minutes ago. By the time he got through the crowd to where our suspect was sitting, the table was empty, but he managed to see him slip into the kitchen. Unfortunately, by the time he made it outside, all he saw was the man jump over a fence and disappear into the crowd." he sighs. "My people found part of his abandoned disguise in the alley."

"How far's this bar from the Pope's stage on the beach?" Nickerson asks.

"It's practically on the beach," Oliviera confirms. "Maybe half a kilometer up the street."

"Set up a ten-block perimeter around that bar. Call in your friends from the National Security Forces and the Military Police to help if you need to. We'll build a net so thick this guy won't be able to slip through," she vows and turns to O'Neil. "Get a picture of every version of Konacher we have to every law enforcement officer in the city. Hell, send it out to every security guard, taxi driver, sanitation employee, and even the damned lifeguards on the beach," she barks and transfers her gaze back to the head Brazilian. "Take us there immediately!"

66

His cover is blown, as evidenced by the increased police presence on every corner. It was stupid of him to run. He was sure that cop hadn't recognized him or even noticed him. He chuckles and blames his nervousness on the tiny little beer.

"Plan B," he mumbles, crossing Duvivier toward his secondary hotel suite. The alternate base of operation is reserved under an alias where he'll swap the priest getup in favor of the brown Capuchin cassock stored in the closet with more of the usual, amusing props. He slows and stops short of the grand entrance seeing a pair of unsympathetic looking Military Police officers patrolling the sidewalk.

He doubles back and hurries up to Barata Ribeiro and ducks into the small café on the corner to get out of sight and gather his thoughts.

He's having stark realizations about his mission, and the penalty he's sure to endure for an aborted plan will be harsh; but his survival instincts kick in, and his mind willingly concedes to the verdict, regardless of the consequences.

He waits his turn in the crowd and nervously orders a coffee, uncertain of his next move. In a moment of clarity, he abandons his black blazer, rips off his white collar and exits the café without taking his beverage.

Dampness stains his black shirt at the pits and collar and sweat beads at his forehead as he assesses his surroundings. He moves quickly and snatches an over-sized papal souvenir t-shirt and a ball cap from an unsuspecting street vendor, and heads east, donning his newly acquired disguise. A local boy who witnessed the theft points him out as he hurries away, and the merchant waves to a police officer standing on the opposite side of the street.

He keeps his head low, bumping into annoyed pedestrians as he navigates the busy sidewalk and avoids eye contact. Minutes later, he reaches Princesa Isabel four blocks away and turns left toward the Marquês Pôrto tunnel.

The avenue is blocked off to vehicular traffic. He presses himself up against the concrete wall of the tunnel, squeezing himself against the flow of boisterous pilgrims marching past him on the sidewalk and the street inside the long, dark stretch of the tunnel he's reasonably sure isn't a safe place for a solitary tourist on a regular day. He stops for a moment to admire the parade, but is suddenly and violently tackled to the ground by a large, angry-looking black man with a sour attitude.

"How's it going, Strickland?" he hears as the man's weight crushes his ribs. "Or do you go by Konacher when you're down here? Doesn't really matter. I've got your ass now. Oh, by the way, I'm Chief Superintendent Kamarre Toure of the RCMP, and you're under arrest!"

67

Saint Faustina Parish, Toronto, Ontario

"Thanks for the ride, Rafe," Father Jakub says upon exiting the car. "Are you sure you don't need any more of my help?"

"No, that pretty much covers everything I need, at least for now," Kellar acknowledges.

"Well, I guess this is goodbye, then. Please don't hesitate to call if there's anything else you need," Father Jakub offers and turns toward the garage in the alley behind the rectory.

"Will do," Rafe answers and calls out to him again. "Hey! What do you have going on for the rest of the day, now that your sleuthing career is over?"

Father Jakub turns back with a smile. "I have a standing appointment to dine with some of our parish shut-ins at the retirement residence every Friday," the young priest replies. "I thought I was going to have to skip it today, but I'm delighted that I can still make it."

"You could have said no when I called you yesterday," Kellar says.

"I know," Father Jakub affirms. "But I know how important this investigation is. I had Father John on standby to fill in for me if we got here too late, so it wasn't any trouble at all."

Rafe smiles and thanks him. "You were a great help to me."

"I know we didn't really get off on the right foot, but I really enjoyed getting to know you, Rafe," Father Jakub admits.

"Yeah, well, I guess you're not that bad either – for a priest," he grins.

"Please keep in touch," the priest calls out.

Kellar nods his head without a word and waves through the open window as he pulls away, then voice commands the familiar number.

"Hey, Bloom," he says over the Bluetooth connection. "I need your help."

"Sure, what's up?" the tech responds.

"I just dug up some information about our suspect I need you to look into."

"At your service, as usual, Rafe. Happy to help. Where do I start?"

"You can start with what just might be his real name—Brian Konacher," he says.

"How'd you come up with that name?" he asks, attacking the keyboard.

"Monsignor Léopold, who ran the orphanage, said that Thomas Strickland was actually the name of the victim whose charred remains were found in the barn. Apparently, the kid we thought was Strickland might be this Brian Konacher character."

"What's a Monsignor?"

"Don't get me started."

"Okay, so do you believe the old *Monsignor*?" Marty asks with reservation

"He might be old, but if he's right, the years haven't affected his memory in the least."

"Yeah, but I'm looking through the court records here and haven't come across this name," he argues.

"It's a lead I confirmed with the newspaper's old records on a microfilm like you suggested," Kellar replies irritably. "Just run it down and see where it goes. Look up anything you can find on the name Konacher. Look up the name Paula Konacher too, and check if there are any properties connected with that name."

"I'll do it because it's you asking, but don't hold your breath."

"Thanks," Kellar says, ending the call as he merges onto 427 North toward Pearson.

68

Rio de Janeiro, Brazil

"So, Mr. Konacher," Agent Nickerson says politely as she enters the stuffy interrogation room. "You've been pretty busy these last few months, haven't you?" she adds, calmly pulling a chair and seating herself across the table.

"These are too tight," Konacher whines, jiggling the cuffs in the FBI agent's face.

"We can loosen them in a little bit, but first, I need you to tell me why you're here in Rio."

"I'm on pilgrimage," he grins. "And please, call me Father Konacher."

"Oh, really?" Nickerson replies sarcastically. "Since when does the Catholic Church ordain accountants?"

"That's the old me," he yawns.

"How long have you been a priest?"

"I was ordained six years ago, incidentally, on my fortieth birthday," he answers. "Late vocation, you see."

"Which diocese do you belong to?"

"The great Archdiocese of Toronto, of course."

She arches her brows. "Toronto?"

"That's what I said," he nods.

"Are you the pastor of a parish?"

"No, I haven't worked my way that far up the ladder yet. I'm just an Associate Pastor at Our Lady of Grace," he says, recalling the name of the closest Catholic Church to his apartment complex.

"Our Lady of Grace in Oakville?" she beams. "You know, that's the same church I go to when I'm up in Canada."

"Well, then," he smiles. "Perhaps you'll allow me the privilege of hearing your confession the next time you're in town."

"Yeah. I'd like that," she lies, her gentle tone fading quickly. "You do realize that the church you're referring to is not under the jurisdiction of the Archdiocese of Toronto, don't you? That it's under the purview of the Diocese of Hamilton? I would have expected a Pastor—ahem, an Associate Pastor, my apologies—would have known which diocese he belongs to."

He grins.

"So, you're basically just a dirtbag imitating a priest to get closer to the Pope to kill him. Can we agree on that?"

"Kill him?" he gasps, his face paling. "I'm not here to kill anyone. I just got paid three thousand bucks and a return flight to run around Rio this week and keep you guys busy."

"You know, that's exactly what you've done in the past, pay people to do your dirty work while you keep your hands clean. Nice try, but we know you and your methods," the FBI agent states calmly. "We'll come back to why you're here in Brazil in a little bit, but for now, let's just focus on the trail of dead bodies you left in the wake of your killing spree in America and up in Canada."

"Whoa, whoa, whoa!" he shouts, attempting to stand.

"Sit your ass down!" Agent Nickerson shouts.

"I'm a lot of things, but murderer is not one of them!" he contests.

"So, you deny being the serial killer we've been investigating who calls himself the Prophet?"

"Shit, yes, I deny that!" he cries out, his entire body trembling uncontrollably.

"Mr. Konacher," she begins but hesitates. "Is it alright that I call you Mr. Konacher and not 'Father' because we both know that's just a load of crap, yeah?"

He nods his consent sheepishly.

"Great, at least now we're now sifting through the muddy water together, right?" she smiles and continues with the line of question. "Mr. Konacher, we have evidence that places you at several homicide crime scenes in San Antonio, Vancouver, Moncton, Gananoque, and New Orleans, and have recently uncovered evidence of your assassination plot against the Pope here in Rio."

"Not me!" he vehemently denies.

"Evidence does not lie, Mr. Konacher."

"Well, the evidence you have sure as hell does. I didn't kill anyone!" he swears. "And as for a plot to kill the Pope, you have to be crazy to think I'd go that far." He looks around the claustrophobic room as his breathing becomes more labored. "I told you, all I was paid to do was alter my disguises and walk around dressed up like a nun one day and a priest the other. This afternoon I was supposed to join the kids waving Jesus flags and prance down the streets singing Kumbaya on the way to the beach."

"And we're supposed to just take you at your word and set you free?"

"Yes!" he exhales.

"We can't do that, Mr. Konacher. You see, we have all this evidence against you. As we speak, the Brazilian authorities are filing the extradition papers to send you back to America in our custody."

"I want a lawyer!" he insists.

"That *is* your right, but that's going to have to wait till we get you back to your temporary holding cell where it all began, in San Antonio."

"You can't do that," he argues.

"Yes, we can," she insists.

"Then I want to speak to my embassy. I am a Canadian citizen and demand to speak with Canadian authorities."

She cocks her head toward the two-way mirror at her back, summoning Juice into the room.

"Mr. Konacher," she says as Juice enters. "I believe you've already met Chief Superintendent Kamarre Toure of *your* Royal Canadian Mounted Police. The RCMP has been on our task force since they linked you to our crime scenes and Chief Toure himself since the homicides *you* orchestrated in *his* New Brunswick jurisdiction. He's a Canadian authority and would be happy to answer any questions you might have related to your detention and your rights."

Konacher glares at the large Black man and rubs his ribs. "Yeah, we've met," he scoffs. "You know, you probably broke a couple of ribs with that tackle."

Juice flashes him a mocking smile, his expression leaving little doubt of what he thinks of the squirrely little man in their custody.

"Can she really do that?" he asks.

"You're safer with her, you little prick!" Juice spits. "After what you did to my friend's wife, you're lucky I don't pack you in a suitcase and fly you to Ottawa for Kellar to dish out what you really deserve."

Brian Konacher wets his pants, and Juice gnarls at him before leaving him alone with Agent Nickerson in the room.

"Would you like to go with Chief Superintendent Toure, Mr. Konacher, or would you prefer to stay in our custody?" Nickerson asks playfully.

"That's okay," he whispers. "I'll stay with you."

69

YYZ, Mississauga, Ontario

"You sure you're not leaving anything in the trunk?" the kid from the rental company reminds Kellar as he prints the rental receipt and hands it to him.

"Quick trip," Kellar says to him, grabs the small, folded piece of paper with a nod, then follows the overhead signs to the Terminal 1 departures level.

His phone buzzes, and he grabs it from his jacket pocket without slowing his stride. "Kellar," he says crisply.

"Hey, Rafe, it's Marty."

"What'd you find for me, Marty?" he asks, walking briskly.

"Okay, I looked up the name Paula Konacher around that time and didn't come up with anything at all," he sighs.

"Nothing about the triple homicide in Stipley?"

"Nope. If the newspapers have it on microfilm, you already have more than I do. I found nothing about a woman by that name, or a triple in Stipley in July, or any other month in 1979 for that matter, sorry."

"Well, we know how good he is with computers. If he was able to modify law enforcement records, I'm sure newspaper databases are no match for him either."

"True, but he might not have scrubbed as far back as he should have to cover his tracks," Bloom announces optimistically.

"What'd you find?" Kellar inquires as he slows to a stop and steps aside for young honeymooners to get by with their cart loaded with suitcases.

"This might be a long shot, Rafe, but since I was already poking around in the paper's online archives, I took the liberty to search for any and all things Paula Konacher-related."

"Sounds like you might have found something interesting," Rafe says, intrigued.

"I came across a Tribune article from 1963 about a party that got busted with a bunch of underage kids. The crime beat in the paper listed a Paula Konacher as one of the teenagers that were picked up and listed the maternal grandparents as her legal guardians. Names were Thornton and Mildred Wilson."

"Good thing we were less concerned about printing minor's names in the papers back then, eh?"

"Looks like."

"How do we know that it's Konacher's mother?" Kellar probes.

"Because *this* Paula Konacher is basically a ghost. The province has no records of this girl anywhere; no employment history, no driver's license, no medical records, no school records or even a birth record. The only hint she ever existed is in this one single newspaper article, Rafe. That in itself raises a flag."

"Okay, nice work, Marty," Kellar compliments.

"Mr. and Mrs. Wilson died in a car accident about thirty years ago. Provincial land registry indicates they owned property in Halton Hills."

"So, we'll never know if they left the house to the granddaughter even if they had."

"They actually willed it to their local parish, which in turn sold it to build up the pot to build a new church in Georgetown."

"So, another dead end," Kellar fumes.

"'Fraid so, Rafe," Bloom admits regrettably.

"Alright, thanks for checking, Marty. I'll see you tomorrow," he replies, but has a sudden thought. "Marty, Marty, Marty!" he yells into his phone, hoping Bloom hasn't disconnected yet.

"What's up?" says Bloom.

"I just thought of something," he says. "Do you know who bought the grandparent's house from the church?"

Kellar waits as a family passes by with the youngest of three children on his father's shoulders, and Rafe recalls their family trip to Florida when his own son had been about that age.

"Rafe," Bloom says for the second time. "You still with me?"

"Yeah, Marty, sorry," Kellar affirms, returning to the present. "What were you saying?"

"Says here the old house was purchased by an Ernest Montgomery."

"He still the registered owner?"

"Looks like. Property deed is still in his name. Utilities and taxes are paid on time. Nothing to indicate he moved or died and left the house to anyone."

"Marty, how old is he?" Kellar asks on a hunch.

"Don't know. Let me check."

Bloom downloads the information as Kellar waits patiently. "You're never going to believe this, Rafe."

"Try me," he replies.

"Apparently, Mr. Montgomery is a hundred and eight."

"So, a hundred-and-eight-years-old and still healthy enough to live on his own and maintain his home and property, is he?" Kellar chuckles. "That's gotta be Konacher's hideout," he theorizes. "Do me a favor?"

"Sure. What do you need?"

"Text me that address and ask Shirley to book me on the later flight back to Ottawa. I'm gonna take a run over there to check that place out."

"Will do," Bloom confirms. "I'll speak with her first, and then I'll shoot over that address."

"Thanks, Pal," Kellar says, pockets the phone and heads back to the rental counter to retrieve his car for a few additional hours.

70

Toronto, Ontario

To the residents' delight, Father Jakub had held an impromptu Bible study for them after dinner. Unable to get to Mass on Sundays, the shut-ins always appreciate the company and fellowship whenever and however they can.

"I'm afraid that's all the time that I have," the priest apologizes, looking at his watch. "I always enjoy these visits very much."

"Don't forget to come back next week, Father," Pamela warns with a wide grin and a knobby finger.

"How could I forget?" Father Jakub laughs and rises from his seat. "Dinner is always so much better here than at my lonely rectory, and you always have such wonderful stories to share with me. Thanks again. Have a wonderful evening," he waves, then slips away and hurries to his car, shielding himself from the heavy rain with his arm.

As he turns the ignition and the engine comes to life, the priest reflects on his busy day now quickly fading in the dusk and thick cloud cover, just a hint of it lingering to the west. Despite their rocky start, he feels that he and Rafe had established something more profound than a temporary working relationship, perhaps something bordering on friendship, and hopes they will keep in touch.

The wind picks up and rattles his old minivan while the windshield wipers struggle to keep up with the driving rain as he creeps his way down his street, breaking just in time to miss the streetcar coming to a stop in front of him.

"Lord, please slow this rain and let us all get to our destinations safely," he prays earnestly as the cars start to move.

He loops around the one-way streets and turns into the alley behind the church, then parks in the garage, happy to take shelter from the storm.

"I must be getting old," he chuckles. "I could have sworn I closed the garage door before driving away. I sure hope rats didn't get in," he sighs, steps out of the vehicle and depresses the door opener's control panel on the wall. The overhead door's usual annoying hum is quiet, and the door remains motionless above his head as he's plunged into darkness with his delayed headlights turning off.

"That's odd," Father Jakub remarks. He jerks the cord to release the manual door latch and the metal door squeals down the rail and comes to a stop at the floor. "Guess the light's burned out too," he laughs, then reaches for the deadbolt with his keys while Mittens, the fat tabby with solid-white paws, greets him at the door with a friendly purr.

"What are you doing outside the rectory, you little scoundrel?" he asks, picking up the parish's unofficial mascot and rubbing its head between the ears to the feline's enjoyment. "Did Paulina not notice you slipping out behind her when she left this afternoon?"

Clutching the cat under his arm, Father Jakub unbolts the door, enters the rectory mudroom and switches on the lights as he drops the animal onto the floor.

"That's strange," he whispers, flicking the switch on and off and getting no response from the ceiling fixture. "I guess I'll have to change that bulb again," he grumbles, reflecting that he had replaced it only days ago.

He steps into the kitchen and clicks these lights with the same frustrating result.

"The breaker must have popped," he ponders, reaching for the cell phone in his pocket and not finding it.

"Shoot. I must have left it at the retirement home," he assumes and rummages for the flashlight in the junk drawer and clicks it on, then moves over to the window. Peering through the blinds, he confirms the surrounding buildings all have power. "I'll have to check the electrical panel, I suppose."

A dazzling flash of light precedes an explosive burst of thunder, and an alarming crash coming from his office immediately after startles him.

"Is someone in there?" he asks nervously, advancing cautiously toward the sound's origins. His racing heart slows as Mittens joining him in a hurry. He laughs at his uneasiness.

"You up to no good again, you little fraidy-cat?" he grins, bending down to tousle the cat's head. "Come on. Let's get some candles lit, and then we'll go downstairs to check out that electrical panel," he adds, lining up the flashlight under his chin. "Boo!" he cries out in the cat's direction and laughs wholeheartedly.

71

Mississauga, Ontario

Kellar lifts his eyes from his phone and watches as the waitress approaches and sets the steaming cup of coffee on the table with a friendly smile.

"You sure I can't get you anything else?" she asks.

"No, just the bill, thanks," he assures her.

"Alrighty," she says, pulling a pen from her ear and jotting something on the back of the check. "Just pay at the counter whenever you're ready. No rush," she reassures him and waltzes over to the next table. "Hey, welcome to Pearson's Grill Lounge. Can I get you started with some drinks?" she asks sweetly.

"Two house reds, please?" the man answers.

"You guys flying anywhere today?"

"No, just getting in, actually," he replies, but Rafe isn't interested in finding out where he and the missus just flew in from and shifts his focus back to his phone.

He re-examines the map on his phone. According to the app, the property once owned by Thornton and Mildred Wilson is half an hour away, but with nightfall and the weather threatening a turn for the worse, he estimates that time to be closer to forty-five minutes to an hour.

His phone buzzes to life in his hands, and he answers on the first ring. "Kellar!"

"Hey, Arch," his friend says glumly from Rio.

"You don't sound too good, Juice," Rafe chuckles. "Agent Nickerson giving you a hard time?"

"Nah, that's not it. That guy I told you we arrested—Brian Konacher? I think he was just a decoy."

"I told you guys two weeks ago Rio was a countermeasure trick," Kellar gloats.

"I know, I know," he acknowledges. "Still his real name, though. Confirmed this and his address with both Federal and Provincial government records. He's been at that address for five-and-a-half years. Probably why our suspect used him in the first place. Bastard's been two steps ahead of us all along."

"Probably more like four or five, actually," Rafe admits sombrely. "Task force still keeping this one locked up till the Pope leaves for Rome again, though?"

"That's the plan."

"You sticking down there for the duration?"

"Think so, although I'm pretty sure we're just wasting our time down here."

"I told you that too," Kellar rubs in a little more salt in the wound.

"What about you?" Juice inquires, ignoring the jab.

"Well, after you and I spoke earlier today, Jakub and I paid the local newspaper archives a visit and found a story that corroborated the old priest's story. Kid was found home alone with three dead bodies inside, so the cops drove him to the orphanage. Some guy at the paper snuck in and snapped a few pictures that never made the evening edition. I think that's where the kid got a taste for killing. There was a shot of those bloody Roman numerals on a wall behind the bed."

"Whoa!" Juice exclaims. "Has to be him. Any other leads?"

"There's an old house in Halton Hills that used to belong to his mother's maternal grandparents. Not in the family anymore, but I suspect it's where he's hiding. I was just about to head there when you called."

"What do you think he's really up to, Arch?" Juice wonders. "I mean, if he's not here in Rio to kill the Pope or make a mess of this gathering, what's his end game?"

"Don't quite know," Rafe admits, his free hand rubbing his forehead. "If he's still following his original covenant scheme, whoever's cast in the role of Jesus is still the key to where he's headed next as far as I'm concerned."

"Any thoughts on who that might be?" Juice probes.

"I don't know. A Cardinal, or a Bishop here at home?" Kellar supposes. "I remember my mom saying priests represent Christ here on earth."

"But which one?" Juice asks. "There have to be hundreds of priests in Toronto alone."

Kellar cocks his head. "I don't know, maybe a high-profile priest in Toronto," he ponders. "Shit!" he explodes, startling the waitress with the two house reds on her tray crashing to the floor. "Juice, I gotta go. Jakub's in trouble!" he cries out, leaving the bewildered waitress to clean up the mess on the floor as he races out of the restaurant without an apology or paying for his meal.

72

Toronto, Ontario

Mittens yowls hysterically, distressed by the endless sequence of lightning and thunder so intense the entire structure shakes on its foundation.

"I know, Mittens," Father Jakub coos as a long flash illuminates the entire rectory. "Not crazy about this weather either. This storm is quite discomforting."

With the taper candles clutched firmly in his hands, the flashlight tucked in his back pocket, and an anxious feline at his feet, Father Jakub settles his nerves and moves carefully in the intermittent light toward the fireplace. Setting the candlesticks at either end of the mantle, he strikes a wooden matchstick and lights the wicks, the pungent smell of sulphur momentarily irritating his nose.

"There we go," he says with a reassuring smile. "Now we can see. You think the wind just knocked out the power to the rectory, Mittens?" he asks. "Come on, let's go down to the basement and check on the electrical panel to make sure it's not something simple before we call hydro and make fools of ourselves."

The nervous cat yowls hysterically again, and Father Jakub giggles. "Okay, before *I* make a fool of myself, then," he laughs.

The driving rain pummels the large windows overlooking the street as strobes of lightning illuminate the space again, and the wind sends a fallen branch crashing noisily against the rectory's aluminum storm door, startling the pair.

"Just the wind, little one," he repeats the words his father would whisper to him as a child, squatting to lightly pat the cat's head. "Just the wind."

With Mittens temporarily appeased, Father Jakub inches his way down the darkened hallway with his flashlight securely in hand, the beam gradually dimming with the old batteries fading quickly.

"Guess I need to buy new batteries too, now, eh?" he mentally notes.

They reach the basement door as another round of lightning floods the hallway. It opens with a loud whine, and Father Jakub descends into the dark, unfinished basement, walking into loose cobwebs as he reaches the cement floor. Swiping away the cobweb, he spits out what he hopes isn't a dead fly or the spider itself.

"We have to clean this place someday, Mittens," he admits.

He shines the dim beam toward the electrical panel's metal casing and manages a few steps before illuminating the shadowy figure in the corner of the basement.

"Hello, Father," the chilling voice calls out.

"Who—who are you?" the priest falters and drops the flashlight as the cat scampers up the stairs.

"What, you don't recognize an old friend from your old seminary days? It's me, the Prophet," he replies.

Father Jakub reaches deep inside himself for strength and wisdom he can only draw from the grace of God. "In the name of Jesus, get out of my house!" he demands forcefully.

The intruder snickers and slowly inches closer. "Not quite yet, Father. Jesus isn't here to help you, so it's useless to call upon him," he says, wielding an intimidating knife and raising it to the priest's jugular. "I have absolutely no intention of using this knife, but I will if you don't do exactly as you're told."

Father Jakub dutifully submits without a word and internally supplicates God's mercy as his composure gradually returns, and a deep sense of peace overcomes his fear despite his predicament.

"Much better," he grins. Lowering the weapon and clasping the fallen flashlight, he shines it into Father Jakub's eyes. "How much does Inspector Rafe Kellar know about me now?" the Prophet asks in a mocking tone. "Hard to keep track since he had his friend take away my ears."

"It's not my place to say," Father Jakub replies.

"Look, Father. Not saying anything isn't going to change the outcome. You and I are both going to die this evening," he woefully admits.

Father Jakub swallows hard and considers the statement. Drawings strength from his tremendous faith that God has a plan, even one not easily discerned by human intuition, he prays for clarity and is compelled to engage the killer in conversation, despite the internal struggle between doing what he senses to be God's will and betraying his friend's trust by divulging sensitive information.

"We know your name's not Thomas Strickland, but that you were born Brian Konacher," Father finally admits, though reluctantly.

"Could be. I have so many names I can't keep track," he smirks. "What else does he have?"

"We also know about your family history, Brian. I'm so sorry for the loss of your mother and your brother, Peter. I can't imagine how devastating that would have been for you to witness as a child," he empathizes, desperate to reach Konacher's humanity. "Those scars never healed, did they?"

Konacher laughs at him. "You think you can shrink your way into my subconscious?" he cackles. "You think you're smart enough to mess with my head? Try to speak to my heart? Try to make me change my mind?" He lunges into the priest's face and hisses. "Won't happen!"

"I'm not attempting anything of the sort," Father Jakub says calmly. "I'm merely trying to grasp a deeper understanding of the terrible pain and suffering that brought you to this point."

The Prophet steps back and studies the priest for a long moment.

"You're not afraid of me anymore, are you?" Konacher eventually asks, noting the unnaturally serene look on the priest's face as Father gently shakes his head.

"I've only seen that in one other person before you," the Prophet marvels.

A long moment of silence is interrupted by a loud clap of thunder.

"We were under the impression that you were in Rio at World Youth Day and that you were going to assassinate the Pope," Father Jakub utters.

"That was my original plan," he admits. "But that old bastard Benedict had to quit, didn't he?" he spits. "Wasn't worth the trouble going down there to kill the new guy," he shrugs, and his face brightens. "And then, like manna from heaven, you and Kellar show up at my work and provide me with a suitable alternate ending and a trick to distract the manhunt. Sending that idiot in my place with a pre-paid ticket to Rio was genius; plus, it allows you and me to become better acquainted," he chuckles. "Looks like everyone but your police buddy was fooled, well, maybe I fooled him a little too."

"So, how do I fit into all of this?" Father Fischer asks.

"Oh, Father Jakub," the Prophet sighs almost admiringly. "You are so fortunate. So blessed and fortunate indeed. You get to play the best part."

"How so?"

The deranged psychopath draws closer to the priest, and Father Jakub feels the man's moist, sour breath on his face.

"You, Father, will be the crowning jewel of my masterpiece. You, my Roman-collared friend, were specifically chosen by the voice to be *in persona Christi* for real. Only with *your* death can the final covenant be fulfilled, and I be free at last."

A chill runs up Father's spine, but dissipates as quickly as it had materialized.

"Free from what?" he asks boldly.

"My tormentor!" he blares, hot droplets spraying onto Father Jakub's face.

"I am a Catholic priest, and therefore, an exorcist by virtue of my ordination. I can free you of the malevolent forces tormenting you," he urges. "If you let me."

"Quiet!" Konacher barks and silence floods the basement for several minutes except for the occasional rumblings from the active weather outside.

"I need to tie you up now," he announces.

"I understand," the young priest replies meekly.

Konacher chuckles as he wraps the thick, gray tape around Father Jakub's wrists. "You think they had duct tape two thousand years ago?" he laughs.

"Are you going to kill me here?"

"No, I have something more artistic planned for you," he says. "Let's go," he adds, leading Father Jakub up the creaky, wooden stairs with a tight grip on his elbow.

"Where are you taking me, Brian?"

"Where isn't important, Father," he replies as they slowly climb up to the darkened rectory. "Names aren't important either. Stop trying to connect with me."

Mittens joins them as they reach the living room, demanding attention with a series of annoying cries.

"Get away from me!" Konacher howls, kicking at the cat who scurries away from the boot and jumps on the mantle, knocking one of the lit candles to the ground and setting the curtains on fire. Within seconds, the room fills with smoke as the Prophet leads his victim out of the rectory, now ablaze.

73

With their deafening sirens howling and emergency strobes flashing, the three responding trucks from Toronto Fire Services hurry south on Roncesvalles Avenue with the ladder truck stopping in front of Father Jakub's residence, the second halting directly in front of the church, and the third rounding the south-west corner at Garden in front of the alley leading to the rectory's rear entrance as the heavy rain continues to wash over the city.

A team immediately grabs the lines from the trucks as others prepare for their offensive attack inside the blazing rectory from the front and back of the two-story brick structure.

The Lieutenant gives the go-ahead nod to the drivers to pump pressure to the lines once the hydrant and pump panel valves are connected, then cries out to put the wet stuff on the red stuff.

A pair breaches the engulfed structure from the front and confronts the scorching flames in the foyer and living room where the fire appears to be at its worse, while others manage the fire's temperature at the exterior of the building with the curtain nozzle. Menacing flickers from shattered windows threaten their efforts, but the rain helps to contain the flames to the rectory and not spread to the church itself or the connecting Knights of Columbus Hall to the right of the rectory.

At the back, another pair enters the residence through the garage and begin their offense from the rear. Dousing the kitchen walls, the firefighters work their way down the hallway and direct their watery assault toward the source centered in the living room as the flames penetrate through the ceiling and threaten to overtake the living space above.

A stored oxygen tank explodes from one of the guest bedrooms, shattering a second-floor window with flames and hot smoke billowing up into the night sky like incense from a thurible.

"Drown it!" a loud voice cries out. "Get 'em out!"

"On it," comes the quick reply as the ladder truck dispatches a firefighter up above the roof to shoot water from his cannon and converts their efforts into a defensive attack.

Thick, dark smoke illuminated from the flames below rises into the night, casting an ominous glow visible from the Gardiner Expressway several kilometers away.

Rafe curses from behind the wheel as he speeds his way through the wet Friday night traffic toward St. Faustina Parish.

"Get out of my way!" he shouts at the slower car puttering in the passing lane in front of him. "Get out!" he screams, his fist pounding firmly on the horn.

His rental isn't fitted with lights and a siren, but he reflects that most drivers are usually clueless to him and his emergencies despite his own vehicle's equipment.

He exits the Gardiner at Lakeshore and weaves his way through cars and trucks along the roadway, his hand steady on the horn and his emergency flashers hard at work. Heading north on Parkside, he takes a right onto Garden and stops shy of plowing into the parked fire truck.

"Where's Jakub?" he barks, waving his credentials and racing to one of the Toronto Police officers guarding the barricade. "Where's Father Jakub!" he cries out again over the noise.

"They haven't brought anyone out of the house yet," the policeman replies. "I don't think anyone was in there."

Rafe starts for the alley, but the young cop grabs him by the wrist and stops him abruptly.

Eyes boring into the younger officer's, he threatens. "You have less than two seconds to let go of me before I rip your arm off and beat you with it! I'm law enforcement!" he cries out, shoving his credentials into the patrolman's face.

The cop's grip loosens, and Kellar shoves his I.D. back into his inside coat pocket.

"It's not safe yet, is all I was trying to say," the policeman answers sternly. "Building's still on fire. You can't just walk in there."

Kellar knows and takes a deep breath. "Who's in charge of the scene?" he inquires.

"Lieutenant Mitchener of TFS over there," he replies with a nod of the head.

Kellar leaves the cop and marches toward the fireman in charge still crying out instructions over his hand-held radio.

"You guys find any victims in there?" Rafe asks, his raised I.D. confirming his right to be inside the barricaded area.

"No," the Lieutenant affirms. "We've almost got this beast defeated and will have a better idea just what we're dealing with when it's completely out. Can say that we haven't rescued anyone yet, and I haven't gotten word of any victim remains in there so far," he asserts. "I guess that's good news, right?"

"How long before I can get in?"

"Best guess, forty-five minutes to an hour. Still a few hot spots here and there. Not safe for anyone yet."

"Thanks," Kellar exhales. Ambling back to his rental with an air of defeat, he feels powerless and frustrated with himself for having left Jakub alone to deal with a maniac.

74

The rain had subsided by the time they passed the airport off-ramp, but the mist from the speeding motorists cutting in on the wet asphalt ahead of them initiates the intermittent wipers anyway. Sensibly, the Prophet drives below the speed limit hoping to avoid unwanted attention from the OPP while his victim, focusing on the unsteady cadence of the windshield wipers, solemnly prays.

"Where are you taking me, Brian?" Father Jakub eventually asks as Konacher maintains his silence and his eyes fixed on the road. "You know, Brian, you can tell me everything. You're safe here. Who am I going to tell?" he reasons. "You've made it clear that I won't have a chance to speak with anyone else ever again on this earth. It's not as though I can share this with Inspector Kellar. You've not even extended me an opportunity to speak with my family one last time before I die," he adds, searching Konacher's face for a sign of any kind.

The Prophet exhales deeply and slowly turns to face the priest before returning his gaze on the highway.

"I'm taking you to my house," he finally admits.

"Where's your house?"

"Halton Hills."

"Why there? What's significant about that place?"

"It's where I kept her as long as I could," he discloses after a long pause.

"Sister Mary Joseph?" the priest ventures.

"Yeah."

"Tell me about her," he encourages.

Konacher studies Father Jakub momentarily then turns his eyes forward again.

"What's to tell?" he sighs. "She was more of a parent to me than my own."

Father notes the moisture welling up at the corner of Konacher's eye.

"I didn't have a father to defend me. I never even knew him. He was just some cabbie my mother screwed in exchange for a ride home from a party one night. And that bitch!" he spits. "My own fucking mother wanted to sell my brother and me for sex when I was a kid just so she could get high!" he cries out. "Well, I fucking showed them!"

Father Jakub listens prayerfully without interrupting the broken man.

Konacher wipes his face and turns to the priest. "I've never told that to anyone."

Father Jakub nods encouragingly.

"That felt pretty good, strangely enough," he admits.

"Tell me more," Father counsels.

With his eyes focusing on the traffic ahead, Brian Konacher eventually opens up.

"Sister Mary Joseph was a sweet woman. I guess you could say she's as close as I ever came to loving someone. You know, back at the orphanage, she liked to hug me," he reminisces. "And I really liked it when she hugged me. That's what I remember most about her. How safe she made me feel,"

Konacher reflects. "I never felt safe as a kid, you know. My mother's legs were like a revolving door to the many faceless men in the house. Some she'd charge for the sex while others she'd offer up her horny ass for free. When she wasn't whoring around, she was smoking up or taking hits and basically dead to the world. I had to take care of my little brother. I didn't mean to kill him," he sniffles. "He was so little and wouldn't stop crying. I just needed him to be quiet. I didn't even notice I was smothering him. When I pulled him out from under the bed and realized he wasn't breathing, I just snapped. I went downstairs and saw my dead mother on the floor in a pool of her own blood, and it's as though a weight had been lifted from my shoulders. A normal boy would have been devastated, but as for me, I felt freedom for the first time in my life. There was only one other thing I had to do, and that was to kill the son of a bitch I had seen touching my little brother's privates in his bed the night before. I beat that asshole's head in with a rock, and it felt good!" he shouts triumphantly.

"And that's when you were sent to the orphanage?" Father Jakub probes after a moment.

"And that's when I was sent to the orphanage," he concurs with a long breath. "They arrested the dirtbag slumlord for the murder, but of course, he walked; not enough evidence. That's okay, though. We both know he didn't do it, right, Father?" he chuckles. "They asked me a bunch of questions but never really suspected me of anything. Killing a grown man had made me feel strong, but I was never very tall and became an easy target for the bigger kids at St. Vince's, especially Tommy Strickland. But Sister Mary Joseph put a stop to that very quickly. She took me under her wing and protected me from that little shit!" he smiles at the memory, but his face immediately contorts in anger. "Then one night, when everyone else was asleep, I found him looking through Sister Mary Joseph's keyhole while he fondled himself, thinking he was alone and safe in the shadows of the hallway. I showed him, though. The next morning, I told him some of the older boys had stashed a bunch of girlie magazines in the barn and that I'd be happy to show him where they were hidden. He could hardly contain his enthusiasm. Would you believe the little prick already had a hard-on?" he giggles. "I led him into the barn, climbed up to the loft and took him to the far corner. I told him they were just under the last bale of hay. He licked his lips and smiled at me, then turned and ducked to reach for the porn, and that's when I hit him over the head with a shovel," he boasts. "I set the barn on fire and sent that little bastard straight to hell where he belonged."

    Father Jakub closes his eyes and silently prays for the soul of Tommy Strickland as they ride in silence for a while until Brian Konacher feels compelled to open up about his ensuing traumatic upbringing.

75

Milberg Reformatory for boys – November 1980

"You are nothing but slimy, little maggots!" the intimidating warden sporting a military brush cut barked. "Low life, law-breaking malfeasants with zero respect for honest people's property. That's why you're sorry, little punk asses were sent here to me," he continued, parading before the new arrivals standing nervously at attention in their underwear. None of them brave enough to budge from the yellow line on the floor of the reform school's detainee intake hall; most of them believed the end of the world had arrived.

"Your mothers aren't here to wipe your asses," he chuckled as his guards encouraged him with their laughter. "When you eventually graduate from my institution for juvenile delinquents, you will have learned the meaning of consequences. You will have paid your debt to society and will return to the outside world knowing that if you get out of line again, nothing you experienced here in my little slice of heaven will compare to what's waiting for you in a maximum-security prison with hardened criminals and sexual deviants just itching to make you their little playthings."

Ten frightened minors, some with tears streaming down their cheeks, stared at their feet and listened as the warden approached the eleventh and smallest of the group with a sneer.

"My speech doesn't appear to have the same effect on you as it does with the others," he said, motioning toward the other young detainees and returning his gaze upon him. "What's your name?"

"Brian Konacher," the boy answered unafraid.

"Well, Mr. Konacher," the warden replied sternly as he flipped through his folder to find the boy's paperwork. "Seems as though you're a little tougher than these other inmates. You're already a hardened criminal, aren't you? Seems that you've killed one of your little friends at the orphanage. I guess we'll have to make sure you get the message loud and clear as soon as possible, for sure."

The unsettling words sent a chill up the young boy's spine, but he wouldn't give the warden the satisfaction of seeing he was rattled.

The warden handed the clipboard to the guard to his right and continued to pontificate.

"From now on, your names don't mean squat!" he screamed, returning his focus onto the group. "You ladies better learn your assigned numbers by heart because that's all we'll be using here. You will answer when spoken to; otherwise, you will keep your mouths shut! Insubordination and back-talk will not be tolerated. In fact, any unruliness will land you in the box for an indefinite period of time," he warned firmly and maintained a fierce gaze over the terrified boys with slumped shoulders and heads low, his billy club smacking loudly in his leathery palm, emphasizing each blow.

"Those of you who still have parents that want to visit your sorry asses will be allowed to see them for thirty minutes every other month. But be warned that you are not permitted any physical contact with them whatsoever! Your mothers can't hug you, kiss you or wipe your sissy, snivelling noses. My guards will be in the room at all times, and I *guarantee* this rule will be strictly enforced. Do I make myself clear?" he cried out and only endured a few seconds of silence. "I can't hear you!" he wailed louder.

"Yes," the boys stammered in unison.

"Yes, Warden!" he demanded.

"Yes, Warden!" they conformed.

"Now, you're going to follow Guard Bricklin to the shower room where you will strip naked and get under the water and use soap. You'll then dry yourselves off and proceed to the on-duty nurse who will give you a quick physical, after which you'll be issued underwear, socks, slippers, and a jumpsuit you'll be told to get into before you're photographed and printed. You ladies will then be led to your dormitory to meet your new roommates, except for Mr. Konacher. Henceforth known as inmate number 800243, Mr. Konacher will be sequestered in separate quarters under Guard Bricklin's supervision for his first week with us. The rest of you, stay in line and do as you're told, and you might leave here as men instead of the pitiful little snots I have here in front of me!"

76

Brian Konacher lay awake on the narrow bed, alone in a cold and somber dormitory annex being repainted, with the itchy woollen blanket pulled all the way up to his chin, still seething from the afternoon's abuse at the hands of Guard Bricklin. All the other boys had had their photographs taken once they had been fully clothed, and none of them had received the humiliating cavity search they had been forced to witness as an example of one of the consequences the warden had apparently warned them about. Although the other guards hadn't seemed to have agreed with Bricklin's method, none of those bastards had raised a finger in protest.

The ten-year-old remained motionless with his eyes closed as the hulking, shadowy figure of Harvey Bricklin neared his rack.

"Wake up!" the guard snarled, waited a moment and yelled again more forcefully. "I said, wake up!"

"What?" the boy fired back, and an eerie smile formed on the guard's dry, chapped lips.

"I like it when they're feisty," he mocked. "Makes it more challenging."

"What do you want?" the kid demanded.

Bricklin tossed a Polaroid at his head, and Brian's heart sank when he saw his naked figure in the photo. Gathering his courage, he glared into the guard's eyes. "You horny for little boys?" he said with an edge and was met with a hard backhand to the face, which drew blood from his quivering lip.

"You know you're not supposed to talk back!" Bricklin replied. "I'm pretty sure the warden was clear on that. There might have to be more consequences, now," he snickered.

"And I'm pretty sure that's considered kiddy porn," the boy said, pointing to the Polaroid then wiping his mouth with his hand.

"Pictures are going to be the least of your worries," the guard vowed with a nasty smile. "I arranged a play-date for you and a buddy of mine at a hunting lodge tomorrow afternoon. If you behave, he might even pay you. And if you so much as breath a word about any of this to the warden or anyone else—" he warned with a clenched fist as he inched his angry face closer.

In a sudden, explosive motion, the boy lunged forward, punched the towering guard in the groin, and then quickly ran down the row of bunk beds.

Bricklin hunched over and groaned while massaging himself but quickly regained his balance and gathered his strength to give chase to the boy who hadn't gotten any further than the locked exit door. Seeing the guard quickly approaching, Brian turned and ran head-first toward Bricklin, who easily subdued him to the ground and dragged him back to his bed by a leg kicking and screaming, then shackled the child to the bedframe.

"See you tomorrow, Scrappy," he winked before walking away.

77

Smithfield Foster Residence, Windsor, ON – September 1981

"Just put your crap there for now," the tall and lanky Hispanic kid told him as he pointed to a bed not much larger than the one Brian Konacher had used for ten months at the reformatory. "This'll be your bedroom for as long as they decide to keep you, or till you decide you've had enough of those messed up sons of bitches."

"What do you mean?" the young Konacher asked as the oldest of seven foster boys gave his newest temporary sibling the grand tour of his new temporary home, a six-bedroom split entrance with a leaky roof and peeling clapboard siding in one of the city's most run-down neighbourhoods.

Juan looked at him and grinned. "These people are into some pretty weird stuff," he revealed.

"Weird like what?"

"Okay, so Frank owns the house and collects money from the government to keep homeless kids here. Why do you think they have so many of us?" he scowled. "Anyways, his old lady ran off with one of the foster kids when the guy turned eighteen. Guess he was a better lay than Old Franky was," he laughed. "Anyways, he went out and found himself a new chick called Roseline and things got pretty weird, pretty fast around here. Look, we all think it's cool that she walks around the house naked pretending we don't see her, but we also think she's a witch," he said casually as they reached a black metal door at the end of the hall in the basement. "Here. Take a look for yourself." He unlatched and opened it to a dark and musty, windowless room, dimly lit with black candles from a chandelier and sconces flanking an upside-down cross on the wood-panelled walls. A chill ran up Brian's spine as he glanced inside and spotted the pentagram painted in red on the floor in the center of the room.

"Place gives me the creeps!" Juan grimaced as he quickly shut the door, turned and bumped into Frank and Roseline.

"What are you boys doing down here!" Frank demanded angrily.

"Just giving the new kid a tour of his new digs," Juan answered.

"You know this room's off-limits to you guys," Frank complained.

"Let them go in, Honey," Roseline urged as she gave the new addition a light pat on the head. "They're going to be initiated next month anyway," she smiled, her yellowing teeth showing behind her black-painted lips.

"And initiated we were," the Prophet admits. "They slowly introduced us to the occult with their Ouija boards and tarot cards at first, but then plunged us in feet-first on Hallowe'en night that same year with dark rituals and animal sacrifices."

Father Jakub prayerfully maintains his silence as Konacher continues to unload.

"That's the night that I was born, Jakub. That's when the voice began communicating with me," he reflects. "I stayed there till the eve of my seventeenth birthday. They didn't believe in banks because they were afraid the government would grow wise to how lucrative it was to keep kids, so they had plenty of money stashed in a safe in their 'special' room in the basement. That night, on the advice of the voice, I sacrificed them all to him and emptied their safe," the memory drawing a smile to his thin lips. "I swapped my clothes and belongings with another kid about my height and took on his identity. It was a lot easier back in those days, but even now, despite DNA cataloguing, I still manage to get around encrypted databases with surprising ease," he chuckles. "Brian Konacher may have died at the hands of a cult leader who murdered his entire household and set his house ablaze, slaying himself before perishing in the fire, but no one ever bothered to find out or even cared to look."

Rafe Kellar and his colleagues on the task force had referred to Thomas Strickland–Brian Konacher as a monster on several occasions, but as the Prophet steers the car off the highway and north toward Halton Hills, Father Jakub sighs deeply, quietly reflecting on society's blissful ignorance of its culpability in the creation of its own monsters.

"I got tired of hearing the voice and headed west, but the farther I traveled, the more insistent it called me back home," Konacher admits. "And finally, one night, I figured the only way to shut it up was to track down that prick Bricklin and serve him up to the voice as a sacrificial offering, and the voice left me alone—for a while."

"How does Sister Mary Joseph fit into all of this?" the priest questions.

Konacher turns to face him with a despondent look and turns to face the road again.

"I rescued her from her miserable cloistered life," he says glumly.

"But she wasn't a cloistered nun," Father corrects.

"My story!" the Prophet cries out in anger. "If I say she was cloistered, then she was cloistered!" he sulks for several kilometers before taking a breath and resuming.

"She wasn't well. Her health was deteriorating, and they wanted to ship her off to another convent in Pennsylvania."

"How did you know all that?" Father Jakub asks.

"I have my ways," he admits. "But stop cutting me off mid-sentence!" he huffs and frets for another long stretch before going on.

"She always told me I held a special place in her heart and that she wanted to stay close to me, so I reclaimed the old family farm and, you could say, evicted the people living there. Officially, they still live there, though," he snickers. "I made myself a nun's habit, forged some official-looking documents that allowed me to leave with her and I simply rolled her out the front door in a wheelchair," he boasts. "The voice remained quiet until she died. I buried her under a church not far away. She always seemed at peace and the only person unafraid of the real me the entire time we stayed together, so I entered the seminary hoping to find that peace for myself and keep the voice at bay, but things didn't quite work out for me there as you know very well."

"So that *was* you they spoke of," the priest concludes.

"I never should have gone there. The voice made me go through hell for a long time after that move. It was angry with me and demanded blood faster than I could provide it, but I persevered without ever getting caught, and it finally left me alone until those morons dug up the church and found Sister Mary Joseph's remains last year. It promised to finally set me free if I orchestrated this elaborate recreation of the covenants."

The Prophet stares at him, wondering if he's said too much, but Father Jakub encourages him to continue his narrative.

"I needed a massive amount of information from which to select my victims and their killers. In the beginning, I developed mindless little games that people downloaded like idiots and naïvely welcomed me into their lives. They unknowingly handed over all their financial transactions and granted me access to private text and email communications and all the social media data I wanted. It's incredible the deeply personal crap people put out there without giving it a second thought, but despite all the information I had gathered, I soon realized my database wasn't expanding quickly enough for my timeline."

He turns to the priest. "Am I boring you with all this tech talk?" he grins.

"Not at all," Father Jakub replies, so he continues.

"I then initiated a hostile takeover as IT director at Synthesized Logistics where you found me, and my database grew exponentially, allowing me to initiate my plan. And now here we are," he sums up.

"So why the attack on Rafe's wife?" Father Jakub asks.

"Didn't he tell you she served him with divorce papers?" he asks with a raised eyebrow.

"No, he didn't. But what does that have to do with anything?"

"She was a distraction," he replies matter-of-factly. "I needed his full attention. I think I have it now."

"Oh, I think that's safe to say," the priest whispers, and they ride in silence until Father Jakub makes another attempt to reach the boy buried deep inside the monster.

"I can help you, Brian. You know you don't have to go through with this," he says.

The Prophet glares at him with a menacing look of sheer disdain.

"Do not mistake me for one of your weak-minded sheep who lap up your teachings of faith, forgiveness, and brotherly love. You guys are such hypocrites, preaching chastity while preying on innocent children. You guys are the worst kind of cancer ever to roam the earth. If I had time, I'd kill every last one of you."

"That is not at all a fair assertion, Brian. Not all priests are predators and, as small as that number is, you and I both agree that a single one is still one too many. But I am not one of those awful men, Brian," Father Jakub stresses and continues undeterred. "I'm very sorry you were hurt. I know your little brother Peter was deeply wounded too, and there is no excuse for the disgraceful actions taken by adults whose sworn duty it is to protect children in their care, not prey on them—that's inexcusable. But *I'm* not looking to harm you. I'd like to help you heal from the heavy and painful burden you've had to carry your entire life. You don't need to resort to this incomprehensible violence. Enough blood has already been shed, don't you think?"

Father Jakub sees hope that Konacher may be considering his words, so he presses on.

"I can help you to overcome the demons," he insists. "You don't have to kill me."

The Prophet howls a disturbing, guttural laugh in Father Jakub's direction as his pupils dilate and saliva drools from his lips.

"I'm not merely going to kill you, Jakub; that's not what's going on here. I don't simply kill people. I sacrifice them! I can assure you that immolating you will serve a greater purpose than to simply satisfy my pleasure if that's any comfort to you."

"Please, Brian. I'm begging you not to do this," he implores.

"Your fate is irreversible. Our conversation hasn't changed anything except to strengthen my resolve. I need to free myself from the voice, and this is the only way it's going to happen."

"Please," Father supplicates.

"Forget it!" the Prophet glares. "Get yourself right with your god, because you're about to die a slow and agonizing death, the likes of which not witnessed in two thousand years!"

78

Toronto, Ontario

Lieutenant Mitchener waves him over. "Inspector Kellar!" he calls out. "We've assessed the structure and have confirmed that it's now safe for you to go into if you want to follow our investigators in for a look, but just to take a look around," he instructs. "Please don't disturb anything."

"Of course," Kellar replies impatiently and falls-in behind a pair of investigators heading inside the fire-damaged rectory to ascertain the cause of the blaze as a handful of curious neighbors huddle together along the barricaded perimeter to catch a glimpse of the action.

The three men enter through the front door in a single file. The lingering smell of wet, charred wood and burned plastic irritates Kellar's lungs and cause him to cough as water drips from the ceiling onto his head. The two TFS investigators set up their portable floodlights inside the living room and lean in for a closer look at a burn pattern between the fireplace and the window reported in the initial walkabout as a possible point of origin.

"Jakub!" Kellar shouts as he quickly moves from the living room into the kitchen then peers into the garage. "Jakub!"

"There wasn't anyone in the building," the senior fire investigator reports.

"Jakub!" Kellar hollers, ignoring the remark and sprints up the stairs to the second level. "Jakub," he shouts again, entering all three bedrooms, opening up closet doors and ducking to check under each bed. "Dammit!" he huffs and kicks in Father Jakub's closet door in frustration, then heads directly for the basement. Stopping at the entrance, he cries out to the inspectors. "Any of you guys have a flashlight?"

"Sorry, just these things," one replies, motioning to the large halogens on the tripods, so Kellar reaches for his cell phone and fumbles with it until he finds and activates the flashlight app.

"Jakub!" he calls out and descends into the darkness. "Jakub!" he says again at the foot of the stairs, scanning with the light and perceiving nothing out of the ordinary.

"So, you guys didn't find any human remains at all?" Kellar asks the investigators and wipes the water from his forehead as he returns to the main level and joins them in what's left of the living room.

"That's what we've been trying to tell you. No one was home."

"Hard to tell if there was even a struggle with all this damned furniture in the middle of the room," Kellar complains.

"Afraid that's the nature of fighting a fire. Gotta gather all combustibles in one area; otherwise, it's like pissing on a forest fire."

"You find a cat by any chance?" Kellar remembers.

"Nope. Not even a mouse," the fireman replies.

"Thanks," Rafe says anxiously as he waves and rushes out to his car. "Bastard's gonna kill him at his house!" he curses and races away from the scene.

79

Halton Hills, Ontario

The Prophet turns into the graveled driveway, steers the old station wagon behind the house and stops under the carport. He turns off the engine and moves swiftly to the passenger side to collect his victim.

With his wrists bound tightly, Father Jakub struggles to exit from the car, so Konacher reaches in and forcibly yanks him out by a lapel. The priest crashes face-first onto the rough concrete slab, his glasses landing by the rear tire and blood forming on his face and forehead from abrasions.

The Prophet laughs, stomps on the eyeglasses, and kicks Jakub in the ribs before spitting in his face.

"Too bad you don't have a beard for me to pull," he mocks. "Nothing personal, you know. The voice demands this be as historically accurate as possible."

Squinting away his blurred vision, Father Jakub stares up at Konacher and tries to appeal to him once more. "You don't have to do this, Brian."

"Stand up!" he demands.

With much difficulty, Father Jakub complies, and Konacher immediately shoves him forcefully toward the house.

He moves slowly, his broken ribs searing inside his chest and blood dripping from his face onto his white shirt and tattered blazer. He sluggishly climbs the rotting rear balcony steps and waits by the door.

The Prophet ignores the light switch and shoves Father inside the old kitchen. The house reeks of mold and decay, and they amble through the darkness toward the root cellar hatch in the floor by the window. Konacher grabs the round metal handle and swings open the door, then thrusts Father Jakub three feet into the damp obscurity of the shallow clay landing as he emits a chilling laugh.

"Don't go anywhere," he chuckles. "I have to commune with the voice, and then I'll be back for you. You should probably pray, too," he advises. "I believe that's what Jesus did just before his capture. Sorry," he feigns contrition. "I know I didn't give you any time for that before I picked you up, but you have a little bit of time now before I move you to the column and scourge you," he snorts and drops the heavy door over the opening, leaving Father Jakub alone in the dark, fading in and out of consciousness.

80

Toronto, Ontario

Progress is agonizingly slow as Kellar inches his way through Sunnyside, with the city's streets at near-gridlock with heavy construction on the westbound Gardiner reducing it to a single lane.

After attempting to reach Jakub for what seemed the hundredth time, Kellar pitches his cell on the floor and blows a gasket.

"How do you people put up with this crap!" he screams. "Expressway, my ass!" he fumes. Ottawa has its share of traffic woes, but this borders on cruel and unusual punishment.

He finally eases onto the Gardiner and eventually creeps his way past the large crew of men working under industrial portable light towers on the Humber River bridge. He curses them as he passes by, then speeds up as the single lane turns into three, and the traffic opens up considerably . . . but only for a short distance due to a three-car pile-up blocking two lanes just east of the Islington off-ramp.

Kellar exhales a curse and reaches for his phone at his feet.

"9-1-1, what is your emergency?" the emotionless female voice asks.

"This is Inspector Rafe Kellar of the RCMP. I'm in pursuit of a dangerous killer responsible for multiple homicides and need assistance. I'm stuck on the QEW and can't move," he cries out. "I need you to send a tactical team ahead of me to intercept my suspect."

"Are you currently involved in a high-speed chase with your suspect?" she asks.

He stares at his phone with a raised eyebrow. "No, I'm parked on this damn highway and can't even budge," he grumbles. "I don't know, maybe you guys around here consider this a high-speed chase," he says sarcastically. "He has at least two hours on me, and I believe he has a hostage he's planning to execute, so we have to intervene at his location ASAP."

"What's the address?"

"His property is located in Halton Hills on 6th Line. It's an old farmhouse registered under the name Ernest Montgomery."

"So, your suspect is currently there with his hostage?"

"I believe so."

"Inspector Kellar, unless you know he's there for sure, we can't dispatch a tactical unit based on a hunch," she replies with an edge.

Kellar closes his eyes and swears under his breath.

"Are you still there, Inspector Kellar?" she asks after a prolonged pause.

"Look," he sighs. "Can you at least send officers there ahead of me to investigate the *possibility* of my suspect and his hostage being there and then call in the cavalry if they find them there?"

"I'll contact Halton Regional right away and have them dispatch someone to that address," she replies. "Would you like me to give the responding officers your cell number to contact you with any updates?" she suggests.

"Yes. That would be helpful," Rafe acknowledges, surprised by the unexpected courtesy.

81

Halton Hills, Ontario

Father Jakub regains consciousness in a start as a hungry rat bites into the bloody flesh of his cheek. He frantically shakes off the rodent with his head, sending it scurrying away and squeaking loudly in protest.

Taking a deep, uncomfortable breath, the priest squints—a pointless attempt at distinguishing his dark surroundings. The floor is hard and cold, and he pushes his bound wrists against it, awkwardly sitting himself up and wincing from the extreme discomfort in his side. Pain throbs from his head and lances from the sprain in his ankle from the shove and subsequent fall into the dungeon, but he manages to move, propping his back against the wall despite the pain. He draws his hands up to his head and, reaching as far back as possible, rubs the soreness where his skull had connected with the hard clay. Closing his eyes and straining through another deep breath, he prayerfully whispers for strength.

"Are you still down there?" the Prophet chuckles as he pulls open the hatch and springs down onto the landing next to Father Jakub. He crouches, gently lays the door back into place above his head and steps down another foot to reach the uneven floor that slopes to the center of the root cellar. With the help of his glowing phone, he moves quickly to the middle support column and tugs at a string to light the bare bulb dangling from the century-old wooden joists.

Father Jakub looks over to him and gasps at the elaborate Roman Centurion costume Konacher sports with an air of smugness.

"I told you the voice demands this to be as historically accurate as possible," he snickers and allows his victim to soak up the meticulousness with which he has prepared for this momentous occasion.

In spite of his blurred vision, Father Jakub's entire body trembles as he recognizes the long, narrow bands of leather dangling from the side of a small wooden stool at the base of the column.

"Please deliver me, Lord," he sobs loudly.

"There's no one here to help you, Jakub. You know, Jesus died despite his own pleas to his father."

"The Lord is my strength and my salvation," Father Jakub prays, ignoring Konacher's catechetical lesson.

"How do you like my flagellum?" he snickers, approaching the priest and dangling the leathery bands teasingly in his face. "I made it myself," he boats. "I thought better of adding the small shards of bone at the end, though. I just need to give you stripes for the occasion, not make you bleed to death or have you go into shock before your crucifixion."

Father Jakub quietly recites the comforting verses of Psalm 23 from memory.

"Come, it's time to get started," the Prophet declares casually. Brandishing his long knife, he slices through the thick gray tape. "I had these made just for you," he grins, pulling out the heavy shackles from his back and clamping them tightly around Father Jakub's wrists.

The priest winces from the pain as Konacher yanks him away from the wall and drags him to the column, where he hops onto the stool and secures the chain to the hook at the top, then leaps down onto the floor. With his long, sharp knife, he leisurely cuts off Father Jakub's jacket and shirt to expose his bare skin from the waist up. He tosses the shredded clothes to the side and bends to remove his shoe and socks.

"Please, Brian," Father Jakub pleads.

"I told you this needs to be authentic. Jesus was naked for his scourging and crucifixion, so I'm afraid you can't have it any other way."

"But he's always depicted wearing a loincloth," Father Jakub reasons. "Please. I've been cooperating with you fully. I've not fought you or given you any trouble. Please, allow me at least this tiny bit of dignity."

The Prophet ponders the reasoning for a moment and finally concedes. "I don't know why I'm agreeing to this, but very well. I'll only cut off your pants and let you keep your boxers, assuming you don't make a habit of going commando," he cackles and slices through the fabric exposing Father Jakub's legs and tossing the sheered trousers in a heap with the rest of his clothes. Stepping back, he whistles at his impressive work and starts to laugh as his victim shivers from the cold and struggles to stretch his bare feet to the ground.

"I can help you overcome the demons," the priest maintains adamantly. "You don't have to go through with this."

"I'm not looking for your help. I've already told you that," Konacher replies.

"There's still some good left inside your soul, Brian. I'm convinced of that."

The Prophet snickers. "It's funny how you actually believe what you're saying," he scorns.

"It's true," Father Jakub argues passionately. "Why else would you spare that young boy's life in New Orleans?"

"Shut up!" Konacher barks, recalling his weakness.

"You could have killed that boy. You were there to kill his father as a surrogate for King David. His young son would have made a logical substitute for Solomon, but you couldn't bring yourself to raise your knife to him. If you don't have a single shred of love-of-neighbor inside your soul, why do you suppose you spared that young boy's life?"

"I said shut up!" he cries out and punches the priest in the head in a fury as the smartphone on the table chirps and vibrates to life. Clutching it annoyingly, he watches as his surveillance equipment streams the live feed of a police cruiser slowly making its way up the driveway.

"Seems that we have company," he says, regaining his volatile composure. "And would you look at that," he smiles. "Seems the policeman is actually a policewoman," he adds, but his playful demeanor quickly hardens as he issues his victim a stern warning. "If you make a sound, if you give away our position, I will bring that bitch down here and gut her right here in front of you. Is that what you want?"

"No, of course not," Father answers meekly. "Please don't harm anyone else. I won't make a sound. You have my word."

"Good. Then we understand each other."

82

"Hello, Inspector Kellar?" the dispatched female officer says to Rafe over the phone. "This is Constable Maria Mendoza from Halton Regional. I've just arrived at the Montgomery property. There's no visible sign of activity inside the house from where I'm standing, but I'm going to walk the outside perimeter to get a closer look."

"How many are you?" Kellar queries.

"What do you mean?"

"You and how many others are there with you?"

"I'm alone."

"Alone?" he cries out.

"Yes," she affirms. "Dispatch said you needed someone to confirm the possible whereabouts of your suspect, and I was the closest unit, so I took the call."

"Were you on your way to your prom?" he replies sarcastically.

"Excuse me?" Constable Mendoza says with indignation.

"I asked for a tactical unit to storm this location, and instead, they sent a twelve-year-old little girl without backup!"

"I'm not a little girl; I'm a cop!" she fires back. "I get enough shit for being a woman from the jackasses back at

Division. I'm not about to take any from a chauvinistic prick from Ottawa!"

Kellar sighs. "Look, that came out wrong, and I apologize," he admits. "But inside that house, whether you can see him or not, is that sadistic son of a bitch who thinks it's cute to call himself the Prophet. He's not afraid to kill, and you're not equipped to deal with him on your own!"

"I'm a trained, professional officer of the law!" she argues.

"He's going to turn you into his plaything!"

"He's not even in there!" she contends.

"Wait till I get there!"

"Look, you asked for someone to come out here and take a look around. Let me do my job!" Mendoza dismisses him.

"Do not proceed any further!" Kellar stresses. "If you hear anything inside, call in Tactical immediately; otherwise, stay the hell put!" he orders, imagining what Konacher will do to her if she interferes with his plans.

Constable Mendoza terminates the call without another word, then pockets her phone, leaving Kellar to fume in his car, one driver among hundreds of others unable to budge.

Raising her sidearm and ignoring Kellar's advice, she stealthily advances around the outside of the house through the tall, wet grass. Edging the root cellar's bulkhead doors on the far side, she then rounds the rear of the building, crouching between the foundation and the old Buick station wagon under the carport. Her pulse races, and her body tenses as she extends her hand up onto the hood, still warm to the touch. Her phone vibrates silently in her pocket, but she ignores it, fully expecting it to be Kellar again demanding her to stand down.

Given this discovery, though, standing down might not have been such a stupid idea . . . but she's not a rookie, and, dammit, she wants to make detective one day, and detectives aren't afraid of Buick station wagons, are they? Of course not! They face danger square-on without second-guessing their confidence and training. Lowering her hand, she stretches her neck past the rear bumper for a better look at the door at the top of the stairs.

Rising from her crouched position, Constable Mendoza cautiously climbs the back porch up to the kitchen door, her breath quick and shallow and her brows as damp as her single-striped pant legs. It's locked. She exhales and relaxes her shoulders, her fear and her fortitude at odds. Harnessing her assertiveness, she sprints to the front door and finds it bolted as well. She whispers a frustrated curse and absently jiggles the doorknob, which unlocks with remote assistance from the Prophet, observing her movements from the anonymity of the cellar.

She opens the squeaky wooden door and slinks inside the dim living room, her flashlight tightly gripped below her weapon and scans the area. The smell of recently extinguished candles permeates the air, partly covering up the musty smell of mold and dust. To her right, she notes a long mirror resting against the wall with red wax pillars surrounding a pentagram on the worn-out hardwood floor in front of it.

"Well, that's not creepy at all," she swallows.

With the living room cleared, she shifts her attention to the kitchen and carefully scrutinizes the space, spotting old takeout containers in the overflowing trash bin by the pantry and making a mental note of the root cellar hatch in the floor. Despite her light-footedness, the ancient wooden stairs give away her position with annoyingly loud cries as she climbs her way up with her stomach in a knot.

"Maybe I should have waited for Kellar," she admits to herself. "But it's a bit late to change my mind now."

Channelling her inner-strength and dismissing her fears, she scales the remaining three stairs to find the four bedrooms as empty as the rest of the house and lets out another lingering sigh of relief.

"Pull yourself together," she chastises herself and hurries down to the main level, satisfied that Kellar's suspect isn't at home. With the creep factor still on high, she reaches for the door without turning back, rationalizing that a call to Inspector Kellar could wait until she gets into the safety of her squad car. She turns the knob but recalls the hatch to the cellar in the kitchen.

"Shit," she utters, running a hand over her tight pony-tailed hair. "Just one more door, and you can get the hell out of this place," she reassures herself.

With her heart beating loudly inside her chest and her sidearm and flashlight drawn, she inches her way toward the opening. Squatting, she grabs the metal ring with her left hand and lifts the heavy door on its hinges, then quickly returns the light into position and sweeps both beam and barrel into the darkness below. The ignition of a sump pump startles her, but she remains undeterred despite the frayed nerves.

"A detective would not be afraid to go down there," she murmurs unconvincingly.

Drawing courage from her training, she plunges herself into the dark cellar with her flashlight and weapon in position. The bright light momentarily blinds and disorients her, and she has no time to react to the freak in the Roman soldier costume racing toward her with a blunt object.

The Prophet swings the club and connects with the side of her head, rendering her unconscious in a heap at his feet.

"Good of you to drop in," he snickers wickedly as he draws his arm back, eager to take another swing.

"Stop!" Father Jakub says forcefully. "Leave her alone!"

The Prophet drops his arm and turns to the priest in a fit of laughter. "You're in no position to bark orders at me."

"She's only doing her job, Brian. You didn't even have to unlock the door for her; she's not part of your plan. Had you left well enough alone, she would have stayed outside, but now, thanks to you, she's here. You've already incapacitated her. She can't interfere in any way. You do not need to harm her any more than you already have," he insists. "Now leave her alone, and let's get this madness over with!"

Konacher chuckles at him, then returns his gaze to the female officer on the floor.

"Okay, you win," he giggles. "I admire your gumption, for a man who's about to be executed. I'm going to let her live, but not before I'm sure she can't interfere with us if she happens to wake up."

"Fine, just don't strike her again," Father Jakub demands adamantly, making Konacher snicker again.

The Prophet reaches for his duct tape and secures her ankles, binding her wrists behind her back before applying more adhesive tape around her head to cover her eyes and finishes with a strip across her mouth. Tossing the roll aside, he grips her arms and drags her limp body to a corner and grins.

"Now, back to you," he says to Father Jakub.

83

Toronto, Ontario

Kellar presses the button and waits for the prompt. "Please say a command."

"Call Marty Bloom," he enunciates slowly and clearly for the Bluetooth connection to dial his colleague in Ottawa.

"Did you say call Marty Bloom?" the automated voice responds.

"Yes."

"You spoke too soon," she criticizes.

Kellar pauses briefly, then tries again. "Yes," he repeats and waits.

"Are you still there?" she asks

"Yes!" he fumes.

"Sorry, you're having difficulty. Please try again."

"Call Marty Bloom!" he reiterates impatiently.

"Sorry, contact unknown," she announces.

"Are you kidding me? You just had it a minute ago, you piece of shit!" Rafe screams and manually dials the contact from the phone in anger.

"Hey, Rafe," Bloom picks up at his desk on the first ring. "How'd you know I was still here?"

"I didn't. I thought I got you on your cell," he grumbles, still frustrated with technology and his inability to reach Father Jakub or Constable Mendoza. "Anyway, I need some reliable intel on that house. Take that chocolate bar out of your mouth and start typing, please."

"Must be serious," he comments. "You never say please."

"This isn't the time, Marty," he warns.

"Sorry. You haven't reached Father Jakub yet, have you?"

"Negative," he sighs. "That's only one of my problems, though. I can't reach him, and I can't move an inch on this oxymoron of an expressway; plus, locals sent some kid to check out the house instead of Tactical, can you believe that?" he shouts. "I told her to wait for me, but no, she hung up on me, and now I can't reach her either. That asshole's probably already killed her."

"Ah, shit! What do you need from me?"

"I need to know what I'm getting myself into when I finally get there. From my phone, I could only see a blurred image of the property with sucky resolution. Not much of anything in terms of terrain, just a couple of scattered white dots in a green field. Looks like there could be a curved driveway leading to one of the dots. Do you have access to anything clearer?"

Kellar makes out Bloom's pudgy fingers eagerly striking the keyboard as he brings up the satellite images of the property. "I've got it here. What do you want to know?"

"How recent is the image you're looking at?"

"Last week."

"How'd you manage to get your hands on that?"

"Not important."

"Won't ask again."

"I just emailed it to you. You should be getting it any moment now," he says as Kellar's phone dings.

"Got it," he confirms. "Man, you could see a flea on a dog's back in this shot."

"House looks like an old farmhouse with a garage or a carport at the back."

"That must be the carport Mendoza was talking about," Kellar presumes.

"Could be."

"What's that small rectangular shape just off the side of the house?" Rafe asks.

"That looks like a root cellar bulkhead door to me."

"Basement access from outside?"

"Yeah."

"Is that a padlocked chain around the handles?" he notes, zooming in on the image with his fingers.

"Yeah, I think you're right. Must not be able to lock these old doors from the inside. Only way in now is through the house."

"Nope. I've got a bolt cutter."

"You just happen to carry a bolt cutter around with you at all times?" Bloom asks.

"Yeah, I call it my Glock."

Marty laughs. "You need probable cause to get inside without a warrant, don't you?"

"I haven't heard back from Constable Mendoza. That's probable cause enough for me. Besides, when I'm finished with him, he won't be in the mood to ask for a lawyer," Kellar vows.

"It's your neck on the line, not mine," his colleague utters.

"What's that, a barn or something way back behind the house?" Kellar inquires.

"Yeah, looks like it could be an old barn," Bloom concurs. "It's roughly 320 meters away."

"Thanks for the help, Marty," he says, wrapping up their conversation as he moves past the scene of the accident and is finally able to make better time.

84

Halton Hills, Ontario

"Ahhhh!" Father Jakub cries out in pain as the leather thongs connect loudly with his back's exposed skin. His entire body shivers and his lips tremble as he stammers a prayer in a whisper.

"No one's coming to save you," Konacher chuckles, takes a step back and draws his arm for another violent chastising of leather bands into Father Jakub's bare shoulders. The priest screeches louder as the searing pain courses throughout his entire being.

"You can scream as loudly as you want, Father," the Prophet giggles. "No one's coming to save you," he says, draws his arm back, then forth with a powerful strike across Father Jakub's thighs.

"Ahhhh!" Father Jakub cries out again and squirms from the pain.

Konacher smiles. "The voice is pleased with me," he boasts.

"Holy Mary," the priest murmurs hoarsely.

"Stop! Praying!" he shrieks in anger, drawing the leather whips back and lashing Father Jakub's back furiously. "She's not coming to save you either!" he hisses and strikes him with the scourge twice more in quick succession before stepping back to catch his breath.

"Brian," he mutters weakly. "I can help you . . . get rid of . . . the voice."

Konacher shakes his head in disbelief.

"Heavenly Father," he petitions. "Please . . . rescue your son, Brian . . . from the clutches of . . . the enemy. Wash him with your son's precious blood . . . and forgive him this and all his . . . wrongs."

"Stop!" the Prophet demands forcefully and swings the leather straps at Father Jakub's head. "I told you to stop praying!" he screams with tears in his eyes.

Quiet momentarily fills the cellar as Father Jakub recuperates from the last blow.

"It's—it's not your fault, Brian," the priest stammers. "What chance did you have? Just let me help you. What you're doing here, it's—it's not the answer. This won't solve . . . any of your problems. Please. Let me . . . help you."

"I told you to shut the hell up!" Konacher barks angrily in his face, then quickly moves to the female officer, lingering over her. "You want me to string this bitch cop up in your place, strip her and flog her naked body as you watch?"

"You promised you wouldn't hurt her." Father manages to get out.

"And you won't keep your mouth shut!"

"You said you were going to crucify me," Father Jakub says, still struggling for breath to speak. "Are you going to do that here?" he asks, forcing out the last word, desperate to bring Konacher's attention onto him and away from Constable Mendoza, still unconscious on the floor.

The Prophet shifts his gaze to Father, steps around the column, and faces him with a sneer.

"Are you looking as forward to that as I am?" he grins, dabbing his contorted face with the back of his hand.

"Are you going to crucify me here?" he asks more insistently.

"Of course not," Konacher grins and swivels his victim's suspended body a half turn. Taking two steps back and winding up, he assaults Father Jakub's chest with the thick leather strips. The priest howls out in agony for several more minutes until his torso and legs are striped with overlapping, painful welts and the Prophet finally abandons the flogging.

"That should do it," Konacher says with admiration as he looks on with a satisfied grin, his hands on his hips and his pulse racing.

He tosses the flagellum aside and hops up onto the stool to unfasten Father Jakub, who collapses onto the floor. Konacher giggles and disappears into one of the darkened corners, then returns with a purple satin sheet and a crown woven from thorny branches he'd collected from the back of the house.

"Please, Brian," Father implores as the Prophet hovers over him with his intimidating props.

Konacher cackles and drapes the sheet over Father's shoulder, then leans in with gloved hands and presses the thorns into his scalp with blood quickly streaming from his forehead into his eyes and down his cheeks.

"Get up!" Konacher yells and fades into the shadow for the second time, then returns with a long, heavy wooden beam. "Get up!" he barks again. "You were looking forward to getting on with the show; well, here's the crossbeam that you'll carry to your crucifixion site."

Father Jakub painfully rises from the floor and reaches for the wood, but Konacher thrusts it forward into his chest and face. He falls backward on the ground and yelps from the pain as the Prophet doubles over in excitement.

"That's one!" he exclaims in a fit of laughter. "Just two more falls to go," he squeals. "Now get up, we have to go!" he cries out ecstatically.

Father Jakub struggles up and reaches for the beam again, wary of having it violently thrust upon him a second time.

"Follow me," Konacher instructs, then leads them up and through the bulkhead doors and outside in the wet grass with the priest staggering out of the cellar, weighed down by the bulky piece of timber on his tired shoulder.

"We're going that way," the Prophet points toward a structure at the back of the property. "Start walking!"

Father Jakub lowers his head and begins to march, but feels Konacher's heel against the small of his back barely three steps in, forcing him to the ground with the bulky crossbeam landing heavily on his neck.

"Ha-ha-ha! That's two!" the Prophet hoots as he hovers over Father Jakub's body and spits on him.

85

Mississauga, Ontario

Kellar recklessly winds his way around the other vehicles traveling north on Highway 427 a few exits away from the on-ramp to the 401 West and absently taps the dial button on his phone's screen more as a nervous distraction than the expectation of hearing Jakub's voice safe from harm on the other end.

"Hang on, Jakub. I'm on my way," he says to himself as he loops his way to the right of a slow-moving transport and cuts his way back in ahead of the angry trucker on his air horn just in time to swerve left and catch the 401 on-ramp.

His phone rings as he merges into the flow.

"Kellar!" he snaps.

"Arch, it's Juice," his friend announces. "How you making out up there?"

"That bastard took Jakub!" Rafe says. "I'm on my way to his hideout now."

"I know. Marty just called and brought me up to speed. Wish I was there with you, man."

"I know, thanks, Juice."

"How far away are you?"

"That'll depend on traffic," he complains. "GPS puts me there in less than half an hour, but it's been wrong twice already."

"I'm catching the red-eye out of Rio tonight. I'll be there late tomorrow morning."

"Don't quite know what you'll find, Juice," Kellar comments. "Someone's going to be dead, and I'm not planning on it being me."

"Don't do anything stupid, Arch," his friend appeals.

"Is that why you're calling? To tell me not to put a bullet in that son of a bitch's head?"

"No, just looking out for you," he replies. "I just don't think this guy's worth tossing your career over. You're already in Madan's doghouse for that stunt you pulled in Montreal."

"He's a psychotic serial killer who's been at work since he was barely out of diapers!" Kellar cries out. "He's been flying under the radar his entire life, killing innocent people as he went along his merry way. He's thrown us off his track more times than I care to admit. He almost killed my wife, and now he's abducted a friend of mine and is planning on murdering him if he hasn't already done so," he recaps. "He plans to end it all tonight anyway, so if I help him make his wish come true, so be it!"

"Just be careful, Arch," Juice cautions.

"I'll see you tomorrow, Juice," he replies dismissively and ends the call, then pushes down harder on the accelerator with the lights from Mississauga's skyline quickly shrinking in his rearview mirror.

86

Halton Hills, Ontario

Father Jakub staggers through the overgrowth that had taken over the path leading to the old barn over the years, and Konacher giggles as they near the ancient structure and swipes at the priest's heel, sending him tumbling hard to the ground for the third time.

"That's three!" he bursts in laughter.

Father Jakub squints up at him through the bloody tears with a look of despair. With the female constable now at a comfortably safe distance from them, the priest resumes his work of conversion.

"I forgive you, Brian," he says from the ground. "Jesus forgives you as well. Do you want his forgiveness?"

"You don't give up easily; I'll give you that," Konacher admits, then reaches down to grab his victim's arm and gestures him to stand. "Let's go," he insists.

Father Jakub manages to stand but loses his balance and tumbles into Konacher, who catches him in his arms, and their eyes lock momentarily. The emptiness the priest had earlier witnessed isn't quite so evident, and he now senses an inner conflict at work inside the killer's heart.

"You have the power to stop this, Brian. You can make this stop. The voice has no control over you unless you hand that power over to it. Take that power away from it, Brian. Ask Jesus to help you, and he will.

"You're going to have to be quiet," the Prophet calmly advises, releasing him from his grip. "Just—just be quiet and let me finish this," he says, urging the priest forward with a quick gesture of his head. "Watch out for the rotted floorboards," he cautions, almost compassionately. "Wouldn't want you to hurt yourself," he chuckles weakly as Father Jakub angles his shoulders slightly to clear the barn's threshold. The smell inside reminding him of a mix of chicken manure and his uncle's oily garage he recalls from his childhood.

"You can stop now," the Prophet instructs as he turns on the overhead light. "Just drop the beam there."

Father Jakub releases the heavy timber as directed, and it lands with a boom on the floor in a cloud of dust.

"Now lay down with your arms outstretched. I think you've watched 'The Passion' often enough to be familiar with the drill."

Father Jakub hesitates, but the Prophet reassures him. "You'll still have a few minutes to live, I promise. I'm just going to measure out and drill pilot holes for the nails I'll be hammering through your hands," he explains. "Then I'm going to screw in these eye bolts to the beam so that when you're nailed to it, I can hoist it up and hook it onto the stauros behind you to form the cross from which you'll hang. I've already attached the footrest on it, as you can see, but don't get your hopes up; that footrest isn't just for show. I'm going to have to nail your feet to it."

Father Jakub's eyes are desperate. "Do you really think that this is what Sister Mary Joseph would have wanted for you?" he asks poignantly.

"Lay down, Father," Konacher replies mildly.

"I can tell you don't really want to go through with this."

Konacher lets out a deep, frustrated breath and points to the floor. "I said—get down."

Father Jakub complies meekly. "I know Sister Mary Joseph would implore you to stop this if she were here," he says, wincing as he kneels down and turns over, then stretches his body and arms on the floor despite the pain. "Do you really believe this is what your little brother Peter would have wanted for you also?" he asks.

Konacher chuckles. "You really think Peter wouldn't want me to do this?" he asks. "It's his voice that lives inside my head!"

87

Turning off his headlights and steering into the driveway, Kellar pulls in next to Constable Mendoza's squad car and kills the engine. He checks his Glock and assures himself his spare magazine is still inside his pocket before leaving the rental, then races around the front of the house in a crouched position, his sidearm drawn and ready to shoot that little bastard Konacher.

"Shit!" he curses as he rounds the corner and spots the open bulkhead doors.

"Police!" he shouts as he begins his cautious entry down the stairs inside the musty root cellar illuminated by the bare bulb dangling from the ceiling. He spots the flagellum on the floor and the column under the light with the shackles abandoned at its base. His heart races at the similarities between this scene and the familiar movie with Robert Powell where his parents made him watch every year on Good Friday. He swallows hard at the brutality of the punishment his friend had assuredly endured.

Hearing the faint moans, he scans the area and locates Constable Mendoza writhing alone in the darkness.

"Holy shit, she's still alive!" he utters, rushing over to her. "Mendoza!" he shouts, yanking the tape from her mouth.

"He's got the hostage," she says weakly. "I regained consciousness just as I heard them leave. He must have taken him to the old barn that I spotted out back earlier," she speculates. "They must have gone there on foot because I didn't hear a car."

Kellar carefully slices the tape from her head with his pocketknife and frees her wrists and ankles.

"You're lucky to be alive, you know that?" he barks. "Stay here and call for back up! This time, you damned well better listen to me!" he warns sternly, then races out of the cellar and sprints toward the barn.

88

"It's time," Konacher announces solemnly, tossing the antique manual drill aside and glancing back to Father Jakub sitting on a bale of hay with his back propped against one of the horse stalls, the purple sheet still draped across his chest and the bloody thorns around his head. "That's a good look for you, you know," he grins. "Maybe if you'd have dressed like that last Easter, your parishioners would have put more money in the collection basket," he suggests amusingly.

"Did you ever ask Peter for *his* forgiveness, Brian?" Father Jakub inquires with sincerity, ignoring the juvenile attempt at mockery.

Konacher lets out a weak snort. "Forgive me for what?"

"For what happened to him under the bed when you were trying to protect him."

"He doesn't care that it was an accident," he dismisses. "He's made it pretty clear over the years that he's always hated me for suffocating him and not protecting him the way a big brother should have."

"It's not too late, Brian. You can still make things right with him," Father Jakub insists.

"I *am* making things right," he replies dispassionately and, moving toward the priest, pulls the sheet away and gestures for him to take his place on the floor with a wave of the hand. "Let's get this over with," he adds softly.

Father Jakub slowly squats, turns himself over, his broken body in a great deal of discomfort, and stretches out his arms across the wooden beam with an unnatural sense of inner peace and strength.

Konacher collects his hammer and a twelve-inch galvanized spiral spike, then, crouching over the priest, presses the nail deep inside the palm of his right hand, breaking the skin.

"Peter would forgive you, Brian; you have to believe me. What happened to you and your brother when you were a child wasn't your fault," he reiterates. "Sister Mary Joseph was right to want to protect you. What you felt for her really *was* love. You are capable of love, Brian. That says a lot about you. It's just unfortunate that Tommy Strickland disrespected her the way that he did. You were only trying to defend her honor the only way you knew how," Father Jakub maintains.

Konacher's puffy eyes begin to well up, and the hammer shakes in his trembling hand as Sister Mary Joseph's compassionate words resurface, convicting his actions and distracting him from his objective.

"The trauma you were submitted to at the hands of those reform school guards only made things worse for you. I'm so sorry you were raped and beaten there as a boy," Father Jakub weeps. "No one should ever have to go through that. But still, that wasn't enough, was it? Your foster family immersed you in the occult and gave the enemy permission to prey on your wounds the moment you were placed in their care. Of course, you're hearing the voice of your brother. That's the devil disguised as your brother's voice controlling you and seeking the destruction of your soul."

"No," Konacher argues.

"Yes, it is," Father Jakub persists. "You were made by God with the hope that you would love him and love others. That's something the devil hates, and he's never going to be satisfied unless he completely destroys you."

"No," Konacher mumbles.

"With Jesus' help, you're more powerful than the enemy, and you can put an end to this."

"No!" he disagrees more forcefully. "That's not possible."

"Tell Peter you love him and that you're sorry. Order the enemy to leave you this instance and free yourself from his suffocating grip once and for all."

The Prophet's lips quiver. "I'm sorry," he whimpers and raises the hammer just as Kellar reaches the barn with his weapon drawn directly at Konacher's head.

He fires a shot as the rotted floorboard disintegrates under his weight, and he crashes through the floor, landing hard on his back five-and-a-half feet below. The bullet misses its mark, but pierces the killer's leather armor plate and penetrates his chest cavity, shredding his left lung and missing his heart by 30 millimeters.

Hammer and nail drop to the floor in a thud as Konacher slumps forward, topples to the ground, and coughs up blood.

"Jakub!" Kellar cries out from beneath the floor. He winces and shakes off the pain, then fumbles in the darkness for his weapon. "Jakub!" he yells again, struggling to climb his way back inside the barn.

"I'm okay," Father Jakub affirms and slowly crawls toward Konacher, still alive but struggling to breathe.

"Is he dead?" Kellar yells.

"No," Father Jakub confirms, drawing closer to the killer withering in his own blood.

"Get away from him!" Kellar orders forcefully.

"I have to administer the last rites," the priest insists.

"What?" Kellar shouts incredulously from his hole. "Get the hell away from him, I'm warning you. That bastard's going straight to hell tonight!"

"Not if I can help it," the priest protests.

"Jakub!" Kellar barks. "I'm warning you!" he says, firing a shot through the roof.

The priest freezes momentarily. "If you feel you have to shoot me, then you just go ahead and shoot me!" he announces rebelliously to Kellar's amazement. "You do what you have to do, and I'll do what I have to do!" He continues toward Konacher.

"Shit!" Kellar curses as he loses his grip and slips beneath the floor again. With his eyes eventually adjusting to the darkness, he spots an opening at the other end and slowly limps his way out as, above him, Father Jakub defies his command and administers the Apostolic Pardon.

"Brian, are you truly sorry for hurting all the people that you've hurt?" he asks as Konacher's breathing becomes weaker and his bleeding intensifies. The once most-feared serial killer in the country's history nods his contrition weakly and gurgles his indiscernible response.

"Have you forgiven all those who've hurt you?"

Again, his head bobs faintly.

"Do you reject the devil, all his angels, and his lies?"

Konacher takes a breath, closes his eyes and nods once more.

"Do you believe Jesus died for you and that he wants you with him in heaven as much as the repentant thief who was crucified next to him?"

Konacher sighs. After a long pause, he opens his eyes and attests in silence as a warm teardrop streaks his cheek.

With the sign of the cross, Father Jakub pronounces the words of absolution as Konacher takes his last breath.

"So, you manage to save his sorry ass even though I told you not to, didn't you?" Kellar says in anger as he reaches the pair on the floor, his weapon still drawn.

"That's not for me to judge, Rafe," Father Jakub shrugs. "All I can do is assist the dying. It's up to them to believe. I have no way of determining his sincerity. All I can do is pray and let God do the rest."

"It's not fair, you know," Kellar states his opinion as he secures his weapon and takes a seat on a wobbly sawhorse. "It's not fair that he gets to be the murderous bastard he's been all his life and still get into heaven."

"That's not how it works, Rafe," the priest reasons. "That's why it's never too late for repentance."

"I don't buy it!" Kellar fumes.

"No one's forcing you to."

Kellar shakes his head and lets out a deep breath.

"Thank you," Father Jakub says.

Kellar huffs. "For what?"

"For saving my life."

"You're a major pain in the ass most of the time, but I wasn't going to let him kill you," he shrugs.

"You're a good man, Rafe Kellar," Father Jakub acknowledges with sincerity.

"Don't be spreading that shit around," Kellar chuckles, then sighs as he takes a look at the cross and the scourge's welts on Father Jakub's body. "Here," he says, handing him his blazer. "Let me help you put this on."

"Thank you," the priest replies and slips into the coat as smoothly as his broken body allows him to.

"You planning on wearing that thing around your noggin all night?" he asks.

Father attempts a smile but grimaces as he pulls off the makeshift crown from his head. "I'm glad these thorns were a lot shorter than the real ones," he winces through the pain.

"You okay?"

"Yeah. I'm okay," Father Jakub affirms.

"Were you scared?" Kellar asks.

"Shitless!" he says, entirely out of character and with a sly grin that catches Rafe off guard. They share a laugh, and he quickly regains his seriousness. "At first, I have to admit I was terrified. But then I had an overwhelming sense that I was not going to die today."

Kellar smirks. "You know, the world's full of dangerous people, Jakub. You can't go around thinking you can rescue every broken individual on the planet."

"But I can't run away from them either if the opportunity presents itself."

Kellar shakes his head. "Things could have gone badly for you here tonight. You know that, right?"

"Worse than this?" he grins, and they share another laugh. "I know, I could have died tonight," he admits soberly. "But I didn't."

They sit in silence while the wailing sirens from the responding Halton Regional officers grow louder in the distant night and the moon peeks through the dissipating cloud cover.

Acknowledgements

The list of people I need to acknowledge is long, but I especially wish to thank my wife and biggest supporter, Annette, for keeping me on track and making sure the story flows naturally and intelligently. Edith, for your friendship and kind words of encouragement when you were with us. I will always remember you fondly. Father Mark, for ensuring I didn't wander off into heretical territories when formulating Father Jakub's dialogue. Deacon Pedro, for your stories and photos of what World Youth Day in Rio was like as a pilgrim. Serge, for your valuable insight as a firefighter. I would also like to acknowledge everyone who proofread the manuscript and offered constructive criticism and I would be remiss to not also highlight Maylon from Right Your Writing for her keen editorial eye and wisdom.

It had been a desire of mine for many years to write a crime novel. I have always admired police officers and know they face a tremendous amount of pressure these days in the court of public opinion. There are good and bad people in every facet of society, and the few bad ones often make it difficult for the many good ones to shine. To the honorable men and women selflessly risking their lives to keep us safe, I extend my sincere gratitude and profound respect.

Last, but most importantly, thanks to our Heavenly Father for the many undeserved blessings he showers upon all of us.

Printed in Great Britain
by Amazon